THE HAND

THE HAND OF
STRANGE CHILDREN

Robert Richardson

GOLLANCZ CRIME

First published in Great Britain 1993
by Victor Gollancz

First VG Crime edition published 1994
by Victor Gollancz
A Cassell imprint
Villiers House, 41/47 Strand, London WC2N 5JE

A catalogue record for this book is
available from the British Library.

ISBN 0 575 05704 1

Printed and bound in Great Britain
by Cox & Wyman Ltd, Reading, Berks

For Jane Gregory and Lisanne Radice

Three may keep a secret, if two of them are dead

Benjamin Franklin

Poor Richard's Almanack

Book One

Prologue

We are all liars, and the most dangerous lies are the ones that we come to believe ourselves. When we recount our past, the pain, regret, sometimes the disgust at what we did makes us flinch, so we change it to the way we would have wanted it to be; the story becomes the sum of how much we can tolerate remembering plus the deceptions behind which we hide. Even when we try to tell the truth, it can elude us. We can recall conversations, perhaps even remind ourselves of them from fragments recorded in old diaries, but the precise motives behind what was said become lost as we justify and rationalize. Recollection awakens ghosts of people who were once part of what used to be our lives, but now are unrecognizable strangers – and among those strangers may be the young people who had our names.

Naomi, Timothy and Richard Barlow were the children of ordinary middle-class parents, a family who appeared blameless, perhaps dull. They were respectable and well-mannered and there are millions like them. They grew up and married and had children of their own. Those who remembered them from their childhood would say later that Naomi and Richard had done very well for themselves and there was nothing to be ashamed of in what Timothy had achieved. What eventually happened was all the more shocking because it destroyed people so conventional, successful, even enviable. But the outsiders' perception was distorted by surface glitter, behind which lay a contamination of secret guilt, overlaid with untruths and constantly corroding.

Our pasts are recorded without us realizing it. A chipped ornament or piece of jewellery holds memories of somebody we knew;

bundles of letters turned out unexpectedly from the backs of drawers bring with them a faint miasma, faded as an old perfume that once was vivid; photographs show how people looked. But these are fossils, not the living reality we have lost. The photograph reveals only an image of a brief moment on a certain day, poses for the camera as fleeting as the shutter, and underneath we may not have been smiling.

Newspapers also provide records, although they are probably the most inadequate of all. The majority of people hardly appear in them, except when they pay to have personal notices inserted or are caught up by chance in some newsworthy event. The births of the Barlow children were not announced, even in their local paper, because that was not the sort of thing on which their parents chose to spend money, but later their names were printed from time to time, usually in connection with something they had done at school, a sporting success or examination results; such tiny cuttings were treasured for a while, then became yellowed and tattered before being mislaid or thrown away. It is more than thirty years since their names appeared in connection with the single event that was the defining moment in their lives. It was published in the *Wilmsford Messenger* of 19 June 1959.

DEATHS

BARLOW – Harold Edward, aged 58, on 17 June 1959, peacefully at Wilmsford Cottage Hospital, after a long illness. Beloved husband of Florence and father of Naomi, Timothy and Richard. Funeral at St Luke's Church, Wilmsford, 2 p.m. 23 June, followed by cremation at Southern Cemetery. All enquiries to William Duncan and Sons, 28a Birchwood Road.

A week later, the following appeared:

ACKNOWLEDGEMENTS

BARLOW – Florence, Naomi, Timothy and Richard wish to thank all their friends for the kind messages of sympathy they have received on their sad loss. Special thanks to the staff of Pennine Ward, Wilmsford Cottage Hospital and the Directors of Coombes Bros Ltd.

And a year later came:

IN MEMORIAM

BARLOW – Harold Edward, in loving memory of a dear husband and father who passed away 17 June 1959. Florence, Naomi, Timothy and Richard.

Similar announcements appeared for the next two years, then they stopped. Cuttings specifically about Naomi began on 4 January 1967 when another notice appeared, again in the *Wilmsford Messenger*:

ENGAGEMENTS

BARLOW–STANSFIELD – The engagement is announced between Miss Naomi Jean Barlow, only daughter of Mrs Florence and the late Mr Harold Barlow of 17 Tattersall Close, Wilmsford, and Mr Charles Stansfield, only son of Mr and Mrs Henry Stansfield of Temple Manor, Dollington, Bucks.

Then, on the Weddings Page of the *Buckinghamshire Courier*, with a photograph, of 15 July 1967:

BARLOW–STANSFIELD – The marriage took place at St Michael's Church, Dollington, on Saturday between Miss Naomi Jean Barlow, only daughter of Mrs Florence and the late

13

Mr Harold Barlow of Wilmsford, Manchester, and Mr Charles Robert Stansfield, only son of Mr and Mrs Henry Stansfield of Temple Manor, Dollington.

The bride, who wore a full-length dress of oyster satin with a head-dress of Nottingham lace, was given away by her brother, Mr Timothy Barlow, and carried a bouquet of white roses and lilies of the valley. She was attended by Miss Daphne Booth-Wills, a cousin of the groom, and Miss Helene Staunton, who wore full-length dresses of pink and cream satin and carried posies of carnations. The best man was Captain Gerald St John Waterford, MC.

After the service, conducted by the Rev. Jonathan Hartley, Vicar of St Michael's, the reception was held at the home of the bridegroom's parents. Among the guests were the Lord Lieutenant, Brigadier Michael Bellamy, and Sir Peter Carey, Junior Minister at the Home Office, and their wives.

The couple, who are spending their honeymoon in the United States, will make their home in Hertfordshire.

On 18 August 1969 a notice in *The Times* read:

BIRTHS

STANSFIELD – On August 17th to Naomi (née Barlow) and Charles, of Brookmans Park, Hertfordshire, a daughter, Roberta Diane.

Then, from the same paper of 9 October 1971:

BIRTHS

STANSFIELD – On October 7th, to Naomi (née Barlow) and Charles, of Brookmans Park, Hertfordshire, a son, David Edward, a brother for Roberta.

Meanwhile, the *Wilmsford Messenger* had reported the engagement and marriage of Timothy Barlow to Claire Hopkins in 1963, and the birth of their son, Harry, in 1965. Harry's death was reported three years later. Richard Barlow's marriage to Katherine Eastwood was announced in both *The Times* and the *Daily Telegraph* in 1970 and the births of his daughters, Katherine and Emma, in the same newspapers in 1971 and 1975.

These cuttings were the sort that virtually every family collects, and after the birth of Emma nothing else of importance concerning Naomi, Timothy or Richard was published until 27 December 1992; throughout that day they were the lead story on the television and radio news and filled most of the front pages the next morning. The following are extracts from the Press Association news agency service to national and provincial newspapers and broadcasting companies.

HSA589910 PASNAPFULL PA   09.03
POLICE Bodies
Police investigating discovery of two bodies in Hertfordshire house.

HSA589914 PASNAPFULL PA   09.08
POLICE Bodies
Bodies of a man and a woman found in house in Devon Lane, Bookmans Park, Hertfordshire. No identities as yet.

HSA589922 PASNAPFULL PA   09.20
POLICE Bodies
A spokesman for Hertfordshire police said deaths were being treated as suspicious.

HSA589926 PAHOME   PA   09.29
POLICE Bodies CORRECTION
In 2 POLICE Bodies timed at about 09.06 read 'Brookmans Park' for 'Bookmans Park'.

HSA589947 PAHOME   PA   09.54

POLICE Bodies

Police arrived at the house at 8.30 a.m. following a telephone call. The bodies were in a downstairs room and a spokesman said they were treating both deaths as suspicious.

   The house is the home of Charles Stansfield, a merchant banker in the City of London, and his wife, Naomi. The couple have two grown-up children.

HSA589966 PAHOME   PA   09.59

POLICE Bodies Advisory

ATTENTION NEWS EDITORS AND CHIEF SUBS

Not for publication. Bodies in Hertfordshire double death case believed to be members of the same family. We are trying for pictures.

HSA589978 PAHOME   PA   10.18

POLICE Bodies (reopens)

Det. Chief Superintendent Michael Dundee of Hertfordshire CID said: 'We received a call to the house at about 8.15 a.m. and found the bodies in a downstairs front room. Both victims had died as a result of shotgun wounds. We are interviewing other people who were in the house at the time of the incident.'

   He added that police hoped to release the identities of the victims later today. A shotgun is believed to have been taken from the house for forensic examination.

HSA589999 PAHOME   PA   10.32

POLICE Bodies

Roberta Stansfield, daughter of Charles and Naomi Stansfield, works for BBC Radio news. The couple's son, David, is an architecture student at Leeds University.

HSA581013 PAHOME   PA   10.37

POLICE Bodies Advisory

ATTENTION NEWS EDITORS AND CHIEF SUBS

We are trying home addresses of Roberta and David Stansfield.

POLICE Bodies (reopens)

Both bodies were taken by ambulance to the Hertfordshire police mortuary.

Mrs Jocelyn Harmer, 46, who lives near the Stansfield home, said: 'Mrs Stansfield's twin brothers and their mother were staying at the house for Christmas, and other members of the family were there as well.

'My husband and I went in for a drink on Boxing Day night and everything appeared perfectly normal. It is a terrible tragedy. They were a very well liked family.'

Charles Stansfield is a senior partner with City of London merchant bankers Kennet Bolingbroke. Company chairman, Sir Malcolm Kilmartin, said: 'We are all dreadfully shocked by what has happened.'

Sir Malcolm added that Mr Stansfield had not been in touch with him.

Police are interviewing other members of the family who were in the house at the time of the tragedy. A spokesman said that at this stage they were not looking for anyone else in connection with the incident.

POLICE Bodies Advisory

ATTENTION PICTURE EDITORS AND CHIEF SUBS

We will shortly be transmitting a colour (horizontal) picture of the house in Devon Lane, Brookmans Park, to go with POLICE bodies.

POLICE Bodies

Hertfordshire police to hold press conference at noon today on two bodies found dead at house in Brookmans Park.

POLICE Bodies Advisory

ATTENTION NEWS EDITORS AND CHIEF SUBS

Police say noon press conference on Hertfordshire double deaths will release names of victims. Trying for pictures of family. No response at home addresses of Roberta or David Stansfield. Round-up lead will be running shortly.

HSA581197 PAHOME   PA   11.14
POLICE Bodies Lead

FLEET STREET NEWS EDITOR IN DOUBLE-DEATH HOUSE

A Fleet Street news editor was one of the family guests at a house where the bodies of a man and a woman were discovered early this morning. The police, who are to release their names later today, are treating the deaths as suspicious, but not yet a case of murder.

Officers arrived at the exclusive £750,000 detached house in Devon Lane, Brookmans Park, Hertfordshire, at 8.30 a.m. following a telephone call and found the victims in a downstairs front room. Both had died from gunshot wounds.

The house is owned by City of London merchant banker Charles Stansfield and his wife, Naomi. The couple have two children, Roberta, an editor with BBC Radio News, and David, an architecture student at Leeds University. Neither were at their homes today.

Neighbours said that members of the Stansfields' family had been staying with them over Christmas. The guests included Mrs Stansfield's brother Richard Barlow, news editor of the *Post* newspaper, and his twin brother, Timothy, a teacher. Their mother, Mrs Florence Barlow, was also staying at the house after travelling with Timothy Barlow and his wife, Claire, from her home in Tattersall Close, Wilmsford, Manchester.

Detective Chief Superintendent Michael Dundee of Hertfordshire CID said that police were not looking for anyone in connection with the incident. Other people who were in the house at the time are being interviewed.

The Rev. Piers (correct) Lumley, Vicar of St Matthew's Parish Church, Brookmans Park, said: 'Everybody is utterly devastated at the news. Mr and Mrs Stansfield are regular worshippers at our church and attended our Watchnight service on Christmas Eve with Mrs Stansfield's mother. I spoke to them after the service and there appeared to be absolutely nothing wrong. It is unbelievable.'

A spokesman for the *Post* said that they had not heard from Richard Barlow (49) since he began his Christmas break on 23 December. Mr Barlow, who has two daughters, is separated from his wife and lives in Eagleton Mews, Paddington, London W2.

```
HSA581239 PAHOME        PA        11.26
```
POLICE Bodies Advisory
ATTENTION NEWS EDITORS, CHIEF SUBS
Press conference on Hertfordshire deaths put back to 1300 hours.

```
HSA581287 PAHOME        PA        11.47
```
POLICE Bodies (reopens)
Katherine Barlow, the estranged wife of Richard Barlow, was collected from her home in Chard, Somerset, by police early this morning and taken to Hertfordshire.

'She was very distraught when she left,' said a neighbour, who did not wish to be identified. 'She just got into the police car and didn't say anything.'

Mrs Barlow lives alone, but her elder daughter, also called Katherine, was spending Christmas with her. She accompanied her mother on the journey to Hertfordshire. The couple's younger daughter, Emma, is believed to have been among those staying at the murder house.

```
HSA581291 PAHOME        PA        11.51
```
POLICE Bodies CORRECTION – URGENT
ATTENTION NEWS EDITORS AND CHIEF SUBS
In POLICE Bodies timed at about 11.48 delete phrase 'murder house' in third paragraph. At this stage police are only treating deaths as suspicious, although it is expected to become a murder inquiry.

There was a great deal more as newspaper reporters and photographers, television and radio crews descended on Brookmans

Park, asking questions of the police, the neighbours and anyone else who might be able to tell them anything. With such a sensational story breaking on a traditionally slow news day, editors were demanding every scrap of information, however tenuous, and, in many cases, however inaccurate. Fact, fiction and fantasy became inextricably confused as the media chafed with impatience for the press conference that would reveal the identities of the victims and confirmation that they had been murdered.

But this was a story that no journalist was going to be able really to tell, because, as is invariably the case, they were starting at the end, and none of them knew when, how and why it had begun. The morning after Boxing Day 1992 was the climax of something that had happened when Naomi, Timothy and Richard Barlow had been teenagers more than thirty years earlier. Something that had taken place in total silence and had lasted less than five minutes, but had determined almost everything they did afterwards and affected the people whose lives had become woven into their own. Stories should not be told from the end, but no single person can tell this one from the beginning. Somewhere in what follows is the truth – or at least what the people most directly involved persuaded themselves to believe as acceptable versions that they could live with.

Chapter One: Naomi

My whole life would have been so much easier if I could simply blame Richard for the fact that we killed our father, but I have to accept that all I can accuse him of is being the one who initially suggested it. He was very clever, at first making no more than speculative comments about how death would solve so many problems for all of us, appearing genuinely distressed that such an awful thing seemed the only answer. Then he began to drop oblique hints that if it didn't happen naturally, perhaps we could . . . I should have seen right through him, of course; he was forever hatching things in his own interests. But in this case it could only happen if Tim and I went along with him, and the terrible thing is that we eventually did. Why? After spending most of my life deliberately erasing so much of the past, that question can still stab and torment me, because the reasons were not enough, they just seemed to be sufficient – and defensible – at the time.

It was a period in which we all subconsciously regressed, becoming again what we had been before we had inevitably started to grow apart. At the moment our father died – it was exactly half past three in the afternoon; I heard the hospital clock striking – we were as close as the times when we were pretending the garden shed into a castle or a pirate ship or standing in Mrs Wolstenholme's corner shop planning which fireworks we would buy for November the Fifth. In order to kill him, we reached back into childhood to act as one again, putting aside the differences between us that had been stretching wider. The inseparable twins had started to become individuals who were almost strangers to each other, and I was persuading myself that I had become a woman, suddenly wiser than a pair of fifteen-year-olds giggling smuttily about sex. Anything either of them suggested I usually dismissed with impatient eighteen-year-old contempt. But not this.

Having planted his idea, Richard, with typical cunning, left it with us; he knew he could not force us and we had to come to him by finding our separate justifications. We kept our thoughts to ourselves for a while, then started cautiously to discuss it, now persuading ourselves to carry it out, now recoiling in horror and guilt that we could even contemplate such a thing. We would give it substance by tentatively putting forward ways it could be done, then rejecting it as unthinkable and cruel. Finally we decided to . . . no, I want to start with my own justification and that means I must try to explain the feelings I had towards my father.

It might help if I begin by describing him. He was some years older than my friends' fathers because he had been in his late thirties when he married. He was six feet tall and had been strikingly good looking as a young man. His face was long with a naturally stern expression, accentuated by severely short hair and the little moustache that had been fashionable before the Second World War but by the fifties looked slightly ridiculous. And that's a word that would really have made him angry, because he was pompous and opinionated, very conscious of his dignity.

He enforced his will upon us and was a powerful influence in our lives, proud of what we achieved, bitingly critical of failure; he saw life in unequivocal terms, black and white, right and wrong, done and not done – that especially. There were no qualifications, no allowances, only certainties, attitudes that he had inherited from his own childhood. I couldn't see that then of course. It's only since then that I have understood – or at least tried to understand – what it must have been like to be an only son of parents who could never have known the concept that children could be damaged by their upbringing. My father was born in 1900, the climax of more than sixty years of increasing imperial confidence. Britain ruled all the parts of the world that mattered – America was still the lost colony, not an important nation in its own right, certainly not a superpower – and the sad little queen had been there for so long that the great majority of people would not have been able to remember or imagine life without her.

The result was that Victorian attitudes clung on, as stubborn as their architecture, antique certainties in a changing world. My father's father I can just remember, still wearing stiff wing collars and waistcoats when I sat on his knee and he would let me play with the golden spade ace guinea hanging from his watch chain. He seemed incredibly old, much more than my friends who are grandparents do today. But when I was a child, people *were* older, or at least behaved as if they were; by the time they reached forty, that was it. Husbands accepted that they would work for the same firm until they retired, wives had been conditioned not to question the limitations of their existence, the legacy of a society that had been ruled by a woman but was totally dominated by men.

When you're very small you have no way of comparing your parents with others. We were fed and clothed, given presents at birthdays and Christmas, and accepted the spankings we received – always from Father – because we knew we had done something wrong and therefore deserved them. But once the tears and the pain were over, we loved him again in the unquestioning way of little children who need objects of love. He did not forgive, but punished – with all the best intentions; he would never have seen himself as a cruel man – and brutal justice was part of his duties as a parent. If the world had not changed so much, perhaps we would always have accepted his standards and not become the people we are – or did what we did.

I was born in December 1940, just before the first of the German blitzes on Manchester. My earliest memory is of being woken by the howl of the siren and seeing the white bars of my cot in the half light as I heard my mother running upstairs. Being hauled out of the warmth and along to the brick shelter at the end of the road was a normal part of infancy. I can also remember my father in a tin helmet – not an Army one because as a skilled engineer he was involved in war work at home, building machine guns or something, but as the air raid warden for Tattersall Close. As Mother carried me through the darkness wrapped in a blanket, I saw him shepherding our neighbours along with an air of self-importance that I came to recognize years later.

After VE Day the war hung on for a while in our house, because I wouldn't go to sleep on summer nights when light seeped in through my bedroom curtains. I'd been accustomed to the darkness of blackout, so Mother brought the material down from the attic – you didn't throw anything away in those days – and put it up again for me. Thanks to Hitler, I've never been afraid of the dark.

Anyway, the point I want to make about the Second World War was that it caused the final death throes of Father's rigid and certain values. He worshipped Churchill, of course, an embodiment of the nineteenth century who had taken part in the world's last great cavalry charge ordering squadrons of bombers over Dresden and Berlin; but afterwards came Attlee's post-war Labour government. Playing with my dolls (still in their thirties clothes), I remember him writing down the 1945 general election results as they were announced on the radio, ranting at Mother that it was the end of Britain, the Empire, the entire world, that it was only a matter of time before the Bolsheviks were marching up Whitehall, you mark my words. Nationalization of the railways and the mines, the Welfare State and the start of the National Health Service all fed his prejudices – although he was quite happy not to have to pay doctors' bills any more. For a few years he lived with a sort of grumbling, self-satisfied pessimism, gloomily warning that Labour was planning to make first George VI then Elizabeth II abdicate and turn Buckingham Palace, Windsor Castle and Sandringham into council flats, following orders from their masters in Moscow. Then the Russians didn't come, Attlee fell and Churchill and the Conservatives returned to power in 1951. It had been a narrow escape, Father told everyone; had the vote gone the other way, democracy would have been lost for ever within a year. And, miraculously, everything changed for the better in his eyes. Rationing was eased, people had more money in their pockets and for a

24

few years the remains of my father's ordered and secure world flickered before it finally died. The irony was that its end was not brought about by some insidious revolution spawned by wicked Communists, but by America, which, after it had become one of our wartime allies, Father had condescendingly acknowledged as a sort of associate member of the British Commonwealth. And they did it not with guns but in a crash of wild guitars.

I must have been about fourteen when I heard my first rock and roll record. I've tried to explain to my children just how shattering that sound was, but it's so much a natural part of their lives now that they can't comprehend. Suddenly there was this music that belonged to us, to our generation, owing nothing to anything that had gone before. It was loud, defiant and blatantly challenging – and my father hated it. Jazz had been bad enough – 'Damned jungle bunny music!' he would snap if he happened to pick it up inadvertently when tuning into the old BBC Third Programme – but it had not invaded his own home, not contaminated his family. It had not threatened him. But I secretly adored those early rock records that I heard at the homes of friends whose parents appeared unbelievably tolerant and liberal. And I wanted to own one myself as part of my little rebellion, although I didn't see it in those terms at the time.

For three weeks I saved part of my half-crown-a-week pocket money, then after school one day I went into the music shop in the high street. They really were music shops then, selling instruments and sheet music which you bought to play on the piano; on the cover was a picture of the singer, the nearest thing we had to pin-ups. Mr Prendergast, who ran the shop, had seen what was happening and had installed booths down one wall in which you could listen to a record before buying it. I spent twenty minutes having them play a whole selection before deciding against 'Blue Suede Shoes' (I wasn't sure why, but I realize now that Presley's overt sexuality was more than I could cope with at the time), everybody had 'Rock Around the Clock' and that the one I really wanted was 'Rockin' through the Rye' by Bill Haley and the

Comets. Even when I'd made my mind up, I almost asked them to change it for Frankie Lymon and the Teenagers singing 'Why do Fools Fall in Love?', but Bill Haley won. It was a 78 r.p.m. of course, thick, brittle and heavy, in a plain brown envelope with a hole in the centre to show the label and cost ... I think it was about two shillings.

An important part of the plan had been choosing the right day, when the house would be empty. It was half past four when I let myself in; Richard and Tim were still at school for a play rehearsal, Mother would be back just after five from her weekly visit to Auntie Eleanor, Father not until six o'clock. I dropped my satchel and coat on the floor of the hall and ran into the front room. In one corner stood our pre-war gramophone – not record player, this was the Stone Age – a wooden cabinet larger than today's automatic washing machines with a fretted pattern on the front behind which was the fabric cover of the speaker. It had a turntable covered in grey felt and a metal playing arm shaped like a question mark, hinged at one end and weighing God knows how much. I opened the little blue tin that was always kept inside and replaced the steel needle – if you're younger than about thirty-five, they were like the end of thick darning needles and played havoc with the surface of the record. Then I took out my precious, precious Bill Haley record and put it on, closing the lid to deaden the scratching. That gramophone had never played anything livelier than selections from *Oklahoma!*, but after a few seconds of hissing it exploded into the room and I sang in my chains like the sea. (Dylan Thomas' poems was one of my O-level set books, and I suddenly felt I understood what that line meant.)

Oh, it was glorious, a wonderful alien presence shouting triumphantly across the ancient three-piece suite, bouncing off the mirror hanging from its cord above the mantelpiece with its pair of ebony elephants superstitiously positioned as if walking out of the house. It sounded to me like a joyous shout of youth and independence, ripping away constricting layers of years of conditioning. All right, of course I know it was only a pop record –

and not even one of the classics – but for the first time I was rebelling, uncertainly grasping the concept that there were other values I could explore for myself, that life did not inevitably operate according to rules that my father laid down.

I didn't think all this at the time, of course. I just closed my eyes – and I know I was smiling – and let my body move to the rhythm. For the first time, I was completely alone and could hesitantly feel what it might be like to be me. The record finished and I put it on again. And again. And ... the clock showed ten to five, time for two more before I would have to hide the record in my room. I had started to concentrate on the words so that I could sing them to myself until I next had the opportunity of playing it. They were banal and repetitive, but after nearly forty years I can still remember them, because they represented something I instinctively knew but was too young to understand; what would now be called my own thing. I sang along with the record, snapping my fingers, shaking my head until my alice band slipped loose and my hair fell across my face. I was gone. It was so silly and childish, but oh, so wonderful. It was freedom. It was me.

Then my father walked in. I'd not heard him open the front door and I can't remember now why he was so early. He brought a terrible, crushing silence into the room, so that the Comets suddenly seemed to retreat into the gramophone in the face of an enemy. He was still holding his briefcase and looked as though he had discovered a gang of Teddy Boys vandalizing his house. He crossed to the gramophone and I winced at the piercing screech as he wrenched the arm off. Then he turned towards me, holding 'Rockin' through the Rye' as though it smelt.

'Who gave you this?'

'Nobody did. I bought it.' I should have said that defiantly, but that was impossible. I mumbled, red-faced and ashamed. I'd been myself for twenty minutes; now I was his daughter again.

'What with?'

'My pocket money.'

'You are not given pocket money to spend on trash. You'll have

27

no more for the next three weeks.' He broke the record in half. 'Come into the other room.'

Out of sight of anyone passing the front window, he put me across his knee and spanked me again; it had not happened since I was about ten and the excruciating humiliation was made worse by the discomfort and searing embarrassment of one of my first periods (something about which my father knew absolutely nothing, and would have recoiled from in distaste). As far as he was concerned, I was a disobedient child who had to be taught, not a fourteen-year-old, hesitantly becoming a woman and confused by what was happening to my body. As each deliberate, angry slap belittled my dignity and battered my timid individuality, the screams inside me spluttered out in bitter, choking sobs. It was degrading and shameful and unforgivable. It was child abuse and he was convinced it was the right thing to do. Then it stopped.

'Now go to your room,' he said. 'You can come down again when you've had time to think about what you've done and are ready to apologize.'

I straightened up, breath gasping out in bitter gasps. Dear God, if there'd been a knife within my reach at that moment ... Smothering tears of pain that was much more agonizing in my mind than my body, I ran upstairs and hurled myself across the bed, muffling screams into the pillow. It was impossible to articulate what I was feeling then, but now I can do it. You cruel, unforgiving, merciless, unloving, stupid, ignorant ... But inside all my rage and resentment there was still that insistent, insidious voice saying you mustn't defy your parents, they knew what was best for you. The rigid shell of my conditioning had only been cracked that afternoon.

I turned over and stared at the ceiling, sniffing and wiping away tears. I thought of all the other girls I knew whose parents weren't fossilized remains of the past and asked God why mine couldn't be like that. I remembered fathers I'd met who understood, who talked to their children, who had something with them I wanted ... relationships was a concept totally outside my experience then, so I couldn't find the word. I wanted to run away, but life outside home was inconceivable; there was nowhere to go. I was Rapunzel in her tower and there were no princes to climb my hair. It would be seven years before I was twenty-one and even he would have to recognize me as an adult; would the spankings go on until then?

Downstairs I heard Mother arrive, expressing surprise at finding Father home. I couldn't make out what he said to her but his voice was still angry, then there were her footsteps on the stairs. I turned my back to the door, concentrating on the little faces I could see in the floral pattern of the wallpaper. She came in and stood right next to the bed, but she didn't sit down and cuddle me, she didn't even touch me.

'Your father's very cross with you, Naomi. He's waiting for you to go down and apologize.' Then she went away.

I lay unmoving and wept with despair. That was it. Physically and emotionally violated by my father, confused and furious, and that was how she handled it. I love her – I really do – but she was always his wife first and our mother a bad second.

I stayed where I was until my brothers came home and I heard Father telling them they had to leave me alone, but after a few minutes Tim came quietly into the room.

'What have you done, Nimmy?' Nimmy was the nearest he had been able to manage to my name when he was little; he still uses it.

'Go away.'

'Not until you tell me what you've done.'

If it had been Richard, I would have yelled at him to get out. He would only have wanted to know so he could gloat over the incident and see if there was anything in it for him. But Tim felt sorry for me.

'It doesn't matter,' I mumbled.

'Yes it does, 'cos you're upset. You've been crying.'

God, he's always been so *nice*. Helpless, incompetent, vague, pushed about by everyone who takes advantage of him, but always kind, always trying to understand. I can never reject him; it would be like refusing a blessing from a bloody saint.

'I bought a Bill Haley record.'

'Rock and roll?' He was impressed and shocked at the same time. 'Gosh. Which one?'

'It doesn't matter. He broke it.' I was certainly not going to confess to the spanking.

'Why did you tell him you'd bought it?'

'I didn't tell him! He came in while I was ...' The mental pain that had started to subside came back, and I curled up on the bed with my back to him. 'Just leave me alone!'

'Dad says he's waiting for you to come down and say you're sorry.'

'Then he can wait.' I curled up tighter. 'I hate him!'

It was a bad moment for Tim, that. He'd have been only about eleven and he and Richard had always seen Father completely differently from how I did. He took them to cricket and football matches while Mother and I went shopping; he let them help when he was working on the car, then they'd all come in and expect me to make them a cup of tea; he bought them a marvellous model yacht and sailed it with them on the pond at Llandudno, where we always went on holidays, while I played on my own on the beach with Mother reading in her deckchair. Tim couldn't hate a father who treated him like that.

'You don't mean that,' he said. He sounded as though he didn't want me to mean it, because he couldn't cope with it. Gently, he put his hand on my shoulder. 'Come on downstairs, and ...'

'No!' I kicked backwards savagely and he fell off the bed. 'It was mine! I bought it. With my money. And I wanted it, because ...'

Because what? Because I was a teenager shedding her skin and the real Naomi Barlow was struggling out. I didn't know who she was, but the half-formed thought that I did not have to be condemned to a life as Harold Barlow's obedient little girl was taking shape. Everyone must find it difficult letting go of the security of being a child, but it helps when your parents recognize what's happening and make their contribution towards releasing the bonds. My father's response had been to force me back into the mould of his prejudices.

30

'Leave me alone,' I said. 'I'll be down in a minute.'

I could feel Tim's confusion and concern as he left me and I was alone again, but not with the magical sense of individuality that Bill Haley had brought; this time it was the loneliness of resignation and defeat. I sound appallingly wet, don't I? Don't mock me for it. Unless you had a father like mine you can't know what it was like for me. And it was the start of a learning curve I had to go through, a process that taught me how parents should behave; my father never knew my children, of course, but he did them a lot of favours.

He was sitting in the living room reading the *Manchester Evening News* when I went down again. I'd washed the tearstains off my face, combed my hair and put the alice band back on; the little rebel he'd come home to was restored to the passive schoolgirl; pale blue blouse and pleated navy skirt, black shoes and white ankle socks.

'Well, Naomi? What do you have to say for yourself?' He did not look up from the paper.

From the kitchen, I heard Mother pause as she prepared our evening meal, and knew she was listening for my response. Tim and Richard were upstairs in their rooms. I lowered my head and became conscious of a scuff mark on the toe of one shoe, thinking irrelevantly of how I'd have to disguise it with polish before school next day. That made me remember my maths homework, and the formula for a quadratic equation irrationally filled my head ... x equals minus b, plus or minus the square root of b squared minus 4ac, all over 2a. Resenting what I knew I had to say, my mind only seemed able to concentrate on anything else. J'ai, tu as, il a, nous avons, vous ...

The newspaper twitched slightly. 'Naomi! I'm waiting.'

'I'm sorry.' Just saying that hurt.

'And you won't do it again.' Not a question, a statement of simple fact. Still bowed, my head shook, but I did not speak.

Now the paper was lowered. 'Look at me, Naomi. Say you won't do it again.'

For one mad moment I nearly screamed and ran from him again.

How much humiliation did I have to choke down? I controlled a shuddering surge of anger and raised my head.

'I won't. I promise. I'm very sorry.' Behind my back I crossed the fingers of both hands. Childish defiance was the only weapon I had.

'So you should be. Now go and do your homework.'

You weren't expecting some magnanimous gesture, were you? A forgiving smile, some brief kindness of words to take away the sting and bitter degradation? If you were, then I can't have explained properly what he was like. Or perhaps he's now so unbelievable that it's impossible to do more than draw the outline and ask you to imagine the whole. According to his values he met his responsibilities as a husband and father conscientiously. He was a good provider, he taught us manners and discipline and many things that benefited us. But while he thought he was producing perfect, obedient children for whose virtues he would be admired he was repeatedly failing to understand us at those very moments when we most needed it.

Whenever they play an old Bill Haley record on the radio today – it doesn't matter which one it is – I have to turn it off, and I'm starting to cry however quickly I reach the switch. There were other incidents, of course, but that memory remains the most powerful and coruscating, because I later came to recognize it as one of the first steps that led to his death. The immediate effect was that I ceased to like my father, while remaining helplessly caught on the emotional hook of loving him; but as I became more conscious and critical of the sort of man he was, love began to rot. Either he was wrong or I was, and for my own salvation he had to become the monster. That afternoon he had started the process by which I would eventually accept that Timothy, Richard and I should kill him, and could even persuade myself it was his own fault. But I know now it wasn't; it was mine.

Chapter Two: Richard

It's not that I don't like talking about my father; the fact is that I don't want to remember him at all. Anyway, if I am going to talk about him, let's get one thing straight from the start; I wasn't the one who suggested murdering him. Whatever else I might have forgotten, I'd remember that. All right, you can accuse me of being an accessory, because I was there when it happened – you can even argue that I could have stopped it – but I didn't *do* anything. I stayed right where I was on that chair until it was over. I didn't even look. So which of the others suggested it? It can't have been Tim, he hasn't got the bottle, so it must have been Naomi. Does it matter? He still ended up dead, nobody found out and none of it is anything to do with the way I am now.

My childhood's irrelevant as well, but if you really want to know, I've got the usual jumble of memories and obviously the old man is in there somewhere. I expect I must have admired him at one time as the sort of male role model you accept without thinking about it. He taught us to bowl offspin, even allowed us to buy the old *Eagle* comic once he discovered that it was edited by a Church of England reverend and Dan Dare was obviously based on an RAF Spitfire pilot. And he made us feel that men were superior to women; he'd have seen feminism as a classic KGB plot. Do I think that way? You'd better ask my editor – she's a woman. He went to work in the morning, came home in the evening, was around at weekends when he wasn't playing golf, fixed things in the house, showed us how to mend our toys when they went wrong, bought the Christmas tree, organized summer holidays . . . the usual things. There was nothing to complain about – or get excited about.

Naomi seems obsessed with the way he punished us as children; when she's going at full throttle you'd think we were abused. But so what? I gave both my daughters a few slaps when they asked for it, but that doesn't mean I don't love them. And they've turned out all right – well, Emma is a headache sometimes, but Kathy's up at Oxford. Bright kid, got it all together. Anyway, that sort of thing wasn't the problem with the old man; you survive being hit – it might even do you good. What got me was his bloody endless rules about how you had to behave. You'd have thought he'd received them personally from God, written on tablets of stone. He was paranoid about doing the right thing. You walked on the outside if you were with a woman on the street; I learnt later that this went back to when women wore crinolines and the man was meant to prevent mud from a passing hansom cab splashing over them. He said it was a courtesy, but I think he really wanted the hansom cabs back. Everybody was Mr This or Mrs That or Miss The Other; the Barracloughs lived next door to us for years, but he never called them Donald and Cicely. At work, the chairman was always Mr Douglas, to differentiate him from his son, Mr Frank, or his cousin, Mr Arthur. How feudal can you get? But he was a hypocrite. I found that out early on, but I'll do some background first.

To give him his due, the old man had done well for himself. Started at Coombes Brothers as an apprentice, went to night classes at the tech, kept his nose clean and his head down, worked his way into middle management. The war helped, because he was in a reserved occupation (knowing him, he probably arranged that) and a few who were standing in his way didn't come back, so by the early fifties he was technical director – or perhaps it was head of research, I can't remember – with a staff of nearly forty to boss about. Money was never really a problem, however much he grumbled about taxes and the cost of living ruining him. He'd have been perfectly comfortable until they gave him the gold watch and illuminated testimonial to hang on the wall.

What I resented most was the bottom line – he had to be right, whatever you were talking about. As I grew older I would try to argue with him, but could never win. There was a classic instance when there was the threat of a strike at Coombes Brothers.

'The Communists are behind it, of course,' he told Mum one night. 'The management should just sack the lot of them. That'd sort them out.'

'They only want another five shillings a week,' I said. Some of the boys I was at school with had fathers who were involved and we'd been talking about it. 'The management and office staff have just had a rise, haven't they?'

He looked at me as if I'd sworn at him. 'Who's told you that?'

'Someone at school. He says that—'

'What's his name?'

'Stuart Campbell. His dad's—'

'Campbell!' I thought he was going to explode. 'Is he the son of that blasted shop steward?'

'Yes, and he says—'

'Now listen to me. Campbell's a troublemaker. He's out to destroy the company I work for. You're too young to understand any of this, but you're to have nothing more to do with his son. Is that understood?'

'But he's a friend of mine,' I protested.

'Then find some other ones. I didn't send you to school to become friends with the children of anarchists.'

'You just said they were Communists.'

'They're the same thing and—'

'No they're not! You might as well say that—'

'*Yes they are!* Don't argue with me. Anarchists, Communists, Fascists, Socialists. They're all out to destroy the country you're lucky enough to live in. Just you remember that. We fought a war against those sorts of people.'

'You didn't.' I instantly realized that was not a bright remark, but I was so appalled at what he was saying that it just came out. For a moment I thought that he was going to hit me. But I was big for my age, and he obviously thought better of it; he was a coward as well.

'I'll speak to your headmaster tomorrow and ask him what sort of education he's giving you, young man. And I'll suggest he adds a few lessons in manners.'

I'd discovered his hypocrisy about a year earlier. One of the most important done things was going to church, with him probably secretly praying that the Labour Party would be wiped out like Sodom and Gomorrah. Just before the sermon all the kids would troop out to Sunday School, and as we walked home – the church was about a mile from the house, but not using the old Wolseley must have made him feel pious – we would be grilled on what we'd been taught.

He knew his Bible – correction, he'd read his Bible but never thought about it – and when one of us started telling him which story we'd heard he'd take over, throw in a few choice quotes and adapt it to some moral lesson that was meant to make us feel holy or humble. Jesus, of course, was Superman in a white robe. The Son of God, meek and mild, Redeemer of all Mankind (except Socialists). I'll swear his voice took on a hushed tone when he spoke his name. But one point was never mentioned – he was Jewish. And the old man was a member of Wilmsford Golf Club, which didn't allow Jews to join.

I stumbled across this minor contradiction by chance. One Sunday we read a passage in which someone called Jesus rabbi. We had our books on our knees as we listened and I'd seen the word coming and started giggling because I read it as rabbit; I nudged Naomi, who was sitting next to me, and pointed it out and that started her off as well. The teacher – it must have been Miss Simpkins, who smelt of camphor – told us to be quiet, but at the end I stuck my hand up and asked what a rabbi was. A teacher, Miss Simpkins said. No, not a Sunday School teacher, Richard, a religious teacher. No, not like the vicar ... well, yes, something like him. A Good Man. I had the feeling she was dodging round something, particularly when she obviously dropped the subject. Looking back, that must have been one of the first moments when the journalist in me started to surface. I'd asked a question and been fobbed off and I wasn't satisfied.

On the way home I raised it with the old man. Without realizing it, I did it rather cleverly (another lesson for the embryonic reporter) because I just asked what a rabbi was without linking it to Jesus. He wasn't pleased. Where had I heard the word? From Miss Simpkins? Why had she mentioned rabbis? That was nothing to do with the church, he'd have to have a word with her. I realize now of course that he suspected her of sullying our minds with Zionist heresy, but at the time I was just intrigued. Here was something that had come up at Sunday School and two adults were ducking questions about it. Back home, I looked the word up in our dictionary. It still didn't register when I read the definition, except that I couldn't understand what there was about it that had made both of them try to put me off. But that evening the old man had a phone call from the golf club secretary and I heard him say, 'What's the name? Goldstone? Damned nerve making an application. Of course I'll vote against it. If the Sons of Abraham want to play golf, they can buy their own course. Let's face it, they've got enough money to do it. As long as it's nowhere near ours.'

It took me a few weeks to stick all the parts together, but then the penny dropped. I was too young to challenge him about it, but I stored it away and never saw him the same way again.

That hypocrisy didn't matter very much, but the next time it did. In the summer holidays one year he arranged a temporary job for me at Coombes Brothers, part of his masterplan to have me follow him into engineering – fat chance – and I spent three weeks making the tea, running errands, nipping out to buy someone's cigarettes. You know the sort of thing; I learnt damn all about the business. One of the people who caught my attention was a secretary called Megan Williams, bottle blonde, make-up out of a red light zone and tits like matching Snowdons; ideal fantasy woman at my age. Just before I left, I was on a tea break with a group of shopfloor workers in the canteen when she walked in. One of them made some comment about what he'd like to do to her then George, the foreman, said, 'Wasting your time there. Got a taste for management, that one.'

He glanced across the table at me. 'You know all about that, don't you, Dick?'

'What?' I didn't understand him.

'Don't act daft, lad.' He nodded towards where she was paying the girl on the till. 'She's your dad's bit on the side. Has been for a long time.'

'No she isn't,' I replied instinctively. They'd been taking the piss out of me since I arrived – one of them had sent me to the stores one day to ask for a left-handed screwdriver – and I'd learnt to deal with it.

'You can believe that if you want to, lad.' George swallowed what was left in his pint mug. 'Come on, time to get back.'

As we left the canteen I looked at Megan Williams again, unloading her tray on to a table as she chatted to another couple of girls. I couldn't believe my father would have anything to do with someone like that – but George had been the only one who had never had me on. When I next got him on his own, I asked if he had meant it.

'I wouldn't have said it if I hadn't . . . pass me that wrench, will you? Thanks.' He continued making some adjustment to a piece of machinery.

'How do you know?'

'I've got eyes in my head.'

He obviously wanted to end it there, but I pushed him. 'So what have you seen?'

'This and that.'

'Like what?'

He finished with the wrench and began rolling a cigarette. He was obviously thinking about what he should say.

'I've got a dog and every night I take it for a walk round the edge of the common, right?' he told me finally. 'One evening I saw your dad's car parked near the trees over towards the railway. About nine o'clock, it must have been. It was light enough for me to see who was with him. And I recognized her.'

'But what were they doing?'

'He certainly wasn't dictating a letter.' He paused as he lit his cigarette. 'I'm sorry, Dick. I've seen a few other things as well and it's been going on so long that I thought you must have known. I should have kept my mouth shut, but it's too late now. Just forget I spoke, will you?'

At first I wanted not to believe him. I felt bad about Dad cheating on Mum, I despised him for preaching morals to us while he was knocking off a girl young enough to be his daughter; perhaps my own frustrated sex drive made me feel envious. The worst thing was that I could do nothing about it. If I'd challenged him he'd have denied it, played hell with me and probably had George fired; there was no way I could tell Mum and I couldn't bring myself to talk to Naomi or Tim about it. I had to carry it on my own. I coped with it – it taught me a lesson in how to handle things – and all of a sudden he was despicable. So when it came to killing him, I had a reason already in place, even though I wasn't the one who suggested it.

When we talk about him – and it was years after his death before we really did – Naomi and Tim keep raking up all sorts of incidents from when we were kids, but I can hardly remember anything. There was that fight with Tubby Key when I beat seven bells out of him with everyone gathered round in a ring in the playground cheering us both on; he was a year older than I was as well. Putting an air pistol pellet smack through the eye of that magpie on the greenhouse roof. Groping Susan Young's tits – or was it Jill Maitland's? – while she was going out with Ian Barker. Winning the inter-school mile race and collecting the cup. Tim says I once burst into tears when I was told off in front of the entire school after being caught smoking behind the bike sheds, but I stopped crying when I was about eight years old. It's like Naomi insisting I wet myself when we lied about how old we were to go and see that horror movie; I told her I'd spilt my orange juice.

Anyway, this is meant to be about the old man. I must have loved him when I was small, the way that all kids love their parents; later on I despised him and I'm not going to pretend I was sorry when he died. He was like a news story, interesting for a while then forgotten. Of course, if the real story had ever come out, his death would have been foot-in-the-door stuff, front-page splash, follow-up interviews, snatch pictures, great quotes, 96-point headlines. I STILL LOVE MY CHILDREN SOBS MURDER WIDOW ... THE FACE OF A DAUGHTER WHO MURDERED HER FATHER ... WE KILLED HIM, THEN KISSED HIM GOODBYE ... HE WAS OUR DAD, BUT HE HAD TO DIE ... CHILDREN OF THE DAMNED.

But if it had all come out and they'd started investigating, they wouldn't have found my fingerprints where they shouldn't have been. So which one of the others was the actual murderer? Sometimes I think Naomi, then I think it must have been Tim; perhaps it was both of them. For Christ's sake, it's thirty-odd years ago. Perhaps he just died. The doctors had said it could have happened any time. And I was the one who went racing out to call the nurse. I wasn't scared, I just knew someone had to be told in a hurry. And I cried – all right, I'll admit that – I cried. But it wasn't because I was sorry, it was because I ... It doesn't bloody matter.

And if you're going to argue that there's a difference between your father dying naturally and you being involved in ... oh, I'm sick of this! He's been dead since 1959. The funeral was at St Luke's and he was cremated at Southern Cemetery. What the hell's it got to do with anything now?

With Naomi living in Hertfordshire I can see her whenever I feel like it, but Tim's still in Manchester; he's never moved more than five miles from where we were born. The only time we're all together these days is at Christmas when Tim brings Mother down to Brookmans Park and I put in an appearance. The trouble with Christmas is that you can spend a fortune getting together all the members of the family that you try to keep apart the rest of the year, then wonder why it goes wrong. A couple of years ago I took

Stephanie with me for the first time and overheard Roberta – that's Naomi's daughter – tell her mother that she must keep her brains in her bra. Then on Christmas Day night Tim drank too much and started getting maudlin. Everyone else had gone to bed and there were just the three of us.

'Dad would have been ninety next week,' he said, right out of the blue.

'He'd never have made it,' I told him.

'We made sure of that, didn't we?'

Naomi, who was filling a tray with used glasses, stopped and looked at both of us.

'Do you still think about it?' she asked.

'Every day,' Tim replied.

'Balls.' If there'd just been the two of us I think I'd have hit him. 'Nobody remembers something that happened so long ago every bloody day.'

'I do. And so does Mum.'

Naomi caught his tone faster than I did. 'What do you mean, Tim?'

'It doesn't come up as often as it used to, but she still mentions it sometimes. It was Roberta who started her off.'

'Roberta?' Naomi looked puzzled. 'How?'

'You know she's got this thing about the family. Wanting to be told the whole history and—'

'That was when she wanted to be a writer,' Naomi interrupted. 'She grew out of that years ago.'

'Maybe she did. But you know how Mum thinks the sun shines out of her. Once Roberta started her thinking about Dad again she kept coming back to it.' He looked at us uneasily. 'Sometimes I think she knows.'

'Knows what?' I demanded.

'Don't be stupid, Richard.' Naomi sat down next to Tim on the sofa. 'What's she said?'

'Just bits and pieces. How she was so worried about how we were going to manage and then it happened like a miracle. How he died on the one day of the week when we went to see him on our own. How the specialist seemed surprised it had been so sudden . . .' His voice trailed off.

'But she's never . . .' Naomi hesitated. 'She's never given you the idea that she suspects anything?'

'Not in so many words.' Tim swallowed the last of what must have been his fourth large whisky. 'But she wonders.'

'Then let her.' I stood up. 'And be bloody careful what you say to her. I'm going to bed. Goodnight . . . and Merry Christmas.'

I must have eaten something that didn't agree with me, because when I got into bed I felt hot and started shaking. I was due in the office the next day, so it was no time to be ill. Stephanie was asleep, but it didn't take long to wake her up; there's nothing wrong with me.

Chapter Three: Timothy

For the first few years of my life, I was allowed to blow out the candles on my cake seven minutes before Richard because I'm that much older than he is; it stopped on our sixth birthday when he lost his temper and screamed so much that we did it together. After that, we were brought up in exactly the same way. When we played dressing-up games with Nimmy she would make us twin soldiers or doctors or whatever. Neither was favoured over the other, Mum dressed us alike until we were seven or eight and, as we got older, always made sure that if one of us had something, the other had the equivalent. Teaching us to play cricket, Dad would organize it so that we had equal turns with the bat, and took us both with him to watch Lancashire in the summer and Manchester United in the winter.

Today, you wouldn't think we were even brothers, let alone twins. We don't look alike – Richard favours Dad, I'm a sort of male equivalent of my mother – and we make chalk and cheese look almost the same thing. Richard's become a caricature of the hard-bitten journalist, the sort who fires a reporter from time to time because he's decided his or her face suddenly doesn't fit; tragedy and human pain are no more than the raw material of news, however much it hurts people; it's terribly important that the *Post* story is better than the one in the *Daily Mail* or *Daily Express* and accuracy is not a consideration; personal privacy is an offence against the freedom of the press. On this last point, he can be utterly hypocritical. When Emma, his younger daughter, was involved in a drugs scandal at her private school, her name never appeared in any of the shock horror exposés. He had no trouble keeping it out of the *Post*, of course, and a few phone calls to senior journalists he knows made sure it didn't appear in other papers. In return, he let them have some exclusive quotes from one of the girls the *Post* had tricked into talking; beating the opposition didn't matter when he wanted to protect his own. A few weeks later, when he was called by the frantic wife of a clergyman who was dying of cancer, he said there was no way they could drop the story about her son shoplifting, even though he had been undergoing psychiatric treatment. The public had a right to know.

So that's Richard, and what he was going to become emerged in our childhood. Of the two of us he became the natural leader, and I followed until he left me behind. He was cunning where I was innocent, he learnt the value of lies, I instinctively told the truth, not always for my own good. Nimmy recognized the separation of our personalities and began to act towards us differently; Richard had to be watched like a cat that could unexpectedly spit and scratch, I was still her little brother who needed looking after. The situation hasn't changed much even now we're all middle-aged. But however much we've grown apart, we are bound together by Dad's death. See how I try to make it sound better by saying 'Dad's death'? That event happens in all families. What I really mean, but find it so hard even as I'm about to write it, is Dad's murder. The one that we committed.

I want to be as honest as possible (and I can hear Nimmy saying 'There you go again. Mr Clean') and the truth is that I can't remember so many important details now because I drove them out of my mind very soon afterwards. But one thing I'm certain about; it was Richard's idea and he came up with it months before we did it. The sequence of events is confused in my mind now, but first of all he worked out all the arguments, then began dropping hints to Nimmy. As she began to come over, he started on me, knowing that with Nimmy supporting him I would agree. I was at that difficult stage – stupid remark; they're all difficult stages and continue for years into adulthood, perhaps all through your life – of dying boy and unborn man, the period when you keep examining your face in the mirror and try to convince yourself that you ought to start shaving. But I was still Nimmy's baby brother and Richard's bewildered acolyte. I'm not going to blame them for persuading me against my will, I have to accept my share of the responsibility, but I was the most reluctant of the three of us.

The most telling weapon they used – correction, Richard used – was Mother. There would soon be virtually no money coming into the house and it was unthinkable that she should have to work. Dad had always looked after her and would want her to be looked after now, but if he was no more than technically alive ... accepting charity would be a terrible humiliation for her ... she'd have to sell the home she loved so much where she had spent all her married life ... move away from her friends ... perhaps she would end up in a council flat. As my initial resistance was undermined, tiny twists of my emotions unfastened what defences I had. But I came to the decision myself one night, lying awake in the dark, when I began to think about Dad and realized that I loved Mum much more.

It had been so gradual a process that I had not been aware of it until that moment. It was not that Dad had started to prefer Richard to me, even though they had so much more in common, it was simply that the gap between the sort of man he was and the children we were had grown so wide that contact had been lost. The others realized this and, if it had not been for his illness, would have started to rebel, questioning his rules and convictions which we had all accepted for so long, arguing, defying him. Being so unlike them, I would have been confused both by their behaviour and what I wanted to do myself. Because I could not have defied him, the conflict caused by that inability would have been eased by long talks with my mother, her sympathy and understanding protecting me if not really helping. Finally, I was her favourite.

Having got that far, I had to look at my father very hard and decide exactly what sort of man he was. At school we were reading *Barchester Towers* and one night's homework had been to draw up a list of the virtues and shortcomings of various characters; Mr

Harding was gentle but naïve; Archdeacon Grantly honest but impatient with others' weaknesses; Obediah Slope was thin on virtues but was industrious; Signora Neroni was mischievous but perceptive. It struck me that Dad was almost like a Trollope character; in many ways he almost seemed to belong to Trollope's century, so ... virtues first. Honest, hardworking, respectable, responsible, conscientious ... I was drawing up a list an employer would like, but what about a family? Try again. He was ... all I could come up with were negatives; he didn't drink or gamble, was faithful to Mum and we had never gone hungry. It wasn't as much as I had expected to find. Shortcomings? This was more difficult, because it was the first time I had ever tried to look at him in such terms. He was fixed in his ways, often to the point of bigotry, had little imagination and no sense of fun; he was old-fashioned and pompous. It struck me that if he hadn't been my father he was the sort of adult I'd have found boring and wanted to avoid. There was nothing I could condemn him for, but nothing I could admire ... and nothing I could love. At that point I stopped thinking about it and tried to go to sleep because I felt as though I was betraying him; but I had taken another step towards Richard and Nimmy and what they were saying we should do.

Over the following weeks I swayed between horrified rejection of the idea and concern for Mum. I knew she had been talking to the bank manager and was worried about money and how we would manage; Nimmy wanted to go to university, but it would be so difficult. I was torn in half, desperately seeking an impossible compromise between tangled emotions towards my father and concern over how his condition was affecting everyone. Then one afternoon, about a year after he fell ill, Mum sat us all down in the front room when we came home from school and told us that the doctors had said there was nothing more they could do. He might recover, but ... somehow she stopped herself crying and suggested that we should all pray for him. It must have been another week before Richard mentioned the murder again; he's always known how to time things like that for maximum effect. I cried myself to despairing sleep that night, then the next day I overheard Mum and Nimmy talking in the kitchen.

'Your father hadn't made arrangements for anything like this,' Mum was saying. 'It's not the sort of thing you expect to happen.'

Nimmy said something I didn't quite catch, but it was to do with Coombes Brothers, where Dad worked.

'I went to see Mr Douglas,' Mum replied. 'It's been discussed by the board and they're very sympathetic, but the company won't keep up his pay for much longer. They say it would set a precedent, although after all these years you'd have thought they could make an exception. All they're prepared to do is repay his pension contributions, which isn't very much.'

She sounded resentful, which was unlike her. She was as correct as Dad about what is now a lost, slightly obsequious, level of respect for an employer; Coombes Brothers' actions were never to be questioned. I felt awful, not only for her but for my own instant reaction. If Nimmy couldn't go to university, what chance did I have of becoming a teacher? I told myself that was selfish, but it brought home to me that if it was bad for me, it was worse for Mum. It was so long since Dad had last been in the house that our lives had rearranged themselves around his absence almost to the stage that his return would be an intrusion we would have to accommodate. Despite what had seemed his previous importance, we had discovered that we could manage without him – even Mum in her way – but only so long as the financial support he represented was maintained. Richard had explained to me what life assurance meant and how Dad had always believed in it; I had some trouble understanding policies and premiums, but had grasped the fact that he had taken certain steps to ensure that we would be all right if he should die. But these things only worked when he was dead, not now that he had lapsed into some twilight existence that couldn't be called life. I heard Nimmy comforting Mum as she started to cry, telling her it didn't matter about university, that she could get a job and the boys would be able to leave school soon and chip in their bit as well and we'd all cope somehow. I knew she was lying, at least about it not mattering about university; she wanted that desperately.

Quietly, I left the sitting room and went upstairs to find Richard. As I walked in he was reading something which he hurriedly closed and covered with some papers. (I searched for it later out of interest. It was a copy of *Health and Efficiency*, the nudist magazine with unprovocative black and white photos of naked women, the nearest thing you could get to *Men Only* or *Rustler* in the fifties; it was so tattered, it had obviously been going round the school for weeks.)

'I want to talk to you,' I said.

'What about?'

'About ... about what you mentioned. What you and Nimmy have been talking about ... about ... you know ... about Dad.'

He's so clever, Richard. He knows exactly how to play people, even giving the impression of incredible understanding and sympathy when it suits him. He instantly saw how near I was to coming over and led me through the last few steps brilliantly. He stood up and put a comforting, brotherly arm round my shoulders.

'Hey, come on. It's OK. Let's talk it through.'

Slowly and patiently, he let me – no, made me – put it into my own words, making occasional comments of encouragement or subtly undermining any misgivings. When I mentioned my concern about Nimmy not being able to go to university, he nodded approvingly.

'You're right,' he said, as though the thought had never occurred to him. It probably hadn't; he'd have considered nobody's interests but his own. 'All her teachers say she ought to go, and you know how much Dad wants her to. But if there's no money ... I'm not bothered. I'd leave school now if I could and get a job on a newspaper, but Nimmy really wants to ... and you want to go to teacher-training college, don't you?'

'Yes.' The question surprised me because I'd never mentioned it to anyone. But I should have known that Richard would have worked it out and was using it to manipulate me.

'Well, I think you should. You've always been cleverer than me.'

Only in the classroom, Richard, because you couldn't be bothered doing any work. But outside in the real world, where you could outwit and deceive, where it helped to be what they now call street smart, where you could twist the rules and cover your lies, you were brilliant and I was helpless.

Anyway, that's how I joined in with them, not completely that day, but I passed a point of no return and afterwards Richard was able to keep me in line with occasional twitches of the lead he had me on. He and Naomi seemed very close during those weeks. They shared a common aim, even if it was for different reasons, and just needed to make sure I didn't start letting my doubts get the better of me. I could so easily have stopped them, because it was either all three of us or none at all. If I'd said no and threatened to tell if anything happened, they'd have had to abandon it. It was the one time in my life that I had power over them, and I didn't have the courage to use it. I wasn't brave enough to save my father, so I ended up helping to kill him.

I find it very hard to talk about the actual murder. I try not to think about it, but it's like having a permanently lame leg that makes you walk crookedly; however much you adapt and learn to live with it, you subconsciously know all the time that you're crippled. And because it doesn't show in any physical sense, which would attract sympathy, it's a disfigurement of your personality that nobody sees and you have to bear in secret.

What I can talk about, because I recall it so vividly, is what happened immediately after we'd done it. I was just numb. Nimmy seemed miles away, smiling at Dad as though she loved him very much. But Richard panicked, which was so out of character that I can still see his face now, white and horrified. For a moment he looked as if he was going to burst into tears, not of sorrow but terror, before he dashed out of the room and we heard him shouting for a nurse.

'It's all right, Tim,' Nimmy said quietly. 'That's exactly what one of us would have done if Dad had ...' She turned and looked out of the window at the hospital grounds without finishing the sentence.

Moments later the staff nurse ran back in with Richard, followed by the ward sister. Tall and gaunt, she'd always given the impression of running the place like a very strict public school in which it was her duty to make sure all the rules were obeyed. Mr Barlow's children visiting unaccompanied had not been approved of – there should always be an adult present, particularly with a terminally ill patient – but she had not been able to prevent it. She took no more than one quick glance at him, before brusquely taking us out of the room with a sort of kindly bossiness.

'Come along,' she said. 'The doctor's on his way and we'll telephone your mother.'

The doctor raced into the ward from the corridor just as she was ushering us into her office. I was last and she almost pushed me inside then asked us to wait for a moment. Richard immediately started blubbering, and, while I can't remember everything we said, I know that he suddenly denied having anything to do with it. Naomi told him not to be stupid and to stop crying.

He glared at her furiously. 'I'm not crying.'

Stunned and somehow detached from everything by what had happened – by what we had done – I was still able to register amazement at Richard's behaviour. His sniffly, resentful denial was like a little boy pretending. I couldn't understand it then, apart from putting it down to the sort of shock I was feeling, but at that moment he revealed something that he's spent the rest of his life covering up. Underneath all that apparent strength, deep below the surface of that ruthless exterior, is a pocket of cowardice. He knows it's there and all his toughness and self-confidence is a lie that he presents to others and persuades himself is real. The greatest danger we were in for weeks after the murder was that he would break down and blurt everything out.

When the sister came back I had the feeling she was uncomfortable. She must have known how to break the news of a death to adults, but she seemed out of her depth with three teenagers. Naomi made it easier for her by asking straight out if Dad was dead and the sister was obviously relieved. She said something about it being very peaceful and for the best. Then Naomi said we were sorry that Mum hadn't been there as well. I remember thinking how that was exactly the sort of thing to say. Responsible. Concerned. Regretful. What you'd expect from children who had been brought up to behave properly, particularly from the daughter who was the oldest. We must have presented the perfect picture of stoical youth, lips trembling but held firm, accepting the sorrow that we had known was coming. As we were leaving the hospital later, I heard the sister quietly saying to Mum how proud Mr Barlow would have been of his children, how proud she must be. That was another of the endless hurts of that day, but the worst had been when Mum arrived and comforted us and said we should say some prayers. That was bad enough, but when we all went through to see him . . . Strangely it wasn't the guilt that was the worst thing for me, it was the realization that a man who had been a natural part of my entire life had gone away for ever. I'd enjoyed my childhood with its security and Dad's reliable rules; I couldn't imagine what life would be like without him there, explaining things, helping me to understand. It was the first glimpse of a hole in the centre of myself that I have never been able to fill.

We didn't speak in the taxi home. Mum sat in front with the driver and the three of us were in the back, Richard in the middle. We passed the road that led to Coombes Brothers, and I had a vivid memory of Dad driving Richard and me along it when we were about twelve and he had taken us in one day to see something he was working on. I'm not quite sure why he did it; perhaps it was to show the people he worked with what his sons were like. I suddenly realized that he had been proud of us and I felt at that moment as low and dreadful as I have ever felt in my life. He had not been a perfect father – there's no such thing – but he had never done anything for us or to us that he did not believe was right. He was too practical to dream, but if he had it would have been a dream that we would be successful, that we would pass on to our children values he had taught us, that as an old man he would be satisfied that he had carried out an important duty in life properly. It seemed a very decent ambition.

But I would never know him as an old man, at least no older than fifty-eight. The terrible thought came that he might have recovered, however unlikely it had seemed, that some miracle would have brought him back to us. But not now that he was dead. Not now that we had ... I still have to force myself to say it ... now that we had murdered him.

Richard had started sobbing again and Naomi took hold of his hand as Mum looked round, concerned.

'Home in a few minutes,' she said encouragingly and smiled, although unwept tears were etched round her eyes. Her grief would take second place to her care for us; she would pick up Dad's share of the burden of bringing us up and add it to her own. And we would lean on her for a while, seeking comfort that she would believe was for our sorrow but was really for our guilt.

Chapter Four: Florence

Even now, after all these years, there are occasional traces of Harold. Living in the same house has a lot to do with it, of course, because I still have many things that he knew. I threw out some museum pieces and replaced them with contemporary furniture, but the grandfather clock that belonged to his parents still ticks and chimes in the hall, I've still got his beautiful rolltop desk, and the framed set of bird pictures – made from real birds sort of sliced in half – still hangs up the stairs, even though Roberta, my granddaughter, makes pretend sounds of vomiting when she passes them. In the garden, the apple tree he planted the year before he died produces pounds of lovely cookers each autumn – even though I really can't be bothered doing anything with them – and I've always put French marigolds along the side of the drive just like he used to. But it's a strange feeling, almost as though I live in the ghostly company of a complete stranger. I know his name and his face, I know so much about him, but was he really married to me for nearly twenty years? Was he the father of my children?

We had what was considered a very good marriage, although I can't imagine many wives today would see it like that – and knowing what I've learnt since, I certainly wouldn't accept it if I could have my time over again. But I bowed obediently to the standards of the time and Harold's own behaviour without questioning it; things were like that then. They're teaching my youth as part of history lessons at school, which makes me feel a real antique, so perhaps I ought to begin by explaining something about myself, how I met Harold, and what he was like.

My family was my parents, my older sister, Eleanor, and myself.

Father would have liked a son, but after I was born the doctor said there were to be no more babies. Father was an assistant bank manager and, with just two children to provide for, was comfortably off. I won't bore you with my childhood; it was completely ordinary, north of England middle-class. We lived in Wilmsford on the south side of Manchester in a detached house and had a maid; people in our social position did in those days. I finished school at sixteen although, without wishing to sound conceited, I could have gone on to university. But the thought never occurred to me because that was not what young women in my situation did. I had been brought up to accept that my natural ambition must be marriage to a responsible man who would provide me with a home and I would bear his children. Some sort of job was permitted for a few years after school, but it was not to be regarded as a career; that was for women forced by necessity into earning a living, which was properly a man's role.

Coombes Brothers held their account at Father's branch and he knew several of their senior financial people. One day he announced that he had been told about a vacancy in their typing pool and had arranged for me to have an interview the following week. It sounds incredible now that an intelligent young woman had no say in the matter, but I accepted it without question. I wouldn't have known where to begin when it came to finding a suitable job and relied on it being arranged for me – like virtually everything else in my life. I could type and had started shorthand lessons (interestingly, that had been at Father's suggestion) and here was an ideal opportunity. The interview was a formality, and I began work at the princely sum of twelve shillings and sixpence a week and met Harold on my second day. I thought he was rude and, at thirty-five as he then was , incredibly old. Working in the research and design department, the typing pool was a foreign country to him – I can't remember now what brought him there – and he stood just inside the door looking unsure before speaking to me because my desk happened to be nearest.

'Where can I find Miss Butterworth?'

I blushed. He could have been the managing director for all I knew and Father had drilled into me that Coombes Brothers was a company run on very proper lines. All the men – except for the factory-floor workers with whom I would have nothing to do – were called Sir, or Mr Whatever if your status allowed such familiarity, which mine certainly didn't.

'I don't know,' I blurted out. 'I'm sorry.'

'Don't you work here?'

'Yes, but I . . .'

'I'll ask someone else.'

Not the most promising beginning to what was to be twenty years of marriage and three children. But after that bad start things improved. I found my feet and my confidence was boosted by compliments from the head of the pool. I was what would now be called a gopher, running round the works – getting hopelessly lost at first – taking memos and letters for signing to all sorts of people. When I passed anywhere near the factory hands there would be the occasional wolf whistle, but that was the nearest to what Roberta now calls sexual harassment. It never occurred to me in such terms; sex was not so much a closed book as a volume that I didn't know existed. Inevitably, I met Harold – Mr Barlow, of course – again and was relieved that he appeared to have forgotten the incident when we first spoke. He was always impeccably correct, but after a while he began to take a moment or so to ask me about myself, which I put down to nothing more than casual politeness. Gossiping with the other girls in the canteen, someone would occasionally mention his name and I began to learn something about him. A bachelor – with no suggestions of any scandalous overtones; even the most racy of my colleagues were totally ignorant of that sort of thing – who lived with his parents not far from where I did. Bit of a cold fish, apparently, but always the perfect gentleman. I had no especial interest, and never thought I would have.

Then came the firm's 1936 staff Christmas dance, held at Milton's Restaurant in the Parade. Staff only, of course; those who actually made the machinery we sold received nothing more than a bonus in their pay packets and an impersonal, printed note from the directors thanking them for all their efforts throughout the year and wishing them the compliments of the season. That's how it was, blue collar, white collar. Four of us from the typing pool went together with the fiancé of one of them acting as chaperon. We sat at a table next to the dance floor and he asked what we would like to drink. Naturally he would pay and we each politely said we would have a fruit juice which was (a) the least expensive and (b) not alcoholic. Then we sat and waited to be invited to dance, chatting brightly and not doing anything that would be considered fast, such as looking at any unaccompanied man for too long. It was all as formal as a minuet, except that the band was playing foxtrots and quicksteps. After about a half an hour, the master of ceremonies invited us to take our partners for 'Tiptoe through the Tulips' and suddenly there was Harold standing in front of me with a slight bow and courteous request. I was startled, but I couldn't refuse. We were long past the days when you carried a card marking to whom you had promised each dance, and his approach had been perfectly proper. I agreed, and he stood to one side so that I could step on to the floor ahead of him.

He danced atrociously, in that he had obviously been to classes to master what was then an essential social grace, where he had learnt the steps but not how to move. He was stiff and self-conscious and, I felt, slightly uncomfortable at doing something beneath his dignity; it turned out to be a correct assessment of him. He complimented me on my dress, which sounded genuine, and made some remark about the excellence of the band, which didn't. When we finished, he escorted me back to our table and asked if he might join us. I was uncertain because he was so much older than any of the rest of the party, but it would have been impolite to say no. One of the other girls raised her eyebrows at me when she and her partner returned to the table and saw us together, and as Harold went to buy more drinks she leant over and whispered to me.

'I didn't know you knew Mr Barlow.' She sounded impressed.

'I don't,' I protested. 'Apart from meeting him at work.'

'Well, I think he wants to get to know you.'

In the few minutes before Harold returned with the drinks, I rather agitatedly reviewed the situation. He could have asked me to dance out of no more than politeness, but why me? There were plenty of other unaccompanied young women to choose from, including many he must have known longer. I remembered someone saying that he was always very deliberate in everything he did, which could mean that ... well, Florence Metcalfe, you'd better start thinking about this. I could see him from where I was sitting and began to look at him more closely. He was tall with very dark hair, cut short and shiny with Brylcreem; all men's hair looked much the same in those days. He had a small moustache rather like Ronald Coleman, who was one of my heroes from the cinema, and while he was not good looking in any extravagant sort of way he had a face you could feel comfortable with, square set and dependable. And I noticed that he had very good teeth – often a considerable bonus in the days before free Health Service dentists. How did I feel towards him? I wasn't sure, but I certainly wasn't antagonistic. He was an older man, but that was no handicap. As he returned to the table, I decided it would be interesting to find out more about him. There was no sudden feeling of attraction, nothing even remotely like my heart lurching as I fell in love; not then, not ever. Harold courted me in the same way that he designed machines, meticulously, one stage at a time; it was to be many years before romance came into my life.

We danced again several times that evening, and I was aware that it was being commented upon round the room. After the last waltz, he returned me to my party and said goodnight; it would have been improper of him to suggest that he saw me home on so brief an acquaintance. I thought about him in a vague sort of way before going to sleep, but at work next day our relationship appeared unaltered, although the other girls kept asking me about him. I told them it had been nothing important, but then realized that I felt disappointed, which surprised me. I felt he had paid me a compliment and that I had done nothing to put him off, so why wasn't he following it up? Then I realized that he was waiting for me to take the next step. You must remember that he couldn't just stroll into the typing pool and ask me to go out with him; perhaps other men could in those changing times, but not Harold. Apart from Coombes Brothers, we had nothing in common, and I couldn't wait until Christmas 1937 when we would be together again at a social gathering outside the regimented atmosphere of work. The Wilmsford Amateur Operatic Society offered an opening; I was appearing in the chorus in *The Maid of the Mountains* and my parents were coming on the last night. I cautiously suggested to my mother that there was someone I had met at work – I stressed that he was a gentleman – who might like to see it as well and if I invited him as their guest ... Looking back, I needn't have worried that she'd start asking awkward questions; I think she began planning what she was going to wear as the bride's mother the moment I raised the subject. Father approved as well; I'm almost certain that he made discreet enquiries about Harold's character as soon as I mentioned his name.

So Harold came and did all the right things, presenting Mother with a small posy of flowers when he arrived at the house, discussing Coombes Brothers and his position there over a glass of sherry and a cigarette with Father before we set off. I wasn't with them for the evening, of course, but Mother told me later that Harold had created a very good impression and that they had asked him round to Sunday tea the following week. Frankly, my dears, after that I didn't stand a chance; without my knowing how it happened, my parents and Harold rapidly reached a tacit understanding. By the time I woke up it was too late; everyone at Coombes Brothers was talking of nothing else – Mr Barlow getting married was sensation enough, let alone the fact that he had chosen a girl eighteen years his junior from the typing pool – and I could find neither the courage nor the reason to escape. And I didn't even know that I might want to escape; I'd been subconsciously conditioned. Do you know that line from *The Importance of Being Earnest*? When Lady Bracknell tells her daughter 'When you are engaged, your father, should his health permit, will inform you of the fact.' It really was horribly like that.

We were married at St Luke's Parish Church on 16 August 1938 with all the trimmings. Harold wore a morning suit and top hat and I had a silk bridal gown made specially for me by Kendal Milne's in Manchester; the reception was at Milton's Restaurant, where he had first spoken to me. The *Wilmsford Messenger* reported it on the front page in complete detail, including all the presents we received, making particular mention of the canteen of Sheffield cutlery from Coombes Brothers (they were important advertisers), Harold's father's civic record (he was an Alderman and years earlier had been Mayor of Wilmsford), and my father's position at the bank and as a leading Rotarian (the editor was also a member). The sacrificial virgin was given a mention as well. It all seemed perfectly acceptable, even happy, at the time, but now . . . well, let's say that I'm sorry I hadn't been brought up in an age when I could have been more self-assertive, not to say downright difficult.

Then there was the Wedding Night, spent at the Great Orme Hotel, Llandudno, for which, according to her lights, Mother had prepared me. It was not quite the 'nice girls don't move' approach, but not a great deal more advanced. First we went through the part of the service that dealt with the happy pair having children, followed by a little sermon about how God had ordained marriage for many reasons, one of which was that children should be born into good Christian homes. But children didn't just arrive, of course, there were certain things . . . she became elliptical. There were certain . . . physical things; a man had natural instincts – and there was nothing wrong with them, of course, when observed properly – and it was a woman's place to submit. There was a passing reference to some initial discomfort and the clear suggestion that one should avoid indulgence, however one might eventually come to feel inclined. Because one thing was absolute; instigation was the husband's prerogative. If my mother were alive today, she would be nearly a hundred, an unusual but not impossible age. And she'd have to come to terms with a great-granddaughter now living

59

with a third man and having a very good time indeed between the sheets – and she certainly doesn't wait to be asked. Mind you, my mother would have to come to terms with me as well.

Confused and apprehensive about what I was in for, we caught the train at Exchange Station and travelled to North Wales. A taxi dropped us off at the hotel, I smiled self-consciously as Harold signed 'Mr and Mrs H. E. Barlow' in the register, and we followed the porter carrying our cases up to our suite overlooking the Conway estuary. The porter closed the door behind him and, for the first time since the vicar had given him permission at the end of the ceremony, Harold kissed me. Somehow, I had imagined it would be different when we were married, but it wasn't; his moustache tickled a little like it always did, and there was nothing more than the kiss. No caressing, no urgent pressing of our bodies together, no hunger. Just a brief, if very affectionate, kiss, then Harold said we should unpack. I took my nightgown (Kendal Milne's again) from my suitcase and stopped as I turned towards the bed; I hadn't any idea on which side I should lay it. Harold at least understood that little confusion, placing his pyjama case on the left; it could have sparked a joke, which would have broken the ice, but he didn't say anything. After unpacking, we walked up part of the Marine Drive for a while, talking about the day, then returned to the hotel for dinner. A string quartet amid potted palms played selections from Sigmund Romberg and Gilbert and Sullivan while we ate, then we went through to the lounge for coffee. It was the height of the season and the hotel was full, so we had to share a table with a couple from Birmingham. She and I chatted about the entertainments Llandudno had to offer while her husband and Harold discussed the Test match. Neither of us said anything that might betray we were newlyweds; in those days, honeymoons were very private affairs, a brief interlude between the public wedding day and the years of respectable marriage that should follow. So strange now.

And so to bed – and what a performance that turned out to be. We smiled and said goodnight to everybody as we left the lounge, then went up the wide staircase and along the corridor. Harold unlocked the door, then stepped aside to let me enter first. I walked over to the window and looked at the moonlight splintered across the sea, which surged gently out of the estuary. I thought how beautiful it looked with the dark mountains of Penmaenmawr and Llanfairfechan on the far shore as a backdrop – and that I wouldn't mind staring at it until breakfast time. Then Harold reached across and closed the curtains.

'I think it's time for bed. You use the bathroom first.'

He went into the little sitting room from where he would not be able to see me. I picked up my nightgown and went into the bathroom, where I stared at my wedding ring for a long time before taking my clothes off. There was a full-length mirror in a wooden frame and, for the first time in my life, I looked at my naked body, I mean really looked at it. I had nothing against which to judge it then, but I know now that it was very good, narrow waisted, full bosomed (not breasts; much too physical word, virtually indecent), well-shaped legs. My hair was blond then and had been shingled for the wedding and one of my best features has always been my eyes, large and pale violet. What I saw, without being able to recognize it, was a desirable woman; what I felt was a wish that whatever was going to happen would all soon be over. With its sheen of peach-coloured silk, the nightgown made me even more sensuous, but I didn't look in the mirror again. Harold was still out of sight as I hurried into bed.

'The bathroom's free,' I called as I pulled the bedclothes up to my chin.

He smiled at me as he walked through and I lay looking at the ceiling, wondering if I ought to pray. What for? Peace in our time wasn't a bad idea; even I had gathered that there was trouble in Europe, despite the fact that my father thought that women should take no interest in the masculine world of politics. I thought of my sister Eleanor, still unmarried and probably envious of me, safe at home. My room would be empty – but it wasn't my room any more. In fact, there would never be another 'my room', just ours –

mine and Harold's. My husband. To love, honour and obey ... I stiffened under the sheet as he came out of the bathroom. He was wearing new pyjamas and the white cord tied in a bow at the waist caught my eye. Just beneath it, the blue stripes of the pattern were out of shape and it looked as though he had something underneath. I was feeling nervously excited, but my apprehension had developed almost to panic. If only my mother had been more specific about certain things. After our conversation, I'd looked at an illustrated book about Italian art in Wilmsford Library, examining a picture of the Boy David, trying to equate what she'd hinted at with what I could see. Harold certainly didn't look anything like the Boy David ... I laugh at the memory now, of course, but I really was that innocent and it was terrifying at the time. He turned off the light and climbed in beside me, putting an arm around my trembling shoulders.

'It's not been too tiring a day, has it?'

I think if I'd said yes, he'd have waited until the following night, but I whispered that it hadn't. Anxious to play my part – and desperately wanting to show my feelings for him – I put both my arms around him and kissed him again; the image in my mind was of Clark Gable and Jean Harlow in ... I can't remember the film now, but when they kissed, they meant it. Hollywood stars were hardly role models for nice girls, of course, but it was the only example I had. I deliberately held the kiss for a long time, partly out of longing to demonstrate that I loved him (which I had convinced myself I must do), partly to delay whatever was going to happen next. His hand reached down and pulled my nightgown up off my legs and around my waist – yes, that was expected – and he moaned slightly, very unlike Harold. Then he began to fumble beneath the bedclothes and I felt a naked leg against mine; it was surprising, but rather a pleasant sensation. His hand returned, this time rubbing my body (top half) and I felt something I couldn't identify pressed against my hip. I kissed him again, then gasped as he moved on top of me, panting urgently; he was heavy and I felt trapped. Whatever I had felt against my hip was still there, Harold relentlessly, clumsily moving it about; even at thirty-seven he was a virgin as well, you see. Then I cried as he began to force me open and it suddenly felt all sticky; he had climaxed at the moment of entry. (All this is wisdom after the event, of course. Now I know what was going on – I know very well, as a matter of fact – but then I was just hurting, scared and bewildered.) What was most confusing was his immediate reaction. All the tension went out of him and he rolled off me. Then, sounding embarrassed, he apologized.

I can't remember his exact words, but I know they didn't help very much. Within a few minutes he was asleep – at least he didn't snore – and I lay wide awake listening to the distant sound of the waves. Was I pregnant now? Was that all it took? Was this marriage? I was half aware of having felt a momentary sense of strange physical pleasure, but it had been so brief that I thought I must have imagined it. I turned my head and looked at my husband. In sickness and in health, for richer, for poorer, for better, for worse, till death do us part. Earlier that day I had stood in church and made those vows, convinced that I meant them.

We had two weeks of glorious weather, one evening at a concert and another at the show on the pier, walks up the Great Orme and afternoons in Happy Valley with Harold taking snaps of me with his box Brownie, two coach trips, one to Snowdon, the other across the Menai Straits to Anglesey, a visit to the cinema to see Charles Laughton and Vivien Leigh in *St Martin's Lane*; as we walked back to the hotel I was humming the tunes played by Larry Adler and the Carroll Gibbons Orchestra, but Harold had found it all too frothy for his taste. The couple from the Midlands came with us to Anglesey, and Harold and the husband – I can never remember their names – struck up quite a friendship. I appreciated that the wife must have guessed we were honeymooners, but she never said anything to show that she did. Except for one moment when we were waiting for our husbands to rejoin us on the coach. She'd been asking polite questions about my family and probing more deeply than I realized, extracting information about me without appearing to.

'Won't you miss them now you're married?' she asked. 'Your parents and your sister?'

'Pardon?' The question caught me off guard. 'Oh no. Our house is quite near theirs and we'll be able to see each other all the time.' I knew instantly I'd given the game away and went very red.

She patted my hand reassuringly. She and her husband were Harold's contemporaries and I was little more than a child by their standards.

'I'm sure you'll be very happy,' she said. 'There's a lot of adjustment at first, but then it's all right. Oh, look! Isn't that sunlight beautiful against the mountains?' She never made any reference to it again, but always gave me a warm and encouraging smile at bedtime every night after that. I should at least remember her name; she was my secret ally.

On our last evening Harold had two extra drinks after dinner. Don't misunderstand me; he wasn't drunk and certainly not objectionable, but when we reached our room that night he kissed me as though he really meant it and for the first time we made love with some level of success. Afterwards, I snuggled up against him, feeling warm and fulfilled in a way that I couldn't explain but liked, and went fast asleep. Early in the morning I cautiously slipped off my nightgown and lay on top of him, stroking his face until he woke up ... and he was shocked. I'd already begun to leave him behind.

Even so, I became a most satisfactory Mrs Harold Barlow. I cooked his meals, darned his socks, washed his clothes, minded my house, nursed him on the very rare occasions he was ill. As he rose through the ranks at Coombes Brothers, I attended more and more company functions and was a credit to him. I nodded obediently when he was expounding about politics and accepted his opinions without question. In the evenings we listened to the Third Programme or he would play his classical music records while I embroidered or knitted. I bore his children and passively submitted to his rules of how they should be brought up. Because he was a good husband, true and hardworking, responsible and correct, sound as a rock. I had chosen — or rather had had chosen for me — a man to replace my father, and was able to persuade myself that I was content, indeed that I was fortunate. For twenty years I accepted what something inside me increasingly insisted was not enough, and nobody suspected.

Till death do us ... Harold died on 17 June 1959 when my children were alone at the hospital with him. Naomi the restless, ambitious one, Richard the hard one, Tim the gentle one. They have become so different that I have to adjust the direction of my love towards each of them. But they are linked together because they were there that afternoon and saw their father die. And, for all their grief, I know that moment brought a sense of salvation to them and they still feel guilty about it. I've told them they shouldn't, but they do, which concerns me. You see, what I've never been able to admit to them is that I cannot feel guilty about that sensation I had when I replaced the receiver after the hospital rang and asked me to go there immediately; they didn't tell me exactly what had happened, but I knew. And as I phoned for a taxi there was an almost painful consciousness of freedom, and relief that my dear, faithful, boring Harold would never know how much I had betrayed him.

Chapter Five: Family Tragedy

Harold Barlow collapsed over a drawing board on 14 March 1958 as he was adding a detail to a half-completed plan; the point of the pencil he was holding leapt upwards off the rule in an uncontrollable, insane sweep, then gouged into the cartridge paper and snapped against the wood beneath. He was unconscious when the Coombes Brothers' company first-aider raced into the room; when his eyelids were lifted the pupils were dilated and only his sloweddown pulse and shallow breathing indicated that he was still alive. An ambulance took him to Wilmsford Cottage Hospital, where X-rays revealed that a blood vessel had burst into an unsuspected tumour on the meninges, the membrane between his skull and his brain.

He was placed in a side room of Pennine Ward, its high sash window overlooking the grounds. The floor was covered in linoleum that echoed the colour of the pale olive green walls; the furnishings were three steel tubular chairs, the red plastic seat cover of one split slightly, and a steel bedside cabinet on top of which was a vase of flowers that his wife, Florence, replenished regularly from their garden, cards from his sister-in-law, the directors and staff of Coombes Brothers and his fellow churchwardens, and a photograph of his children. On the bottom of the iron bed hung a chart recording his temperature and pulse rate. By one side of the bed was a stand holding an inverted bottle from which a tube stretched up through his right nostril and into his stomach, its slow drip feeding him. On the other side, another, thicker, tube led from a black metal cylinder to a mask attached to the lower half of his face. What looked like a pink rubber football bladder hung from the cylinder, expanding and shrinking to the rhythm of his artificially controlled breathing. In the silence of the room, the bladder's gentle sighing was the only sound.

He lay motionless beneath the sheet and biscuit-coloured cotton counterpane with the name of the hospital stitched in crimson at one corner. When his wife visited, she would gently lift out his right arm and hold his hand as she quietly told him about her daily life, what the children were doing, the little gossip of their neighbourhood. Twice a week two nurses pulled back the covers and sponged his body before rolling him on one side and applying ointment to his bedsores. Once a fortnight his nails were trimmed and each month his hair was cut. Each week Mr Hardcastle, the specialist, looked in during his rounds and asked Sister Poole if there had been any signs of response to sound, light or other stimulus; the answer was always no. The tumour was an unbreachable barrier that had cut off his conscious mind. After he had remained in this state for nearly a year, the specialist's house surgeon spoke to Florence Barlow in the ward sister's office.

'Mr Hardcastle has asked me to talk to you again,' he said. 'Last week we had a Harley Street specialist examine your husband and his conclusion is the same as ours. An operation is much too risky. It's been tried in similar cases, but the results have always been that the patient has either died or lapsed into permanent coma.'

'My husband's in a coma now.'

'Of course he is, but . . . Mrs Barlow, I don't want to raise your hopes, but there have been cases where patients have made at least a partial recovery. There was a report in *The Lancet* recently about a lady in America who regained some powers of speech.'

'After how long?'

The doctor looked uncomfortable. 'It was a long time, I'm afraid. About seven years, as far as I remember.'

'And then she could only speak a little.'

'Yes, but the brain is a part of the body about which we still have a great deal to learn. In your husband's case . . . well, I can't make forecasts, but almost anything is possible.'

'Including, of course, that he might remain exactly as he is.'

When the house surgeon had first met Florence Barlow, she had not been what he was expecting. Her husband was in his late fifties; she was well under forty, attractive and clearly intelligent. He had immediately recognized that she would know if he ever offered bland platitudes or false hopes, so he had never done so.

'The position is that we can keep your husband alive, Mrs Barlow. I cannot promise anything more.'

'And how long can you keep him alive?'

'That's impossible to say. Apart from the tumour, his general health is excellent for a man of his age. His heart's sound and we've found no signs of any disease.'

'So he could live to ... what? Seventy? Eighty?'

'Frankly, yes, Mrs Barlow. Or he might die tomorrow. We simply don't know. But there is nothing more we can do for him.'

She looked down at her handbag on her lap for a few moments, then raised her head and nodded. 'Thank you, Doctor. I appreciate your straightforwardness. I'd like to go and sit with him for a while now.'

'Of course.' Regulation visiting hours had long been abandoned for the family.

'Can I just get one thing clear,' she said as they both stood up. 'Are you saying that there is some possibility – however slight – that my husband could make a complete recovery?'

The house surgeon spread his hands out. 'Mrs Barlow, there are circumstances in which it would be very wrong for a doctor to make prophecies. I've never heard of it happening, but I can't say it's impossible. Perhaps you'd like to discuss it with Mr Hardcastle?'

'Would he tell me anything different?'

'No ... I'm sorry.'

'Then I won't trouble him. He's a busy man.'

Florence sat beside her husband for more than an hour. What she had just been told had not shocked or frightened her; she had already recognized the position and, in many ways, had come to terms with it. But now it was confirmed, she had to place the possibility of Harold's permanent total incapacity into the context of the rest of her life. She had always been a practical woman with the ability to separate her emotions from the everyday domestic demands of a wife and mother. She would have to make an appointment to see Mr Douglas, Harold's chairman, and explain the situation to him; that was a courtesy as much as an occasion to discover what Coombes Brothers' attitude would now be. So far, Harold's salary had continued to be paid, but ... the bank account was solely in his name, which would mean seeing the manager, and probably her solicitor. The children's headteachers must be told, although of course they were already aware of what had happened. Letters would have to be written; to the president of the golf club, various friends, Harold's cousin in Toronto, the man — what was his name? Summers or Summerville — in Southampton with whom he had started to play chess by post and who had taken such a sympathetic interest. Then there was the holiday she had booked months before, partly in an effort to inject normality into the abnormal, partly as a desperate dream that Harold would recover as suddenly as he had fallen ill. It was not too late to cancel it ... no, that would only add to the children's feelings that their lives had been thrown into chaos. She could still take them as long as the hospital knew where to contact her; she had to carry on as normally as possible.

As practical questions piled up, they became too much to think about all at once. She put them from her mind for the time being as she reached forward and stroked her husband's forehead, quiet tears slipping down her face. She often felt that she had married — had been married — in haste, but Harold had been reliable and true, predictable and pedestrian, of course, but never anything other than absolutely correct. He had not provided any excitement, but neither had he been the cause of any pain. He had never shared her continuing involvement in amateur operatics — apart from dutifully attending a performance of each show she had appeared in — but had never tried to stop her. There was a terrible irony in that just before he fell ill she had played the leading role in Lehar's *The Merry*

69

Widow – with Donald Barraclough playing opposite her. Dear Donald, who had been so concerned and understanding when he had heard the news, who had so considerately kept away, even though he only lived next door ...

Oh, there was confusion. There was guilt, there was remorse, there were beckoning promises, as tempting as they should be forbidden, now additionally agonizing. If Harold had not fallen ill, what would have happened? What *had* happened? It had all begun so innocently, with pleasant, easy talks and laughter, before gradually moving into something deeper, unknown and captivatingly new. His remarks about Cicely, at first no more than oblique indications but which had led to fuller confessions of an unhappy marriage. Her own gestures of sympathy that had become more involved without her realizing it, until the night he had kissed her as they sat in his car. The next time they met, he had apologized and said they must revert to their former state of friendship, but (and Florence recognized her responsibility here) they had continued to the point where throughout every rehearsal – it had been for *Iolanthe* – she had only half listened to the producer and musical director, waiting for it to end and for Donald to drive her home. It had been the romance that Harold had never been able to provide, like some operetta courtship, its delight grasped at and heightened as justification for its sense of nervous wrong. Physically it had been no more than embraces filled with a sense of relief and finding, but each one had been warmer and more urgent than the one before, each another step towards what would inevitably happen; what Florence, as she adjusted to each stage, increasingly knew she wanted to happen. Donald had unlocked a need inside her, a need she had not recognized.

Florence tucked her husband's arm beneath the bedclothes again and kissed his forehead. First she must see Mr Douglas, then the bank manager, then ... no. First she had to tell the children that after months of raising hopes with talk of further tests, specialists, signs that were 'interesting', the sense of rising to a medical challenge, the doctors were giving up. All that was left was a chance that their father might recover because something inexplicable unlocked his personal prison. Haphazard and blind fate, which had reduced him to what he was, had become his only saviour.

Sitting on her father's workbench, Naomi stared out of the window of the garden shed at the roses on the trellis behind which lay the vegetable plot, long since gone to seed following her father's illness. The shed smelt of oil and sawdust but was impeccably tidy, well-used, with dependable tools stored in their proper places, lengths of spare timber left over from various household jobs stacked in one corner, nails, screws and washers in tins labelled according to size on the shelves, rake, spade, fork and hoe hanging from their hooks. When she and her brothers had been small they had been allowed to use the shed for games as long as they promised not to touch anything; Naomi could not remember when they had last all been there together. But now they had instinctively returned there, Richard and Tim sitting next to each other on the ancient black travelling trunk in which their father kept partly finished pots of paint. Afternoon sunlight flooded through the open door, a mist of slow-moving dust gleaming in its beams.

'When is he going to die?' Tim asked quietly.

'Mum said the doctor told her that he might just suddenly get better,' Naomi replied.

'But they also said he might never wake up again.' Tim began to sob and Naomi suddenly became conscious of being the oldest; she responded in imitation of her mother as comforter to her husband.

'Come on, Tim.' She dropped off the workbench and knelt on the floor beside him, pulling up her skirt to keep it clean – they were all still in school uniform – and took hold of his hand. 'It's no worse than it was before.'

'It's no better, either. The point is, when are we going to do something about it?'

Naomi glared a warning at Richard. 'Not now.'

He shrugged. 'Tim knows what I'm talking about.'

His brother howled and leapt up, running out of the shed and back to the house before Naomi could stop him. She closed her eyes and sighed wearily as she stood up.

'Have you got no idea at all of when to keep quiet? I know what we've talked about – and I know you've spoken to Tim as well – but to mention it now . . .' She turned away from him, disbelieving and furious.

Richard ignored her mood. When their mother had told them the news from the hospital, he had immediately decided it was important to take advantage of the moment. Now that the doctors had given up any real hope was the time to press his arguments about their father's death. Once he won Naomi over – and he knew she had begun to move towards him – then Tim would inevitably follow.

'I'm only being realistic,' he argued. 'It makes even more sense now . . . doesn't it?'

'It's not the time to talk about it,' she repeated. 'I don't know what to think.'

'Are you going off the idea, then?' he asked.

'Just . . . just don't ask . . .'

Too eager not to lose the momentum he had carefully built up over several weeks, Richard made a mistake. 'You mean you don't want to face the fact that you hate him.'

He yelped as Naomi, breathing very fast and deeply with rage and anguish, kicked him hard on the shin.

'Never say that again, Richard!' He flinched as she pulled her foot back again threateningly, then nodded. 'Understand?'

'OK,' he mumbled. She saw tears start from his eyes in the instant before he lowered his head.

'You'd better. What we've got to do at the moment is concentrate on helping Mum.'

'How?' He dragged his sleeve across his face before looking back up at her. 'The only thing that's really going to help her is if he dies. We all know that. And if he lives like he is for years—'

'I've told you, Richard,' she interrupted sharply. 'Not today.'

'Tomorrow, then? Next week? Unless you've got some other suggestion about how we can really help Mum.'

'Just leave it alone for the time being. Perhaps we'll . . . I'm going to see how Tim is.'

As she left, Richard rubbed his shin as he pulled a crumpled packet of five Woodbines from his pocket with his other hand; nobody was likely to come to the shed and find him smoking. Convinced in his own mind, he was impatient with the others' hesitation. Their father was as good as dead already; the moment he ceased to represent financial stability, his meaningless existence became a threat. Their mother had said nothing about his job except that she was going to talk to Coombes Brothers, but Richard had long ago worked out that they would not keep on paying him indefinitely. Now he had to keep Naomi and Tim in line until they realized that as well. Naomi wanted to go to university, Tim would worry about how their mother would manage. Richard began to think how best to apply his talent for manipulation.

When Naomi entered his room, Tim was lying face down on the bed, sobbing. One hand clutched a stuffed toy rabbit, ears crushed and body shapeless from years of childish love; even Richard's mocking had never been able to make him give it up. She sat next to him and stroked his hair comfortingly.

'Come on,' she said encouragingly. 'We've expected this for a long time now.'

'That doesn't make it any better,' he mumbled.

'I know . . . but crying won't help Mum, and she's the one we can do something for.'

'Like what?'

'Just being there. Supporting her. However awful we feel, it must . . . all right, not worse for her, perhaps, but just as bad. We mustn't let her down.'

'What about . . .' Abruptly he rolled over and looked at her. 'What about what Richard's been saying?'

Naomi hesitated; she was not sure how far Richard had gone with Tim. 'What do you mean?'

'About . . . about . . . I can't say it. But you know. He's talked to you.'

'You mean about ending it for Dad?'

'Yes . . . to help Mum. It would help her, wouldn't it? If Coombes Brothers stop paying him she'll not be able to manage. She'd have to sell the house and move into a council flat or something. I couldn't stand that.'

'We don't know that they'll stop paying him.'

'Richard says they will. Do you think they won't?'

'I don't know . . . perhaps . . .' Naomi suddenly began to cry. 'Why did it have to happen, Tim?'

'Dunno.' He took hold of her hand and squeezed it. 'I'm frightened, Nimmy. What's going to happen to us?'

'We'll be all right,' she assured him.

'How? Unless . . . you know.'

They looked at each other for a long time, then Naomi said, 'You'd do anything for Mum, wouldn't you? So would I.'

She had meant to do no more than express appreciation of her brother's concern, but it was one of those sentences that one person says and another always remembers because they see it as important. It was a very small moment among many conversations the children had over that period, but it was a critical turning point at which the most reluctant began to make his decision. Left alone again, Tim grasped at the words. 'You'd do anything for Mum, wouldn't you?' Yes, he would.

Florence's arms were folded across her chest as she stood against the kitchen cabinet, as far away as possible from Donald Barraclough.

'How have the children taken it?' he asked.

'Not too badly. I've left them alone to talk about it.'

'And when are you seeing Coombes Brothers?'

'Tomorrow morning. Mr Douglas's secretary arranged an appointment for me immediately.'

'I'm sure they'll do all they can.'

'We'll see. I'm not getting my hopes up. My father always said there was no place for sentiment in business.'

'But Harold's been with them for years. Surely ...'

'I'm not getting my hopes up,' she repeated firmly. 'Harold's always believed that the board's first duty is to the shareholders.'

She bit her lip as he turned his head. At certain moments, Donald looked incredibly handsome, much more a matinée idol than a representative for a drugs company. She ached to be in his arms.

'If there's any way I can help, you only have to ask,' he said.

Florence stiffened as he moved as if towards her. 'No. Please don't touch me, Donald. That would be dreadfully cruel at the moment.'

He stopped. 'All right. I'm sorry, Florence. It's just that it's been so long since we've talked to each other properly and I wanted to ... I shouldn't have come round.'

'I'm glad you did. Just give me time to sort things out and then ... well, just give me time. But I'd like you to go now.'

She turned round and closed her eyes through a long quiet moment, then opened them again as she heard the door close behind him. Through the frosted glass cupboard doors of the kitchen cabinet she could see the blurred outline of the new dinner plates she had bought the day before Harold fell ill. He had never eaten off them and now he never would. Just as he would never again play his Bach and Brahms records, try to reduce his golf handicap, grumble over the bills, criticize the Labour Party, take the church collection, laugh at something on television, write letters that *The Times* never published, weed the flowerbeds, check the cricket scores ... endless tiny things. Some had irritated her, but all had been part of the man who was her husband. Reliable, decent, responsible ... and, in all but the ultimate act of marital betrayal, deceived.

And now helpless, mind frozen in a body that might as well be dead. No longer a father, because he could not carry out what he saw as his duties; no longer head of research at Coombes Brothers because he could not think; no longer a golfer because he could not move, or a music lover because he could not hear. No longer a ... she stopped herself. Yes, he was still a husband. Perhaps he would not be a provider for much longer and she would never again feel his heavy presence beside her in the night, cook or wash for him or submissively agree with his opinions. But he was still her husband – and could remain so for years.

On the wall behind Douglas Coombes's desk hung a portrait of his father, Mr Thomas, who had founded the company in 1902; his son was beginning to look like him, wavy hair growing white, florid features becoming plump, exaggerating the long, thin Coombes family nose. As he listened, his eyes were full of sympathy and attention. When she finished, he shook his head sadly.

'Mrs Bar ... may I call you Florence? Thank you. First of all, I must say on behalf of the entire board – and myself – how shocked and sorry we are. Harold was ... I'm sorry. Harold *is* simply part of Coombes Brothers. When I joined the company my father spoke of him very highly, and then of course he was only in a junior position. Mr Thomas took great pleasure in watching his progress.'

'Harold's always been very happy here, Mr Douglas. Coombes Brothers has always been a very important part of his life.'

'We all know that, Florence, believe me ... You say the doctor told you there still might be a recovery?'

'Yes, but it's only a possibility. And even then it could only be partial. That's why I need to know the company's position.'

'Of course.' He pulled a notepad towards him and took a gold fountain pen from his inside pocket. 'You're very like Harold. Businesslike ... Can you remind me? Exactly when did he fall ill?'

'March the fourteenth last year.'

'The fourteenth.' He wrote as he spoke. 'Just over twelve months ago. As you know, the board has regularly approved his full pay beyond the customary six weeks.'

'Yes.' She lowered her head, hating the demeaning situation she was in. 'I'm very grateful.'

Douglas Coombes leant away from her, revolving his black leather executive chair slightly to one side.

'However, you'll appreciate that we will have to consider the position in the light of what you've now told me,' he said. 'It's already on the agenda for the next board meeting and the directors will want to be completely in the picture. I will explain – and of course we will all hope for Harold's recovery – but in the mean-time ...'

Florence's hands tightened around the gilt clasp of the handbag on her lap as he opened a grey cardboard file.

'Harold became eligible to join our management pension scheme five years ago when he became our research director. He elected to make the middle rate of payments. Normally that would have produced ... well, that doesn't matter. The point is that we have talked to our insurers who say that if he should not be able to return to work his contributions will be repaid to you. In full.'

'And how much will that be?'

'Something in the region of two hundred pounds ... I can ask my secretary to check the exact figure if you wish.'

'No thank you, Mr Douglas. I'm seeing the bank manager later this morning, but I'm sure an approximation will be enough for him to tell me ...' She looked down again. 'I'm sorry, this is very difficult.'

'Please.' For a moment, Douglas Coombes looked even more like his father. 'There's something else you wish to ask?'

'Yes.' She rubbed one thumb against the edge of the clasp. 'I need to know – the bank will need to know – if there will be any more money. I appreciate what the company's done already, but I have to know if ...'

'I realized you'd ask,' he interrupted. 'As I've said, we have already stretched our normal practices in Harold's case. However, in view of the situation now, the board will want to ... can you tell me the name of his specialist?'

'Mr Hardcastle ... I think his initial's G.'

'Mr G. Hardcastle.' He wrote the name on his pad. 'Unless you have any objection, we'd like an official medical report from him.'

'I don't mind.'

'I knew you wouldn't. I'll try to arrange to have it in time for the meeting. After that ... well, obviously it will be the board's decision, but I think – most regretfully – that they will have to consider the position seriously.'

'You mean that his pay will stop.'

He sighed. 'I'm afraid so ... but not immediately. I'll recommend to the board that we continue Harold's full pay for a further three months – if we take it from the date of the meeting, that will be until the end of July – and I'm sure that will be agreed. But after that ... I'm sorry, Florence, but you will appreciate that we are bound by certain rules.'

'Harold's been with you for more than thirty-five years.'

'So have many of our employees. Some of them for longer. We have to be very careful about setting precedents.'

Florence stood up. 'Thank you for seeing me, Mr Douglas. You've made the position perfectly clear.'

He rose as well. 'I'm only sorry I can't say anything different. But in the circumstances ... and, of course, should Harold make the recovery we all hope for we'll be delighted to have him back with us.'

Her mouth tightened. 'I'd be delighted to have him back with me. Good morning, Mr Douglas. Thank you for sparing your time.'

Coombes Brothers' works were set back from the main road where Florence Barlow would catch the bus to the town centre. She walked through the factory gates and alongside the chainlink fence by the new extension, her ears filled with the muffled sounds of pounding machinery and the sudden shriek of a hooter marking the start of the shopfloor's morning break. For more than half his lifetime, Harold had walked, cycled or driven along this road to and from work. He boasted that in all that time he had taken only five days off – one for the birth of each of his children and two in 1948 when he had flu. Now he was worth nothing more than repayment of his own pension contributions and a final three months' salary. And how long would that last with a family still to bring up and the rest of her life to live? Her vision became blurred with tears, not of grief or worry, because she had shed more than enough of those. These were tears of anger and resentment – and a part of that bitterness was terribly, unforgivably directed towards her husband for continuing to live.

Chapter Six: 17 June 1959

When his children had started visiting Harold Barlow on their own, a sense of duty – towards both parents – had been mingled with a conscience-stricken resentment. None of their friends' fathers had imposed such a burden on their families; they were losing the freedom of Saturday afternoons while their mother did the shopping; and what could they do except look at him, silent, helpless and inert? The hour from two o'clock infected the entire day, first with foreboding of the vigil, afterwards with a sense of guilt. During the early visits they sat uncomfortably, frequently taking furtive glances at the creeping hands of their watches; mundane sounds of hospital activity became something to break the deadly monotony, voices in the corridor reminders that there were still living people in the world. Then they began cautiously to talk, meaningless remarks that he looked a bit better that day, wondering how often his air cylinder had to be replaced, what the figures and graphs on the charts at the end of the bed meant. Then familiarity bred acceptance and they took books to read, pocket games, comics, even school homework. They fell into the habit of chatting about other things until the hour was absorbed into a part of their weekends, the man on the bed like a view from a window that they knew so well they did not look at it any more. When they left, Naomi would kiss him on the forehead and her brothers would self-consciously press his hand; Harold Barlow was of a generation in which men were not kissed by their sons. Eventually this became a brief, instinctive ceremony, performed out of some concept of expected behaviour rather than any demonstration of love; during the month before he died it stopped.

The ward staff became so accustomed to their visits that none of them noticed that on 17 June 1959 the children arrived without their usual books. The staff nurse smiled a welcome as they walked down the corridor and went into the side room and Richard closed the door firmly. Naomi had fallen into the habit of kissing her father and whispering 'Hello, Dad' when they arrived, but that day she did not want to touch him. It was several minutes before any of them spoke.

'What if someone comes in while we're—' Tim sounded terrified.

'They never have before,' Richard interrupted sharply. He was on edge. His eyes darted round the room without knowing if they were looking for anything, and there was a knot in his stomach. He had brought the others this far, now they had to cross the final threshold.

There was another silence before Tim quietly asked, 'When?'

Richard looked at his watch. 'In about quarter of an hour. If we do it too soon, somebody might suspect something.'

Naomi went to the window, looking across lawns and flowerbeds that stretched to the railings by the main road. A rotary sprinkler was throwing a cascade of water across the grass and in the distance somebody was pushing a patient in a wheelchair. They were in the middle of a blazing summer that was to stretch deep into the autumn of that year. She saw the 47 bus that they caught to go home pull up outside the gate; carrying gifts for patients, several of its passengers got off and began to walk up the drive. But they would not be going back on the bus today; their mother would be called and she would almost certainly book a taxi for them all. Mum would be called after ... Naomi turned from the window and looked at her father. His arms had been left on top of the counterpane; his hands, which had always been muscular and powerful, were shrinking, the framework of bones visible beneath sallow, waxy skin, the hands of an old and dying man.

'We are all sure, aren't we?' she said. 'It seems so ...' Her voice trailed away.

'We've talked about it for ever,' Richard snapped. 'And you both agreed.'

'I know, but . . . I just wish there was another way.'

'Well, there isn't.' Richard gestured at their father. 'Look at him. He's never going to come out of that. Not after this long. He's not alive any more. All we're doing is what's going to happen anyway.'

'For Mum,' Tim murmured, almost as if to himself.

'That's right,' his brother said encouragingly. 'For Mum.'

Naomi looked away again. Would it really be the wrong thing for the right reasons? What *were* her reasons? That if her father remained how he was she might not be able to go to university? Sheffield had already offered her a place depending on her exam results. She'd worked hard for something she wanted and felt she deserved. She had grown to resent the limitations her father had placed on her life; now his blind, ageing, useless body blocked her hopes. It would make no difference to him when he died, but it would mean an enormous difference to her.

'How do we do it?' Tim asked.

'I've told you. It's easy.' Richard sounded impatient. 'See that tap on the cylinder? If we just turn it off for a minute or so he won't be able to breathe. He'll just quietly die.'

They stared at the dulled brass tap, and the sighing of the bladder seemed to grow louder in the quietness.

'Won't it hurt him?' Tim asked.

'I've told you—' Richard began.

'I'm talking to Nimmy.'

'What?' His sister started out of her own abstraction. 'No . . . it can't hurt him. Mum's said the doctors have told her he can't feel anything, hasn't she?'

Tim nodded. 'That's all right, then.'

Richard began to chew one of his fingernails. If it went wrong now, he might never be able to bring both of them back to this point.

'Let's do it now,' he said.

'You said quarter of an hour,' Tim reminded him.

'It doesn't matter. Come on. The best thing will be if we don't look at . . . if we just look at the tap. You can close your eyes if you want.' He went and stood next to the oxygen cylinder; Naomi and Tim didn't move.

'Come on,' he urged.

'You could turn that tap on your own,' Naomi said. 'We'll just . . .'

'Oh, no . . . we agreed. It has to be all of us.'

The knot in Richard's stomach tightened as he waited. If either of them would join him the other would follow, but if neither of them . . . Tim blinked rapidly.

'All right.' His teenage voice, which had started to break, croaked. 'Nimmy?'

She nodded and the three of them gathered round the cylinder.

'Just don't think about it,' Richard said quietly. He took a handkerchief from his pocket and laid it on the single arm of the tap. 'Just do it like we agreed.'

Naomi took hold of the tap first, then Tim, then Richard; he had argued they should do it in order of age, which meant he was the last.

'I can hardly feel your hand, Richard,' Tim whispered.

'Take hold more firmly,' Naomi said. 'Push down so I can feel it. That's better. All right . . . now.'

Their joined hands twisted, lifted and took hold of the tap again five times. The bladder began to swell and shrink less, then stopped. They all tensed in case any sound from their father should force them to look at him, but nothing broke the utter silence in the room. They heard a bell ringing urgently as an ambulance raced through the gates. Naomi silently counted to one hundred in her head, then added another fifty. Outside, the hospital clock struck the half hour.

'I want to let go now,' Tim whispered. 'Please.'

Naomi shook her head. 'Not yet. We've got to be absolutely sure . . . Richard!' She slapped her free hand on top of his as he began to pull it away. 'Don't you dare! We all let go together when I say so.'

She could feel his hand pushing up against her own until she glared him into submission; silently, Tim started to cry. Naomi began to count in her head again, forcing herself to be deliberately slow. Fifty ... a hundred ... a hundred and fifty ... her own hands were beginning to sweat.

'All right,' she said finally. 'But first we turn it on again.' Their hands moved in unison, and the gentle wheezing of the bladder returned to the room. 'Now let go.'

Richard snatched his hand away and was standing against the wall almost before the others had moved. Tim and Naomi's eyes went straight to their father. His chest was still rising and falling.

'It's all right.' Naomi sensed Tim's dismay. 'It must just be the machine now. He's dead.'

'But how do we know?' he protested. 'What are we going to say? We can't just leave him at the end of the visit as though nothing's happened.'

Naomi hesitated as she thought. They had worked out that cutting off the air supply would kill him, but beyond that they had not been certain what would happen.

'We'll tell them he made some sort of noise,' she suggested finally. 'Like he was choking or something. Then when they come to look at him, they'll ... Richard! Come back!'

It was too late. Her brother had already burst out of the door into the corridor and they heard him shouting for a nurse.

'What's he going to say?' Tim sounded horrified.

'It's all right,' Naomi assured him. 'If he blurts out that Dad's dead they'll think it's just panic. It's what one of us would have done if he'd ... when someone comes, don't say anything.'

Running footsteps sounded outside, then the staff nurse dashed into the room. 'What's the matter?'

Naomi gestured towards her father. 'We're not sure. He just ... we thought something was wrong. I'm sorry to ...'

She stopped as the ward sister appeared in the doorway; there was still no sign of Richard.

'Wait outside for a moment,' the sister said. 'We'll look after your father. It's all right.'

Richard was standing by a notice board in the corridor. There was a pleading terror in his eyes as he looked at them, but none of them spoke as they waited. Within a minute the ward sister came out again.

'Come into my office,' she said and there was a gentleness about her as she shepherded them into the room. 'Wait here and I'll be back as soon as I can.'

'What's happened?' Naomi asked. She found that her mind was working very clearly and knew it was the right question. She noticed that the sister did not answer it.

'The doctor's coming. He'll be able to tell us.'

She smiled, then left, closing the door behind her. For a few moments the only sound was Richard's helpless sobbing.

'Is he dead, then?' Tim asked finally.

'I think he must be,' Naomi replied. 'We'll soon find out.'

'I didn't do it.' Through his sobs, Richard's voice was barely audible, but sounded defiant and defensive. 'You did.'

'Don't be stupid!' Naomi snapped at him. 'We all did it.'

'Only because you made me.'

Naomi stared at him in disbelief. 'What are you talking about? It was your idea in the first place. We wouldn't have even thought of it if you hadn't ...'

'Yes you would. You wanted him dead more than me.'

His sister turned away from him, anger and frustration mixing with her own sense of fear at having done something unforgivable and outside all her values. Suddenly it was like talking to an argumentative child.

'If ... if they start asking questions I'll say it was me,' Tim said.

'No!' Naomi smiled to take the sting out of her violent refusal. 'You can't do that, Tim. We all agreed to do it and we all did it together. All three of us. Including you, Richard. Now we just have to keep very calm. When Sister comes back, neither of you are to say anything. I'll talk for all of us. Don't worry. It's going to be all right.'

In the side ward, the sister and staff nurse watched as the doctor felt in vain for a pulse, lifting one of Harold Barlow's closed eyelids with his other hand.

'What happened?' he asked.

'His children were visiting and one of them came running out shouting for a nurse,' the sister told him. 'When I got here I realized he'd gone.'

'Yes, he has.' The doctor let go of Harold Barlow's wrist. 'But how did they know anything was wrong? Where are they?'

'In my office ... but I don't think this is the right time to talk to them. They're very upset.'

'I realize that, but it would be interesting to know what symptoms they saw. How old are they?'

'The daughter's eighteen, I think, and the brothers are younger. They're twins.'

'Perhaps it will be possible later. We don't know much about this sort of condition, and any information could be useful. Have you contacted his wife?'

'I told Nurse Bolton to telephone her. She should be here soon.'

'Good.' The doctor turned off the air supply. 'Disconnect the drip, please. I'll try to contact Mr Hardcastle. He may want to come in. And will you let the morgue know? Thank you, Sister.'

The sister placed Harold Barlow's arms beneath the counterpane while the staff nurse closed the curtains. As they left, the sister locked the door with one of a bunch of keys clipped to her belt before returning to the main ward.

'Did you manage to reach Mrs Barlow, Nurse?'

'Yes, Sister. She said she'd be here as quickly as possible.'

'Good. Bring her straight to my office when she arrives. I'll be there with her children. Make sure there's some tea. Tell Mr Marshall in the mortuary that we've had a death. The body is not to be moved until Mrs Barlow has been, and Mr Hardcastle may

86

be coming in as well. Doctor Brewis is letting him know.'

The sister left the ward and paused outside the door of her office. However inevitable, breaking the news of a death caused anguish; with adults she would make sure there was a drop of brandy available to supplement the customary hot, sweet tea, but now she had to tell three teenagers. She would have preferred to wait until their mother arrived, but she couldn't leave them alone, distressed and frightened, for that long. Drawing in her breath, she opened the door. The children were standing by the window, taking comfort in the nearness of each other. Naomi had her arm round Tim's shoulders.

'Your mother's coming,' the sister said. She instinctively addressed Naomi. 'She won't be long. We can wait here ... come and sit down.' None of them moved as she placed chairs in front of her desk. 'Come on.'

'Our father's died, hasn't he?' As Naomi spoke, Richard sobbed violently. 'It's all right, Sister. We realized that.'

'Sit down,' the sister repeated. Naomi kept her arm round Tim as they moved to the chairs and the sister took Richard gently by the arm. When they were seated, she felt more comfortable standing above them.

'I'm afraid he has. It was very peaceful and he wouldn't have felt anything. I'm very sorry it was while you were with him, but you knew it was likely to happen, didn't you?'

Naomi nodded. 'But we didn't think it would be so soon. Mum said that the doctor told her he could live for years.'

'That's quite right.' The sister felt she had a duty to protect her profession. 'But some things happen without anyone being able to explain them ... can you tell me what did happen? Before you called for a nurse? I'm sorry to ask, but Mr Hardcastle, your father's specialist, will want to know. If you'd rather not ...'

'It's all right.' Between comforting Tim and telling Richard to stop being hysterical, Naomi had worked out that they would be asked and what she should say for all of them. She was again conscious of being surprised that she could think so clearly.

87

'We were just sitting talking to him – I know that sounds silly because we knew he couldn't hear us, but we always did. Telling him how we were going on at school and how the garden was looking. The sort of things he'd want to hear if . . . well, that's what we did. Then . . . I'm not sure, because it was so unexpected. It was as though he suddenly tried to move and that bladder thing on the cylinder went up and down very quickly, then stopped. It must have lasted – I don't know, it didn't seem very long – then it went back to normal.'

She looked apologetic. 'We should have called someone at once, but we just went to him because we thought he was waking up. We were calling his name – didn't you hear us? – and holding his hand. Then when he didn't move again . . .' She shook her head helplessly. 'We're sorry. We should have called you immediately . . . we're sorry. If we had, perhaps you'd have been able to . . .' The sob that choked off the sentence sounded like guilty grief.

'It's all right.' The sister reached down and took Naomi's hand. 'You mustn't blame yourselves. Your father was very, very ill and there was nothing more the doctors could have done for him.'

'But if . . . when he moved like that, I mean . . . couldn't he have been . . . coming back to life?'

'No.' There was no reason for the firm denial, but it had to be said and reinforced with considerate lies. 'That's impossible. Thank you for telling me, but you must never think it would have been any different. Mr Hardcastle will be able to explain exactly what happened. I'm dreadfully sorry that nobody heard you calling to him, but even if we had there was nothing anybody could have done. You must always remember that. We all knew that your father was going to die and it's awful that you were with him when he did – but it's better than if he'd been alone, isn't it?'

Naomi smiled at her and gave a little nod. 'Yes. Thank you, Sister. Can we see him again when Mum arrives?'

'Of course you can. You'll want to say goodbye.' She straightened up as someone knocked on the door. 'Come in . . . oh, good afternoon, Mrs Barlow. I'm so sorry, but . . . well, I'll leave you with your family for a few minutes. I'll be outside when you're ready.'

As the door closed Naomi rushed across the room. 'Mum!'

'Oh, my darlings.' Florence Barlow's voice was tight with shock as they embraced. 'Tim. Richard. Come here.' They closed together in a group, arms clasped around each other. 'It's all right. Dad's better now. I just wish that I'd been with you all. I'm so sorry.'

'No.' Naomi mumbled into the sleeve of her mother's coat. 'Don't say that.'

'You know what I mean.' Florence stroked her daughter's fair hair as she kissed it. 'Let's say some prayers for him.'

'Not now.' Naomi began to pull herself away. 'We'll do it later ... we ought to go and see him first.'

'If that's what you want. Richard? Tim? All right, let's go and find Sister.'

The curtains in the side ward were of a thin mauve material which turned the sunshine seeping through them into pale purple, masking Harold Barlow's face with lavender. The sister stood by the door just inside the room as his family gathered in silence round the bed. Florence looked at him for a long time, then bent down and kissed him.

'Goodbye, my dear,' she whispered. 'Thank you.'

All the children began to weep.

'We'll leave him now,' their mother said. 'Just say goodbye. He loved you all so very much.'

One by one, they kissed their father, even his sons at the last, then Florence led them out of the room and the sister locked the door again. The tears of guilt and grief spilled on Harold Barlow's face glistened in the soft, sombre light before evaporating in the heat of the afternoon.

Later that day, when neighbours in Tattersall Close saw the drawn curtains they told each other what a blessing it was. So sad. Such a nice family. How dreadful for the children to lose their father. But such a relief for Mrs Barlow. They looked in the *Wilmsford Messenger* for the announcement, then attended the funeral, some from affection, some from a sense of social duty, some because such events filled a morbid need, an acquaintance with grief without the pain of personal loss. It was, they agreed, done properly. Two official cars following the creeping hearse, floral tributes suitably fulsome but not vulgar, dignified. Mrs Barlow in proper black, the children in school uniform with black ties for the boys. In the crematorium chapel, as metal rollers carried the coffin through the doors, they noticed how the children held each other's hands as they stood in the front pew with their mother. So brave, so mature, even though they were so young; Mr Barlow had brought them up so well.

Book Two

Prologue

At 11.30 on the morning of 27 December Daphne Byron, editor of the *Post*, read the latest confused and conflicting information on her computer screen, then turned to Brian Durham, her deputy news editor.

'Have we got *any* bloody hard facts on this?' she asked.

'Precious few,' he told her. 'As far as we can work out, most of the family were in the house, and we know Dick was taking Stephanie with him. The only fact we're certain of is that two of them are dead.'

'And we've still not heard from Dick?'

'No. His mobile's disconnected. In the meantime, the Manchester staff are chasing anything on Dick's mother and brother, and there's a stringer digging around in Leeds. Stansfield's son is at university there. One of Dick's daughters is at Oxford, so we're asking questions there as well. Trevor, Penny and Nick are out on it – incidentally, the police have put that press conference back again – and picture desk have sent Terry and Derek. I've got reporters phoning everyone we can think of, but people are still away for Christmas. That's about it at the moment.'

Gold bangles on Daphne Byron's wrist clinked as she lit a cigarette. She had not planned to be in the office that day but had hired a private helicopter when the paper had telephoned the news to her apartment in Paris. The editor had to be there for such a story, but her position was ambivalent. When Richard Barlow had poached her from the *Daily Mirror* years before, they had had a brief affair which she had used as the first step of her eventual rise to the top. He had not objected – the news desk was as far as he wanted

93

to go – but he had continually played on what he regarded as their special relationship. Too many people on the *Post* knew about that affair and it had become a flaw in her reputation for icy professionalism. Many other editors – even highly successful ones – had been brought down because they had left an exposed weakness, but if she got rid of Dick Barlow, one of the hardest of journalism's hard men, then nobody would dare try to challenge her. She had begun a process of not inviting him to key editorial meetings, overruling his decisions and making sure everyone knew, appointing outsiders who would help in freezing him out. As she had crossed the Channel that morning, she had reflected that his death might be a tragedy for some but would save her a lot of trouble.

'Do we have any idea at all who's dead?' she asked.

'Nothing definite,' Durham told her. 'The *Express* apparently has a line that one of them's the grandmother, but nobody else is saying it and we can't get confirmation. Penny's been leaning on the police press liaison officer, but he's keeping shtum until the conference. We've got someone monitoring Hertfordshire police radio, but they're wise to that trick. Perhaps someone'll let something slip, but everything's being done by phone.'

'What the hell are they playing at? They've said they'll release the names. Why not now?'

'The official line is that they're still making enquiries.'

'Bollocks. It's some bloody copper who wants his moment of glory on television.'

'Maybe.' Durham shrugged. 'It's academic anyway. The names will be announced long before we come out tomorrow. We just need to get our own angle on it.'

'Make sure we do. We can wipe out the opposition without Dick Barlow's help. Right?'

'Right.' Durham was fully aware of the situation. Dick Barlow was yesterday's man and the right sort of result on this story would further erode his reputation for being indispensable – if he was still alive to need it.

'I want all copy of everything we get on this put into my personal queue,' Daphne Byron added. 'Everything. PA, leaks, tip-offs. The lot. The moment it arrives. Understand?'

'OK,' Durham agreed. 'I'll create a file catchlined "Barlow". Everything'll be in there ... and I assume you're taking morning conference.'

'Of course ... what size are we tomorrow?'

'Thirty-two.'

'Christ, that's not enough. I'll get four pages put on.' She gestured towards her screen as she picked up a telephone and started to punch the buttons. 'Splash, turning to page three and a spread on four and five. Centre pages as well if we can get enough copy. Pictures of everyone and quotes from as many as we can get hold of. I do not want to hear that any other paper has signed up anyone from that house exclusively. Forget the budget, we outbid everyone else. Just get on with it, and ... Jimmy?' She spoke into the phone. 'Daphne. I'm putting another four on tonight's edition ... I don't give a shit if we haven't got the ads to cover it. I'll clear it with the sixth floor. What's the print run? How many? No way. Put on another forty thousand minimum. I'll give you the story to sell them ... yes, I'll clear that as well. And I want printed bills for London and the Home Counties ... how do I know how many? You're in charge of circulation. As many as it needs. I'll message the wording to you as soon as I can ... what time? I don't fucking know yet. Just make sure you're ready for it.'

She slammed the phone down and looked at Durham again. 'Big chance for you, this one. Don't screw up.'

'Don't worry.'

'I'm not worrying ... but you should be.'

Walking back to the news desk, Durham knew what he had to deliver. Better angles, quotes and pictures than the opposition, and nobody was going to ask too many questions about accuracy; as long as it read better, that would be enough. And when Dick Barlow came back – if Dick Barlow came back – he would find that the ground had crumbled beneath him a little more.

'New line on PA, Brian,' one of the reporters shouted as he sat down at the news desk, and he automatically hit a pre-programmed button on his keyboard to call up the service.

```
HSA581244 PAHOME        PA              11.39
```
PASNAPFULL Bodies Advisory
URGENT. ATTENTION NEWS EDITORS AND CHIEF SUBS
Not for publication. Two men seen leaving shotgun deaths house in Brookmans Park, Hertfordshire, accompanied by police officers.
Trying for identities.

Durham picked up a telephone. 'What's Trevor's mobile speed-call number?'

'Seventeen, seventeen.'

He punched the buttons. 'Trevor? Brian Durham. PA have got a line on two men leaving the house. Did you see them? You're not there? Talking to who? ... What about? ... shit ... make sure it's exclusive or the editor'll have your balls for breakfast. I'll try Nick.' Durham rang off and called an alternative number.

'What does he say?' someone asked as he waited.

'He's with some woman who's telling him that Naomi Stansfield bought her husband a shotgun for Christmas. Looks like he's got it to himself. Nick's still at the house ... Nick? Brian ... yes, it's just come through on PA. What? Who's saying that? Are they certain? All right. Get back to me as soon as you confirm it.'

He rang off again. 'Nick saw them leave. He says one's Stansfield, but he isn't positive about the other one. Might have been his son or Dick's brother. They were straight out of the house and into the car. However, he's certain neither of them was Dick.'

'Where did the police take them?'

'Headquarters, apparently. Penny's got that staked out.' A phone rang and he snatched it up. 'Penny? Good timing. Stansfield's apparently alive and he and another man have been seen leaving the house. Any sign of them with you? What? But Nick's got a positive identification on him! Jesus Christ! Bend that bloody press officer's ear again. Promise to sleep with him if you have to. I want to know exactly who—'

'PA again, Brian.'

'Hang on, Penny,' Durham snapped as he called the agency service up on to his screen again.

```
HSA581280 PAHOME          PA           11.44
PASNAPFULL Advisory urgent
POLICE Bodies
ATTENTION PICTURE EDITORS
Picture of two men leaving Hertfordshire double-death house now
available on PA Pictures. Still seeking confirmation of names.
```

'PA have got a pic at the house,' Durham said into the phone. 'We'll check against that. Keep chasing your end.' He crashed the phone down and shouted across to the picture desk. 'PA pic of two men leaving the house. Where the hell is it?'

'Coming over now, but it looks as though it was taken from the next county. What does Penny say?'

'She's been told that one of them's Dick.'

'Did she see him?'

'No. They whipped them in the back way. Bastards. But a copper at the house hinted that one was Stansfield. That's all we need, the police pissing us about ... are they sending that pic by fucking carrier pigeon?'

'Two minutes.'

The picture had been hastily snatched from the gate, nearly twenty yards from the front door; the figures were slightly out of focus and one was half hidden by the winter leaves of an overhanging beech tree at the side of the drive.

'What do you think?' Durham held the result up to one of his colleagues who had been peering over his shoulder. 'Could that be Dick behind the tree?'

'It's such a crap image that even the one you can see could be anybody.'

'Has anyone ever met Dick's brother or his brother-in-law?' Durham shouted across the news room.

'I met Stansfield at a press conference once,' a reporter called back.

'Come and look at this . . . is that him?'

The reporter held the picture close to his eyes and squinted. 'Possibly. He's about the right height. But I'm not positive. Sorry.'

'Have photographic blow both of them up,' Durham ordered. 'Get them round to anyone we can find who works for Kennet Bolingbroke and wire it up to Manchester so they can check if anyone recognizes Tim Barlow.' Two telephones rang on the desk simultaneously; he grabbed the private line as somebody else answered the second.

'Durham . . . yes, Penny . . . who did you hear it from? . . . anybody else got it? . . . what's the address?' He grabbed a piece of paper and began to write. 'Twenty-seven what? . . . Colander Drive? . . . spell it . . . Holland Drive . . . got it . . . OK . . . no, you stay there. Just make bloody sure he doesn't talk to anyone else. Hang on.' He turned to the reporter who had been trying to identify Stansfield. 'Penny's had a tip from some kid on the local paper that Naomi's been having it off with some Tory councillor. That's the name and address. Get out there and talk to him . . . and make sure nobody else gets a sniff of it.'

As the reporter hurried away, Durham spoke into the phone again. 'OK, Penny, we're on to that. Any more on who they've taken from the house? Well keep chasing it.'

He rang off as Daphne Byron appeared at the news desk. 'I told you to keep me informed.'

'I haven't had time and all hell's breaking loose here. Two men have been seen leaving the house, but God alone knows who they are.'

'Is either of them Dick?'

'Penny's been told he is, but we're not certain.' He offered her the wired photograph. 'Have a look for yourself. That damned tree makes it impossible to identify the one on the left and the one you can see isn't much better.'

'Are we positive it's two men?' Byron asked. 'The one behind the tree could be a woman wearing trousers.'

'Let's have a look ... Christ, it could. I'll have Penny check it out. Incidentally, Trevor's got a line that Naomi bought her husband a shotgun for Christmas. Pick the bones out of that. And Penny's been told she's been having an affair with a local councillor. Mark's just gone out to talk to him.'

'Anybody else got either of those?'

'Not as far as we know.'

'Keep it that way. Everything into my queue. Now.'

As the morning passed, fact and fiction, rumour and speculation mixed together while frequently conflicting information was being gathered by other newspapers. The journalists knew that the truth lay inside the house in Devon Lane, but when that was revealed everyone would have it and it would be worthless. The important thing was the exclusive angle, and they chased anything – unsubstantiated rumour, guesswork, hunches – that promised it. Perhaps many of the things they were being told weren't true, but in a business that succeeds on readable lies, that wasn't particularly important.

Chapter One: Roberta

HSA581300 PAHOME   PA   11.50
POLICE Bodies (reopens)

Steven Boussana (correct), 24, Roberta Stansfield's boyfriend, a student at the London School of Economics, said: 'I was going to go with her to Hertfordshire for Christmas, but my mother was taken ill and I had to pull out. Roberta telephoned me on Christmas Day morning and sounded fine. She certainly didn't indicate that anything was wrong.

'I've tried ringing the house, but the police will not tell me anything. They say they will only give information to next of kin, but virtually all Roberta's family were with her so there's no one I can ask.

'I'm worried sick about her. There's no way she wouldn't have tried to get in touch to say she was safe.'

Mark Dyson, a producer with BBC Radio news, also said that they had not heard from Roberta Stansfield since news of the tragedy broke.

'We can only think that she's too involved in comforting the rest of her family to contact us and say she's all right,' he added.

Two years ago I was so deliriously happy that it frightened me if I thought about it too much. Martin was the centre of my life and I was caught up in a this-is-the-only-possible-man-in-the-world-for-me-and-I-want-to-have-his-babies affair. Shortly after we met he qualified as a doctor, joined the staff of St Bartholomew's Hospital and started to build his career; I was ridiculously besotted. We took holidays in India and California, held hands during concerts, discovered new restaurants, shared private jokes and comments that only we understood; I carried a picture of him in my bag and would just take it out and stare at it. Then one night I had to leave the studio early because I felt ill; when I got home he was in bed with my flatmate. That is what they call a formative experience.

The worst thing was that it made me feel incredibly inadequate; the best thing was that it strengthened my relationship with Mummy and Daddy. I went running home and they listened as I sobbed my heart out and talked until all hours of the morning, understanding attacks of hysterics or depression, just being there. I'm not sure how I'd have coped without them – even if I'd have coped at all. And when I stopped being semi-suicidal they let me go with no guilt and no debts. I like to think that one day I will feel secure enough to fall desperately in love again and this time I won't get smashed down, but, whoever he is, he'll have to accept that however much I give him there'll always be a part kept back for my parents. At this stage of my life they are my closest friends; it's not a Freudian hang-up, just a recognition of what they did to help me. It's an attitude that will change, of course.

I'm over the self-pity now and live in another flat in Muswell Hill (no flatmate this time). Steve's my second boyfriend since The Disaster, but I think he's getting too close, so bye-bye time could be approaching; I'm simply not ready yet. I'm an assistant news producer with Radio Four, having sort of drifted into it when a second-class degree in medieval European history at Somerville offered limited career openings; frankly I wasn't mad keen on the subject but wanted to go to Oxford. I'm not sure what I want now; for obvious reasons I'm cautious about any form of commitment. I'm twenty-three years old, five foot four and very slim – skinny if you want to be blunt about it. I have what romantic writers would call a heart-shaped face and the less poetic describe as having a wide forehead and pointed chin; my lips are thin, my eyes hazel and my hair reddish brown in a pageboy cut. I have a 32-inch bust – dammit – but good legs, even though they spend most of their daylight hours in tapered trousers.

When Mummy and Daddy first let me go again, I kept returning home to recharge my confidence batteries. As I crawled to my feet – and realized I was in danger of becoming selfish – that eased off, but I still see them regularly; they're less than half an hour's drive away. And because they were so good to me I felt a need to take a closer interest in them. So how do I see them? If you think that people's personalities are reflected in their appearance, perhaps I ought to begin by describing them.

Mummy started making slightly self-deprecating jokes about her age after she turned fifty, but she's still very attractive, taller than I am, blond hair – largely natural, but with a bit of help – good figure. Her face is . . . well, that depends how you catch her. She doesn't laugh enough; when she does she's incredibly pretty as her sky-blue eyes sparkle. But she suffers regular attacks of what my brother David and I call Mother's Great Sorrow, when she looks as though she's chief mourner at a mass funeral of everyone she knows. We've never understood what causes it. She and Daddy are happily married, David and I are not the sort of children to give her grief – not now, at any rate – and she has everything she wants, hordes of friends and plenty to interest her. But it's as though . . . I'm not sure if I can explain it . . . as though just beneath the surface there's something permanently worrying her. I've tried to talk to her about it, but she won't; she says it's nothing important. But she's lying, and after all I've admitted to her I wish she'd confide in me.

Daddy is a merchant banker, organizing the finances of small governments or international conglomerates. He's one of those people who's aged very well – men are often luckier than women like that – and his face is . . . it's so difficult to describe faces . . . it's lean and urbane, like an athlete with a degree in philosophy. I hate to say I'm closer to him, because I feel I'm betraying Mummy, but it's true. I can remember when I was tiny, waiting to hear his key in the front door when he came home and running to meet him; it probably didn't happen as often as I think it did, but it's one of those memories that colours how I still relate to him, that enormous smile as he puts down his briefcase and bends to scoop me into his arms and raise me up above his head, laughing, the safest hero figure of all. Don't get any stupid ideas; it's a love without shadows and I value it.

So I've been lucky in my parents and reasonably lucky with the rest of my relatives, in that none of them is totally awful and they're all interesting in some way. I still enjoy it when we're all together – usually only at Christmas now.

David is two years younger than me and studying to be an architect; he's disgustingly good looking and conceited with it. I take a malicious pleasure in telling his endless girlfriends that he's got false teeth (he hasn't, of course). We get on very well with each other in a love–hate sort of way.

The extended family is just on Mummy's side because Daddy was an only child and his father is in a nursing home now, suffering from bloody Parkinson's disease. That's heavy for me, although I try to keep it to myself. When I was small, Grandpa was an absolute sweetie, spoiling David and me rotten, incredibly patient and perceptive. I learnt everything I know about wine from him, he was the first person to take me to Paris, where we spent hours in the Louvre and he bought me my first real drink. Now he's like the ruins of a beautiful house that you loved and grew up in, and every time I see him I want to scream at God for letting that happen to such a lovely man ... sorry, I shouldn't have started on that. Let it go.

When I was fifteen I decided I wanted to be a writer and practised on the family. I described Uncle Tim – I still called him that then – as 'one of those people doomed to play the triangle in the great orchestra of life' (I'd been reading Saki and it was catching). It sums him up, though, surrounded by people doing things, humbly waiting to make his little contribution. He's got an apologetic, hesitant face that you don't know whether to kiss in sympathy or slap in frustration. I'll swear he sleeps in that Harris tweed sports jacket, although he does appear to own several pairs of trousers to go with it. He's a teacher at Wilmsford JMI School, where he himself went more than forty years ago; it's as if he never left it. Claire, his wife, has a scrunched-up personality that makes me think of a rubber toy crammed into a box that's too small, constantly straining to burst loose. It's not just because she's married to Tim; years ago they had a baby who died, and she couldn't have any more. She's a nursery nurse – classic sublimation – and I feel very sorry for her, because I can appreciate how frustrated she is. They both give the impression of being reasonably contented, but I sometimes wonder if they're happy – even if they've ever been happy.

Then there's Tim's twin brother, and we're on another planet. I spent half my time despising and the rest grudgingly admiring Richard. He's an absolute, one hundred per cent, bastard – and a bloody sexist – but as a journalist myself I recognize that he's a brilliant professional. The *Post* is crap, of course, but it's what more than three million people want to read every morning. He has a very hard face – think of James Mason in a foul mood – and his hair is cut short and combed forward; his teeth look as though he chews wood. Since he left his wife, Kate, there has been the usual series of bimbos to fulfil a middle-aged man's case of need, the latest being Stephanie, who has the mental capacity of an amoeba and the combined mammary glands of three normal women. Richard's daughters are chalk and cheese as well; Kathy, his elder one, is reading English at Balliol, but Emma, who's seventeen, is shacked up with a bunch of undesirables in Hackney, into drugs and God knows what else. One of Richard's few redeeming features is that he genuinely loves them, and Emma worries him more than he admits.

Then there's Mummy's mother, whom I absolutely adore. I called her Nana when I was little, then it was Granny for a while, but now it's Grandmama, which is a little posy joke between us; if I'm telling her off, it's Grandmama Florence. She's turned seventy, but you'd never think it, slight, impish – caustic when she wants to be – slyly dropping occasional hints that if she ever told the whole story of her life ... What she's admitted to me in confidence is enough; my sweet little Grandmama was quite a goer in her time. But Mummy and her brothers look on her as the Ageing Parent and she is different with them. It must all be tied up with how they became conditioned to see her when they were young, but there's a lot they don't know – perhaps they wouldn't want to – and I can't tell them. The worst one for this is Tim, who still lives near her in Manchester and calls in at least a couple of times a week. It's so obviously the little-boy-who-never-grew-up syndrome that it's almost funny, but I often think there's something about his behaviour that irritates Grandmama. No, not irritates ... worries her in some way. I sometimes wonder if it's tied up with the thing I've never managed to pin down; what happened to Grandmama's husband.

The basic facts were that he died in 1959 from a brain tumour after being unconscious for about a year. As that was ten years before I was born, he's never been anything more to me than a name and a face in photographs in which he looks dreadfully old-fashioned – like everyone else in them. The first thing that caught my attention was that Mummy obviously found it difficult to talk about him, which was strange because he'd been dead about twenty-five years before I started asking questions; she could hardly still be grieving. The only thing she seemed to remember was him spanking her once because she bought a pop record; getting that out of her was like drawing teeth, and then she didn't want to say any more. The uncles were more forthcoming, but it was as if they were remembering two completely different people. Richard dismissed him as 'a boring old fart'; even for him it sounded well over the top about his own father. Tim was completely the opposite, embarrassingly sentimental, going on about what a marvellous dad he'd been, how he taught them to play cricket, what a pity it was that his grandchildren had never known him. But with all three of them there seemed to be strict limits on how much they were prepared to say; sometimes I felt as if I was intruding.

I half forgot about it until about a year later when I went up to Manchester on my own to stay with Grandmama. One afternoon we were chatting as she did some embroidery when the picture of my grandfather on the desk reminded me.

'What was ... I expect I ought to say Grandpapa ... what was he like?' I asked.

She gave me her 'Now what are you up to, young lady?' look over the top of her spectacles.

'Grandpapa? Yes, I expect you would have called him that. Why do you want to know?'

I shrugged. 'Just interested. We've never really talked about him. Am I like him in any way?'

She laughed. 'Not in the least. You'd have to be a throwback to the last century. I'm not sure that he could have coped with you.'

'You do.'

That seemed to make her think for a moment, then she put down her embroidery, got out of her chair, went to the desk in the corner of the room, opened the top drawer and took out a photograph album.

'Yes, I do,' she confirmed. 'And I'm not sure how he'd have coped with that either. Let's look at these.'

That was the first time I realized what a beautiful woman she had been. There were snapshots of their honeymoon in Wales and she was absolutely gorgeous, with the sort of looks that transcend changes in fashion. Grandpapa – no, I can't call him that; I'll say Harold like she does – Harold was rather handsome as well, but only by the standards of the time, greased hair and little moustache, rather stern and uptight, I thought, for a man who should have been enjoying himself.

'But what was he like?' I asked again as we moved through the years and reached pictures of them with their children. 'He looks horribly pompous in some of these.'

'Yes, he was pompous.' She smiled. 'Although I didn't think of him like that. Not then. He was very correct. Fun wasn't natural to him.'

'Didn't that annoy you? You're fun.'

'Thank you.' She ruffled my hair. 'I try my best. But Harold just wasn't like that. I don't think it annoyed me. I accepted it. He was a very good husband – and a good father.'

She recalled odd stories about him – none particularly interesting – as we turned the pages, then the photographs stopped. The last one had a caption beneath it: 'March 1958: Harold in the garden two days before he fell ill.' Grandmama looked at it for a moment, then closed the album.

'There were never any more, of course,' she said and it was impossible to miss the brittleness in her voice.

'What actually happened?' I asked. 'I know he had a brain tumour, but was there really nothing they could do?'

'Not in those days.' She traced the word 'Photographs' embossed in gold on the album's padded cover with the fingers of one hand. 'Perhaps something would have been possible now, but all they could offer then was to keep him alive . . . if you could call it living. They told me he might live for years.'

'But he died quite quickly, didn't he?'

'Yes. It was . . . let me remember . . . it must have been about fifteen months after he collapsed. Quite suddenly, but very peacefully, in the hospital.'

I squeezed her hand, part comforting, part apologizing. 'Sorry. I didn't want it to upset you.'

'It's all right. You're going through one of those emotional stages where pain's very dramatic. It's perfectly normal, but when you're as old as I am, you'll discover that . . .' She looked guilty. 'Oh dear, I'm being patronizing, aren't I?'

'A bit,' I told her.

'Then it's my turn to apologize.' She took the album back to the desk. 'It hurt an awful lot, of course, but life has to go on.'

'How did it affect Mummy and the boys?' For a moment she didn't reply, and seemed unnecessarily concerned with putting the album back in the drawer.

'Do you mean immediately or afterwards?' she finally asked.

'Both, I expect.'

She looked across the room at me, thoughtful and enquiring. 'Have you talked to any of them about it?'

'Yes . . . well no, not properly. I've asked what he was like, but—'

'What did they say?' Her interruption was unexpectedly sharp.

'Sorry? Oh ... I can't remember all of it now. It was ages ago. I think Mummy still misses him, even after all this time. Uncle Tim told me about him teaching them to play cricket.' I kept Richard's comment to myself. 'To be honest, they didn't seem to want to say very much.'

'Didn't they?' That appeared to interest her. 'Did they say they loved him?'

'Of course they did.' But when I thought about it, only Tim had actually said that.

Grandmama seemed to be thinking again as she went back to her usual chair. 'What about the day he died? Did they tell you about that?'

'I don't think they mentioned it.' I was beginning to wonder what I had got into; looking back, that afternoon was when our relationship began to change and I increasingly became her confidante. 'Apart from saying that he was still in hospital and had never woken up, and ... well he just died, didn't he?'

'Yes, he just died ... did they tell you they were alone with him when it happened?'

'What?' That really shook me. 'No. Were they?'

'Yes. I used to sit with him every afternoon during the week, but on Saturdays they went to give me a chance to do the shopping and other things there hadn't been time for. The hospital called me just after I came home, but when I got there your grandfather had been dead for half an hour.'

'And they'd been there when it happened? That must have been awful for them ... and for you.'

'It wasn't too bad for me. It was a shock, of course, because there'd been no reason to expect it so suddenly, but I'd come to terms with the fact that it would happen sooner or later. As for how they felt ... well, to be perfectly honest, Roberta, I don't know. And if they don't want to talk about it perhaps it's better left alone.' The clock on the mantelpiece struck four. 'Good heavens, look at the time! My hair appointment's at quarter past. I'll be back by five-thirty. Make yourself a cup of tea and watch some television.'

It was a perfectly genuine reason for ending the conversation, but I had the instant feeling that she was somehow grateful for the excuse. She went and put on her coat and told me to help myself to the fig roll biscuits she still thought I enjoyed (I did, but was becoming weight conscious). After she had gone I took out the album and looked through it again, thinking about my mother and uncles at their father's bedside when he died; it was gruesome, but it happened to lots of people. Having never seen a dead body, the thought of one held a sort of repulsive fascination, something you wanted to experience and shied away from at the same time. I tried to imagine what it must have been like. They'd have been teenagers, so I tried thinking of how I'd have felt sitting in a hospital room with my father lying silent and paralysed on the bed. The way he'd been for more than a year. For the first few visits, they'd have been awkward and uncomfortable, unable to do anything, but thinking it was distasteful to try and behave with any sort of normality. After a while they would surely have become accustomed to it, absorbing the abnormal as part of their lives. Then one afternoon they realized that he was dead. How? There must have been something that at least one of them noticed. Then what? Had Mummy thrown herself on him, weeping? Had they all cried? Did they want their mother? I would have.

After that I could imagine how I'd have felt if it had been Daddy, but I couldn't put myself inside their minds. But the thing that struck me most strongly was that there was no way they could have forgotten being there when it happened, yet not one of them had mentioned it. Why not? Because, even after all these years, it was still too painful? Because they still felt guilty for not noticing something was wrong quickly enough so that they could call for a nurse, which might have saved him ... or maybe they didn't *want* him to get better and had seen something was wrong but hadn't done anything until it was too late? And was that what Grandmama suspected? That if she'd been there she would have called instantly for help and he might have lived? But to all intents and purposes he could as well have been dead anyway, so letting him die peacefully would surely have been a kindness. I turned it round every which way without knowing if anything I imagined was the truth, and it was still in my mind when Tim called on his way home the next afternoon. As usual, I was irritated at the way he still treated me as a schoolgirl – he hadn't grown up and seemed to think I hadn't either – and found his behaviour towards Grandmama infuriating. It was as if she were senile, not the shrewd, capable woman I knew her to be. As he was leaving, I followed him out to his car.

'Grandmama's been telling me about my grandfather,' I announced casually.

He paused as he was about to put the key in the door. 'What's she been saying?'

'What he was like. I was interested.'

'I've told you that,' he said. 'He was very nice.'

'We talked about when he died as well,' I added. 'I didn't know that you and Mummy and Uncle Richard were there when it happened.'

'Did she tell you that?' He snapped the question out.

'Yes. It's true, isn't it? There were just the three of you. But none of you mentioned that when I asked you about him.'

'Didn't we?' He looked down as if to make sure he was positioning the key in the right place. 'Well, there are some things you don't talk about.'

'Why not?' I demanded. I wasn't letting him off that easily.

'When you're older you'll understand.' The lock clicked and he opened the car door.

'Understand what?' His pompousness maddened me. 'It must have been awful, but it's nothing to be ashamed about.'

'Of course it isn't.' He sounded defensive. 'But we don't talk about it.'

'Not ever?' I persisted. 'Not even to each other?'

'Well sometimes we ... don't you ever stop asking questions, Roberta?' Before I could say anything else, he was in the car and starting the engine. He didn't wave as he drove away.

Still annoyed with his condescension, I felt slightly guilty, as though I had callously tried to force open an old, very painful wound. Tim can be infuriating, but he has the vulnerability of someone who is very gentle and it had been unkind of me to press him like that. But . . . oh, I don't know what the 'but' was. Because it had all happened so long ago, because they all surely would have come to terms with it by now, because lots of things.

And I remembered how they'd been when I was dreaming of being a writer, trying to draw something out of my own family for raw material and despairing that we were boring, comfortably off, middle-class ordinary, exactly like everybody else. Jane Austen could have done something with them, but not me. I'd wanted Brontë neuroses, Dickensian misfortune, passion like Dante and Beatrice; I'd have even settled for a Somerset Maugham stutter. But all I'd been offered was the mundane and irrelevant, not a single word about that shattering afternoon at the hospital. It's so long ago now, it doesn't matter, of course, but I sometimes wonder why they kept it secret, as though it was shameful.

Chapter Two: Naomi

HSA581309 PAHOME   PA   12.11
POLICE Bodies

Dr Patrick Evans, chairman of the Hertfordshire and North London branch of Child Support, described Naomi Stansfield as one of its most active fund-raisers.

'If anybody has a heart of gold, it is Naomi,' he said. 'Nothing is ever too much trouble for her and she is always conscious of other people's needs. She is one of the nicest people I know and is open with everyone. I cannot believe there is anything about her that anyone could criticize. She has tremendous affection for her family and they are all very close, even though her mother lives so far away.

'These murders must be the work of an outsider. There was an armed robbery in this area only a few weeks ago, and I'm convinced it has happened again with tragic results.'

The most important thing about me – the thing by which I have survived – is that I'm not Naomi Barlow any more. I'm Naomi Stansfield, not just by marriage but by everything about me. It's been like that for so long that it's now completely natural; I am not living a lie, I have become another person. Charles was with Conrad International when we married in 1967, eight years after Father's death, but joined Kennet Bolingbroke in 1983. His job frequently involves social gatherings with the great and the good, foreign dignitaries, diplomats, senior Whitehall economists, even the occasional royal. I have one entire wardrobe of clothes for those evenings when I am the perfect executive wife, polite and slightly deferential to the men, asking the women about their children and where they are going for their holidays. I have an inexhaustible collection of small-talk gambits and always introduce three new topics into any conversation.

At home in Brookmans Park – Green Belt suburban Hertfordshire about half an hour from the centre of London – I do all the right things as well. School governor, active in the local church, organizer of Red Cross and Cancer Relief house-to-house collections, part-time assistant in the Children's Society charity shop, fund-raising coffee mornings for all causes, envelope stuffer and canvasser for the Conservative Association. Charles and I go to a West End theatre at least twice a month and our villa in the Dordogne is as plush and elegant as our home. It's an inconceivable distance from the daughter of a skilled engineer in middle-class Manchester; it has to be. My present friends and admirers – I've been chatted up in the most civilized manner by an Ambassador, an elderly GCMG and, on one nerve-wracking occasion, the wife of a Principal Private Secretary – would raise a very shocked eyebrow if they knew some of the things that happened in that period after Naomi Barlow ran screaming from her father's accusing corpse.

During the year or so when he was ill, I had started finding boyfriends. It wasn't difficult because I was attractive enough, but I had never dared do it while he was in the house; he'd have seen them off and told me to concentrate on my school work. Mother raised no objections – she had more than enough on her mind, anyway – and I embarked on the usual groping in the back row of the cinema, grateful that nylon tops wouldn't show creases when I got home, having my hand firmly moved against the front of bulging trousers, accompanied by urgent muttered requests to press harder. I found it irritating when I wanted to watch the film, but it was expected if he'd paid for the seats. I started drinking cider as well, and it was years later that I learnt it was actually more alcoholic than beer. But, as clumsy male fingers unfastened buttons and fumbled with bra clasps, there were limits to how far I would go, no matter how much effort it took to stop. At extreme moments I found that the image of my unconscious father was a total passion killer and I used it regularly. For reasons I could never understand I lied to other girls at school, in that I gave the impression that a great deal more had happened, but I was still no more than the slightly shop-soiled virgin daughter on the afternoon of 17 June 1959. Father's funeral was a week later and two weeks after that I cried in pain as I lost my innocence – to a sixth former whose name I can't remember, but he had an adolescent boil on his neck – on a warm, dusky evening in dust-smelling long grass at the edge of Wilmsford playing fields. No, that's not true; I'd lost my innocence in that hospital ward.

The following September I started at Sheffield University, reading English; if they'd had a degree course in shagging I'd have come out with First Class Honours (my generation was threatened with the Bomb, not Aids). I can't remember half their names now, and daren't even think about the total number; one week there were four different ones. It was relentless, meaningless, endless sex. Angry, demanding, like a starving woman gorging herself in a food store. I didn't come out of it until early in my final year, when I woke up in my bedsit one morning to find that the latest one-night-stand had already gone. No note, no half waking me for a whispered, appreciative goodbye; just laid and left behind. Something clicked and I cried for the first time since Father's death, then went into purdah to sort myself out.

I accepted the reason for what I'd been doing. Because I'd killed my father, I had to shake him off by behaving as utterly unlike what he'd made me as possible. I'd spent two years defying his ghost. Look at me. I can't be your daughter. This isn't Goody Two Shoes Naomi Barlow. This is a tart who'll strip for any man who fancies her – and there are plenty of them. I've been fucked in bed, on the floor, in the back of a car, against a wall at a drunken party. If you want more proof I'll do it with two of them at the same time, I'll let someone take photographs, I'll even ... Why? Because that means I'm not your daughter, of course, and I've got to have that because if I am your daughter, *I can't stand it!* I can't live with what I did to you! Do you want me to spend the rest of my life feeling guilty! Please. Go away. Leave me alone . . .

Inevitably, I found religion for a while, still running, of course, but this time keeping my clothes on. I dabbled in Buddhism, found a Jesuit priest to talk to, read Dame Julian of Norwich, even attended a Billy Graham revival meeting where I paid ten shillings to be saved. I convinced myself I was stumbling towards some sort of redemption and went through a ridiculous brief period of considering becoming a nun. That phase passed, like everything else, and I drifted back into the familiar, safe Church of England, holding on to a vague idea about some sort of life doing good works as a form of penance. When I wasn't praying I knuckled down to studying and my performance improved dramatically. Then, in my final term, Paul Fletcher, one of my tutors, invited me to his house. My instant reaction was to suspect a pass – I had become hyperconscious of sex and treated it like a devil permanently waiting to trap me again – but told myself not to be uncharitable. He was in his late thirties, married with a family, and there had never been anything about him to suggest he was the sort of lecturer who regarded available girl students as one of the perks of the job. And when he made the invitation, after we'd been discussing one of my essays, he showed an unexpected concern and awareness.

'Is anything the matter?' he asked casually.

'What do you mean?'

'You've become . . . withdrawn lately. I could always count on you to throw out awkward questions, but now you just sit there like a church mouse . . . and you look very unhappy.'

I pulled back sharply; I was still too tender for kindness. 'I'm all right. I've just been working hard.'

'I'm fully aware of that, and I'm glad you have,' he said drily. 'You used only to run on two cylinders. I had the impression that your social life took up a lot of your time.'

'I don't think that's anyone's business but mine.' I wasn't in my confessional mood that morning.

'It isn't,' he agreed. 'However, if you continue putting your back into it you should come out with a decent degree. All right. Same time next week. Thank you, Naomi.'

He started to read someone else's essay, but as I was leaving he spoke again without looking up.

'Are you free on Sunday afternoon by any chance?'

'Why?'

'My wife and I are having a few students and some of the profs round for drinks in the garden. Would you like to come?'

'Oh.' It was the first time he had ever suggested we should meet outside the limits of my studies. 'Thank you. Yes, I would.'

'About three o'clock, then.' He turned a page, scribbling some comment on it. 'You know where we live, don't you? What used to be the vicarage on the corner of Warwick Road. Don't worry if you can't make it for any reason. It's quite informal.'

I walked home pondering the invitation. It suddenly seemed that Dr Fletcher was taking an interest in me because I was doing some work at last. A couple of his colleagues had taken an interest for very different reasons, and I hadn't disappointed them, thus adding adultery to my activities in one case. I decided to go; it fitted in with my new, purer self.

When I arrived – flat shoes, high-necked blouse, crucifix on a gold chain, plain black skirt, no make-up – the front door was open and I could see right through the long hall into the kitchen at the back. Beyond that the garden was visible through the window, mingled voices of the guests clearly audible. I still rang the bell and waited until a woman appeared at the kitchen door, holding a glass of wine.

'Hello! Don't just stand there. It's liberty hall.'

She waited as I walked towards her. She was what we called bonny in the north, a polite way of saying she was overweight, so much so that the billowing cotton kaftan could not disguise it. She had a soft round face and curly chestnut hair.

'Margaret Fletcher.' She held out her hand as I reached her. 'Now which one are you?'

'Naomi Barlow. Thank you for inviting me.'

'Naomi? Oh, yes, Paul's talked a lot about you. Come on and meet everybody. You probably know most of them anyway.'

It was a typical university gathering, intellectual discussion and political polemics mixed in with the small talk. The Fletchers had four young children who raced around shouting and screaming, and there was a constant supply of inexpensive wine or beer. Serious long-haired young men argued obscure points with their tutors, an affected girl in her second year became emotional about Castro, someone tried to persuade the professor of music to recognize a direct connection between Wagner and Stan Kenton, one of my former lovers – surprisingly, the only one there – answered every argument by quoting nihilism until he was told to shut up. It was one of the hottest days of the year.

Dr Fletcher welcomed me and introduced me to people I didn't know. After a couple of drinks I began to relax and join in. Margaret Fletcher turned out to be a graduate in logic and moral philosophy who had put it to one side when the family arrived and clearly welcomed the stimulation of adult conversation and I found I was enjoying myself. I felt a sense of regret that I had not behaved in a way that might have brought similar invitations in the past. At one point I realized that I had stopped self-consciously fingering the crucifix as though it was a talisman to reassure my emerging soul. I can't remember what we talked about, but I was being listened to and presenting myself as exactly the sort of student my father would have been proud of. The afternoon was opening up new possibilities; perhaps I could take a postgraduate course, write a thesis, become a female don, retreat into a life of pure intellectualism . . . then someone mentioned an horrific murder a few weeks earlier in which a man had strangled a child.

The case had revived fierce arguments over the question of capital punishment. There had been a tremendous outcry against it after Ruth Ellis had been hanged in 1955, and Britain was moving towards abolition, although that wasn't to come until the end of 1969. Everyone in the group I was with had passionate views, backed up with prejudices, statistics and moral attitudes; as there was obviously no common ground on such a question, the row became heated and I wished I was anywhere else but in that spot. Face flushed with wine and emotion, Margaret Fletcher was going hammer and tongs at a maths tutor.

'That's crap, Bernard!' She almost spat the words at him. 'We're not talking about absolutes. Two plus two always equals four, but you can't apply that sort of simplistic reasoning to life and death. Hanging – or any other means of execution – is barbaric and a sign of failure by any society that permits it. The law recognizes the concept of justifiable homicide, and you have to extrapolate from there.'

'You're not suggesting that all murders are justifiable, are you?' he asked.

'Define justifiable for a start,' she snapped.

'I'm not sure that I can, but the law seems to manage it.'

She groaned impatiently. 'That's not an answer. Is it, Naomi?'

'What?' I was hoping she'd forgotten I was standing next to her. 'An answer to what?'

'Can the law have it both ways by saying "Thou shalt not kill" and then kill people itself, in whatever circumstances?'

'I . . . I've never thought about it.'

'Then you should. All your generation should. And you should start doing something about it. Because there are plenty of people who are meant to be older and wiser who can't see it for the bloody savagery it is . . . and another thing, Bernard . . .'

She was in full flow again as I stepped away from her. All the voices faded to a hum and the colours in the flowerbed opposite me suddenly began to swim together crazily.

'Are you all right?' Dr Fletcher caught hold of my arm as I swayed.

'Yes . . . sorry, it must be the heat. I just went a bit dizzy.'

'Come and sit down.' He led me to a faded deckchair, half shaded by a laburnum tree. 'Would you like a glass of water?'

'No. It's all right. If I sit here I'll be fine. I'm sorry. Don't let it spoil your party. Please ... if I could just be on my own for a few minutes.'

'Of course. If you want to go into the house and lie down just let me know.' I appreciated that he realized how embarrassed I felt. I closed my eyes and lay back as he moved away.

I know it must seem incredible, but never, never for one moment, had the thought of execution entered my mind; there had been too much to handle, too much to compensate for to leave room for questions of legal punishment. I'd been eighteen at the time of Father's death, surely too young to be ... I gripped the wooden frame of the deckchair as terror and nausea flooded through me, then opened my eyes with a start as the chair jerked violently. One of the Fletchers' children was sprawled on the grass at my feet, looking guilty.

'Sorry,' she gasped hastily, then scrambled up and dashed off again, chased by the others, whooping with delight. I watched them tear down to the wall at the end of the garden, screaming with laughter. She had two scruffy knockabout younger brothers, one of whom she wrestled with for a moment before running away again, shouting 'Can't catch me!' She was me with Tim and Richard, carefree, excited, irrepressible on a childhood day of summer. Only – what? – ten years or so earlier I had been like that. It was a natural innocent happiness that everyone loses, of course, but I suddenly felt I would never be able to replace it with something more durable. At any moment, when I was least prepared for it, what I had done would stab me viciously, my conscience wincing in agony. I would never be able to escape, it would always be there waiting ... I held on to a half-formed realization. When I said *I* would never escape, I meant Naomi Barlow, the girl I'd been trying to deny – trying to destroy – in all those endless beds. I'd been doing the right thing, but in the wrong way; what I had to find was a personality to escape into, one so far beyond any realistic dreams that Naomi Barlow could have had as to be impossible. Unexpectedly, I smiled to myself at the thought that one way would be to marry Prince Charles and end up as Queen. But something as preposterous; the first woman Prime Minister – becoming Queen seemed more plausible than that in 1961 – or ... I told myself not to damage a fragile hope by being stupid about it. I'd seen the way out and felt curiously better, that an impossible torment could perhaps be relieved. I would have to live a deception, but that would be more tolerable than a reality that was crucifying me.

'How are you feeling?' Dr Fletcher's voice interrupted my thoughts.

'Much better, thank you.' I stood up. 'I'm dreadfully sorry.'

'Don't apologize. Come and have something to eat. You students always starve yourselves.'

A couple of years ago I read in the *Daily Telegraph* that he'd died – he was only fifty-seven – and felt very sad. He was a good tutor and a kind, perceptive man. And it reminded me of that moment beneath the laburnum tree. Afterwards, it became not an obsession but a deliberately calculated process. I came out with a decent second in English and had to decide what next. Returning to Manchester was obviously out of the question, so I joined what in those days the social analysts referred to as 'The Drift South' and moved to London, where I landed a job with a public relations agency and found myself a flat in Kentish Town. It was the Swinging Sixties, beehive hair-dos, mini skirts, those gorgeous high leather boots, tremendous freedom and excitement. I was young, single and attractive – but still with one thing on my mind. Wearing the best of Carnaby Street and the King's Road, I enjoyed myself and changed my personality at the same time. Lacking a Liverpool accent – amusingly chic in London then – my northern provincialism had to go. I went to elocution classes, devoured guides to etiquette and bought every fashion magazine I could lay my hands on. I enlarged a very limited sophistication with trips to Paris and Florence, attended the latest exhibitions at the Tate and the National, read and quoted from the trendy books, saw all the right plays and films. Within a couple of years I could pass myself off as a perfect product of the Home Counties, with even a suggestion of Roedean if you didn't look too closely. I kept visits to Manchester to an absolute minimum – 'Sorry, Mum, but you wouldn't believe how busy we are at the moment' – and whenever my father crept into my mind I simply threw him out again.

The next stage had to be marriage. There were plenty of prospects – while I was positively abstemious by my previous standards, I slept with a couple of them – but none was spectacularly different enough. As I pushed my way up the social ladder my expectations rose as well. Then, at Wimbledon in 1966, I met Charles. I'd been involved in organizing corporate hospitality for one of our clients and was there on Men's Finals day, handing round the canapés and champagne. I had carefully selected clothes for such events, not blatant, but elegant and understated sexy; these were the occasions when my antennae were on high alert and I needed to be ready. Charles was with a group of other bankers, several older than Methuselah, which at thirty-six made him stand out; he also didn't have a wife with him and actually went out to watch the tennis. I was stuck in the tent of course while Santana beat Ralston in straight sets, but when he returned I asked if it had been a good match. At first he thought I was just doing my job, but then he seemed pleased to find someone who was interested in what was happening; in fact, I was becoming interested in him.

The details don't matter, but I accepted an invitation to play at his own tennis club – I'd been quite good at school and had kept it up as part of my essential lifestyle – and that led to dinner and eventually to bed. His wife had been killed in a plane crash less than a year after they married, so he was quite free and we fell in love with each other. Simple as that ... well, he genuinely fell in love with me; I allowed myself to fall in love with him because he was exactly what I needed. In the November after we met he took me to visit his parents for the weekend; up to then I'd been increasingly confident, but this was the acid test. They lived in a Buckinghamshire mansion – really; parts of it were Jacobean and it fetched one and a half million pounds when they sold it. I smiled a lot as I pushed down my terror and was evasive about my background, although there was no real need. They accepted me for exactly what I seemed to be – a presentable young woman and someone close enough to their son for him to want them to meet her. Charles's father is turned eighty now and suffers from Parkinson's disease; then he was still vigorous and incredibly nice to me. That first weekend, he showed me round the garden – the grounds, it was more than thirty acres – where there was a mulberry tree which family legend said had been planted by Prince Albert; they had actually entertained royalty. All women make a special effort when they meet the man they know they want to marry; from that moment I went into overdrive, even though I had convinced myself he would eventually propose anyway.

Back in London, I devoted an entire evening to composing a letter of thanks to his parents and sent them flowers. At Christmas I bought his mother an expensive brooch and his father a box of the best cigars I could find. I agonized over Charles's present – he really was the man who had everything – before deciding on what seemed a silly idea at first, but what I realized might have the right effect. We weren't living together – not quite the right move, I'd decided – but I had a key to his flat in St John's Wood and often went there after work to wait for him. On the day before we were due to go to Buckinghamshire for the holiday, I rang him from there at the office.

'Hello, you. I've got your Christmas present.'

'Thank you. I promise not to open it until Christmas Day.'

'No, I want you to have it tonight. See you in about an hour.'

Just before seven, I heard him come in and walk through to the living room. 'Naomi? Where are you?'

'In the bedroom.'

He stopped in the doorway as he saw me, lying on the bed with an enormous wide silver ribbon tied in a bow round my waist; apart from Chanel No 5, that was all I was wearing. I opened my eyes very wide and looked helpless.

'I couldn't think of anything to buy you that would say what I want to say. So will you have me as a present instead?'

For a moment he still didn't move, then the most wonderful

smile filled his face. I knew how serious he'd become after Sarah's death, and that something frivolous would reach him. As he reached the bed I sat up and put my arms around his neck and kissed him.

'Happy Christmas, darling,' I whispered. On Christmas Day he proposed to me; his present was my engagement ring.

The wedding was at his parents' parish church the following summer. They had suggested it should be held in my home church, but that was unthinkable. The last time I had been in St Luke's at Wilmsford was for my father's funeral and I had never been back. I said that theirs was much nicer and had all sorts of family connections that were important to them. I was a bit concerned about how my mother and brothers would handle a wedding that would be reported in the county magazine with a junior Cabinet Minister and a Lord Lieutenant among the guests, but there were no problems. Mother was nervously impressed but carried it off, and Richard was blasé about everything; Fleet Street had already given him a jaundiced view of wealth and fame. I asked Tim to give me away; in some ways I'd rather not have done, but it was his place to do so and Charles's family expected it. He was reluctant at first, but I pointed out that he was – just – my older brother and said I wanted him. He felt uncomfortable throughout the whole event, but he survived.

Dressed by Dior – I'd been saving up for that gown for a very long time – the most memorable moment of the day was not when I walked between the pews filled with morning coats and couture, not when Charles and I stood in front of the rector and made our vows, not when they scattered pink and yellow rose petals that caught in my sunlit veil, but when I signed the marriage register in the vestry. For a tiny moment I paused and looked at what I had just written – Naomi Jean Stansfield – and felt as if I had finally put down a terrible weight that I had been carrying for years. During the reception in the huge, flower-filled marquee that the caterers had set up on the front lawn at Temple Manor, Mother came up to me and took both my hands in hers.

'You look so beautiful and so happy,' she said softly, and the tears began to flow. 'He'd have been so very proud of you.'

Controlling my own tears, I leant forward and kissed her cheek, partly in affection, but mainly so that she would not see my face and the look of relief that Naomi Barlow was no more.

Naomi Barlow comes back occasionally, not somehow as the person I used to be, but like someone I once knew and have forgotten. It doesn't happen as often now, but there are still times when that stranger's face appears before me. I tell her that she's dead, like he is; in different ways, I murdered both of them. And her ghost goes away until the next time.

Chapter Three: Tim

`HSA581322 PAHOME    PA            12.23`
POLICE Bodies Advisory
ATTENTION NEWS EDITORS AND CHIEF SUBS
Police press conference on Hertfordshire double killings has been put
back to 15.00.

`HSA581340 PAHOME          PA       12.29`
POLICE Bodies (reopens)
Barry Hughes (30), headmaster of Wilmsford JMI School, Manchester,
where Timothy Barlow has been a teacher for nearly 30 years, said:
'Everyone is utterly devastated. Tim and his wife, Claire, have taken
his mother to spend Christmas with his sister and her family in
Hertfordshire every year for as long as anyone here can remember. It's
become a tradition with them. It should have been just another
normal, happy Christmas. Things like this don't happen to people like
the Barlows.

 'Tim has been part of this school for so long that it's almost impossible
to imagine the place without him. I've had members of staff ringing
me in tears since they heard the news. All we want to hear is that he's
all right, but obviously something terrible has happened.'

A friend of mine was telling me the other day about when he
returned to his old grammar school because it was about to be
closed. It was the first time he'd been inside it since he left more
than twenty years ago.

'It was as though they'd pulled it down and rebuilt everything
on a smaller scale,' he said. 'I remember the hall seeming as big as

a cathedral when we stood in morning assembly, but now it felt almost cramped. And a group of us wandered round for more than an hour arguing about which had been our classroom in the second year.'

My school – my first school, that is – has changed as well, of course, but I've hardly noticed because I've been here while it happened, little by little. When I was a pupil, it was two schools – infants and juniors – each with separate headteachers, Miss Day and Mr Tonks. Now it's Wilmsford JMI, all under Barry Hughes, and the staff are much younger than the ones who taught me. The reason for that is that during the war a lot of teachers were called out of retirement because the young women were serving with the forces and many of them were still there when I began in 1946. They believed in sing-song chanting of times tables and spelling tests and could impose discipline without any problem; we do things differently now, but I often think we may have lost some virtues from the old systems.

When I joined the junior school staff in 1964 the old teachers had gone; but Mr Tonks was still here, although within a couple of years of retirement. My classroom was what I'd known as Mr Foden's room; there were the same iron-legged sloping desks with holes for porcelain inkpots – they'd gone, of course; ballpoint pens were allowed – and even the blackboard fixed to the wall was the one he had used; the screw in the top-right-hand corner that didn't match the others had still not been replaced. One of the things that intrigued me was the first time I did playground duty. A long brick wall runs down one side of the playground with decorative pillars set at regular intervals, about ten feet apart, forming a dozen sections. A group of boys were playing football and the goal was the third section from the corner.

'Why's that particular bit of wall the goal?' I asked one of them. 'Why don't you use one of the others?'

He looked at me in bewilderment, then shrugged, dismissive of a newcomer's ignorance. 'Dunno. It's always the goal.'

He was right. That's where it had been in 1946, and nobody

ever suggested it should be changed, even though there was no logical reason for it. The school had been built in the 1920s, and some unknown boy had made a decision at the start of one of the first playtime soccer games, probably with an old tennis ball and any number a side. Small children are very conservative, so the goal has remained the same for all the thousands of games that have followed, even now. It's somehow comforting.

Why did I become a teacher? I'm not sure. It was just a job that appealed to me. I knew that my A-level results weren't going to be good enough to follow Nimmy to university, but in those days five or six O-levels were enough to get you into teacher-training college. The job at Wilmsford happened to be available when I finished, and . . . It's not important. I had to do something, and teaching's as good a profession as any. I enjoy it and I'm good at it. My only regret is that I wasn't appointed headmaster here, but that's only because when Mr Tonks retired I was obviously too young and when Gordon Davies, his successor, left, the local authority was Labour-controlled and only interested in someone who believed in that ridiculous initial teaching alphabet and letting children express themselves by screaming a lot. Thank God that stupidity has passed. By the time the job became vacant again, I was considered too old; some of my colleagues – including Barry – are a generation younger than me, and I know that 'Mr Chips' has become a behind-my-back nickname in the staff room, but it doesn't bother me.

I could have moved. I went through a period of applying for other jobs, but none of them came off. I was very close with the last one, though, and felt an unexpected relief when I was turned down after the second interview. Then I realized I didn't actually want to leave Wilmsford JMI – another school would have presented the same problems, I was earning enough for my needs, I was perfectly contented when I thought about it. Claire, my wife, has also lived in Wilmsford all her life and neither of us has ever had any wish to move away. All our friends are in the area, and so are our roots. Nimmy and Richard live the best part of two hundred miles away, so I'm the only one left to look after Mother. She's still perfectly independent, of course, but she's turned seventy now and you never know when she might need ... let's get a few things straight.

First, I'm not clinging to the past; parts of that are too painful and all I want to do is forget. Second, there's nothing strange about how I care for my mother. I'm not criticizing Richard and Naomi for what they've done with their lives – that's their choice and I respect their right to it – but you'll find plenty of families in which one member remains closer to the parents than the others. Third, people who think I'm boring don't know me; in fact, nobody really knows me. They see what looks like a grey man in a rut of the safe and the familiar and think that's all there is to it. At school it's ask Tim if you want something done. He's always ready to cover when somebody's off, doesn't mind taking the first-years on those ghastly day trips or organizing the school Christmas pantomime. Outside, Claire and I are the unexciting couple with the ten-year-old Sierra, the ones who don't give dinner parties or go out very much. There's a degree of sympathy among those who remember what happened with Harry, but it's become patronizing. They think that if you scratched my surface there'd be nothing underneath. They wouldn't believe what there is.

First off, I murdered my own father while he was lying helpless in a hospital bed. That man had never harmed me in his life, he'd never done anything that he didn't genuinely feel would be good for me. Do you know anyone with a hang-up to match that? Do you think that these kid teachers I work with could even *conceive* something like that about me? Second, it's nearly twenty-five years since Harry died and I'm still suffering. Not from grief – however agonizing, that becomes tolerable – but from the fact that Claire and I have never been able to replace him.

There's nothing physically wrong with either of us; it would be better if there was. It's just that I can't have sex with my own wife. It was difficult enough before Harry; afterwards, I found it impossible. We had bitter rows about it when she'd accuse me of denying her another child because I was scared, then began to demand explanations that I couldn't give her. We sought help, of course – marriage guidance, a sex therapist – but nothing worked. One of the counsellors became obsessed with my family. What did I remember about my parents' relationship? Did they show affection to each other? Did I ever see them kissing or cuddling? Did I find it difficult to talk about something like that? Too right I found it difficult, but I couldn't tell her why. I could talk about Mum, of course – that wasn't the problem – but not Dad. I had to back off, and couldn't even explain why to Claire. One thing neither of us would consider was divorce. Claire's not excessively religious, but she said she took her marriage vows seriously, and I just couldn't imagine managing without her. Apart from a brief period when I was at teacher-training college, I've never lived on my own.

So we finally came to terms with it – or at least turned our backs on it – but it's seeped into every corner of our lives. The problem is that sex is so all-pervasive now; you can hardly turn on the television without seeing some couple in bed together, and every time it happens one of us leaves the room without saying anything. I don't know how Claire copes, it's impossible for me to ask her, but I know what it's doing to me. There are times when I want her, but I daren't even make the first move now because I know there will eventually be a brick wall and we'll both be hurt again. For a long time she accused me of being gay, but I'm not. I only find other women attractive – and I'm sure I'd be all right with them. Not that I've tried; I've found other alternatives instead. That's personal and nobody knows about it.

So that's what's beneath the surface of boring old Tim Barlow. Guilt over Dad, which I can understand, confusion over my marriage, which I can't. Claire's become a nursery nurse – there were some resentful comments about needing children in her life when she decided to start the training course – and we both close our eyes to the cracks and hope they won't grow any wider. And apart from that salient difficulty we've hammered out a reasonable relationship. We're both members of Wilmsford Amateur Operatic Society, where we met and in which Mum is still active. We've got a shared interest in gardening and visit stately homes to pick up ideas. We're certainly not rich, but we're comfortable. We've made the best of it, and I can live with myself.

The rest of the family we don't see that much, apart from my niece, Roberta, who often comes up to stay with Mother. I appreciate that, but she's what Claire calls a right little madam. All the latest clothes, souped-up Golf GTi, full of whatever's the thing to do or the place to be seen at in London. We think she's stuck-up and spoilt, but she and Mum seem to get on very well, which is odd because you'd not think they'd have anything in common. I don't like calling when she's there, but I still do, of course.

Christmas is the only time we're all together now and it's always at Naomi and Charles's house because Mum enjoys going there. My brother-in-law's as rich as Croesus, but there's no side to him. For a merchant banker he seems to know a lot about education and we have some quite interesting conversations when we meet. They always have a tree nearly as high as the ones you see in department stores, covered in expensive baubles from Harrods that Naomi replaces every year. We've given up trying to match them on presents; there's no way we can afford the fortune that Naomi spends. Claire used to feel embarrassed about it.

'Look at this,' she whispered to me one Christmas morning – I think it was 1976 – as the parcels were handed round. Naomi had given her a blouse. 'It's pure silk. It must have cost a fortune.'

'I've got a gold-plated fountain pen,' I muttered back beneath the sound of everyone else's voices.

'She's just trying to show us up – to show you up. She'll probably give that stainless steel dish we bought them to a jumble sale.'

'We can't do anything about it,' I replied. 'It's her way.'

As the wrappings were torn open I reflected that flaunting her money had become Naomi's way, not just with us but with everybody. One of Charles's business associates and his wife were spending Christmas with them that year as well and I'd heard Naomi explaining how much it had cost to have the kitchen completely refitted with real oak units specially made for the job. Plus quarry tiling on the floor, double oven, enormous new freezer and one of the first washing-up machines I'd come across. I thought about Mum's kitchen in Tattersall Close. The lino had been replaced since we were children, but she still used the same cooker and Formica-topped table that we had crowded round for breakfast before leaving for school. My sister had become a snob, which was the last thing I would have expected when we were young.

Richard's laugh interrupted my thoughts and drew my attention to him. He was still married to Kate at the time and Emma, his younger daughter, had been born about eighteen months earlier. He was not quite as much a stranger because I'd recognized that ruthless edge in him years before, but in his case too it was difficult to equate what we had all been and what we had become. I don't want to sound pious, but as children we had been brought up according to certain standards, perhaps best summed up by the fact that Dad had enrolled us in the Cubs and later we had been Scouts. You told the truth, promised to live by a decent code of honour, you didn't lie; the sort of thing I try to instil into nine-year-olds while teaching them joined-up writing. But Richard now lied naturally, in much of what he wrote and a great deal of what he said; he'd once told me about how he'd destroyed the career of a rising MP by getting some minor film actress drunk and tricking her into telling him about some mild indiscretion years before. He boasted about how he'd fiddled with the tape recording he'd secretly made so that it all sounded much worse than it had really been. When I said it didn't sound fair, he sneered at me.

'It isn't bloody Wilmsford junior school, Tim,' he said. 'It's the real world and in my job they're all fair game. I got a five-hundred-pound bonus – off the record, no tax – for that little exclusive. Not bad, eh? Bet you wish you could pick up a bit extra like that.'

I nearly asked him what he thought Dad would have said about it, but that's a subject we all avoid.

There was an odd incident that Christmas Day. During the evening the phone rang and Charles returned from the hall to say it was for Mother. She didn't seem surprised and made no reply when one of us asked who was calling her as she walked out of the room. It must have been about ten minutes later when I went into the hall to go to the downstairs lavatory. Mum was sitting on the chair by the telephone table, laughing; the moment she saw me, she said she had to ring off.

'Who was that?' I asked.

'Just a friend.' She stood up and looked in the large, oval gilt mirror over the table, fussing with her hair.

'Which one? Mrs Jackson? Someone from church?'

'No, it was . . . oh dear, this is a mess.' She poked her perm about in apparent irritation. 'I'll just pop upstairs and fix it. Wasn't the turkey delicious? I don't think I'll want to eat again until New Year. I noticed you weren't holding back either. I was glad about that. I sometimes think you don't eat enough. A bit of fattening up wouldn't do you any harm. You should get Claire to cook you some good old-fashioned steak and kidney puddings . . .'

The inconsequential sentences faded as she disappeared round the turn of the stairs. She'd never before shown the slightest interest in what I did or didn't eat, so she had been deliberately changing the subject. It struck me that I could think of none of her friends who would be likely to telephone her on Christmas Day. When I rejoined the others, I quietly asked Charles if the caller had given a name.

'No,' he replied. 'Just asked if he could speak to Mrs Barlow. Said he was a friend and wanted to wish her a happy Christmas.'

'He?' I repeated. 'Long-distance call?'

'Could have been. It was a fairly faint line. Why?'

'I was just wondering who it might have been.'

'Better ask her . . . how's your drink?'

Driving back to Manchester, Mum was full of what a marvellous time she'd had and how generous Naomi and Charles had been and what a lovely house it was and . . . I could see Claire biting her lip in the front seat next to me, and changed the subject.

'So who was your mystery caller?' I asked abruptly.

'Mystery caller? Oh, on Christmas Day. I told you. It was a friend.'

'A man friend,' I added.

'How do you know ...? Yes, Tim, it was. If it's any of your business.' The unexpected sharpness in her voice made me feel uncomfortable.

'We don't usually have secrets,' I said.

'Don't we?' She let the answer hang in the air for a moment, then turned to Claire. 'That book you bought me about the Royal Family is absolutely fascinating. I was reading it in bed last night. You must borrow it back some time. Did you know that ...?'

I stared at the motorway. Who was this man she wouldn't identify? She was ... I had to work it out ... she would be fifty-nine in the coming February, although on her good days she could pass for ten years younger. Someone else in her life? It was unthinkable. She didn't need anyone. I did her decorating and odd jobs, she had her WI and bridge afternoons, coach trips to the Lake District or Blackpool illuminations. It couldn't be someone else she loved; she'd loved Dad. I told myself to stop imagining stupidities. She must simply have met somebody who was lonely and they'd got to know each other and met for coffee a few times, maybe strolled round Wilmsford Park. He'd been on his own on Christmas Day and had rung her because he had nothing to do. It wasn't as if they might have ... No. You see, I know her better than anybody – she's my mother – and she'd never do anything like that.

Then it struck me that by questioning my remark about us not having secrets she could have meant she suspected there were things about me I hadn't told her. About me and Claire, about ... personal things ... about Dad and how he had—

'Mind that car!'

Claire's urgent shout cut through the sudden dizziness of panic and I instinctively swerved into the outside lane.

'Pay attention, Tim,' Mum said crossly. 'We don't want to be killed.'

As the M1 swam back into focus, the momentary terror hardened into a knot of unease that was like a physical pain. I realized that if the unthinkable happened – if Naomi or Richard suddenly broke down and confessed everything – the punishment they gave me wouldn't matter. The terrible thing would be that Mum would know, and I'd lose her.

Chapter Four: Claire

```
HSA581293 PAHOME     PA              12.09
```
POLICE Bodies Advisory
ATTENTION PICTURE EDITORS AND CHIEF SUBS
Colour pictures of Timothy and Claire Barlow and Charles and Naomi
Stansfield (both upright) to go with POLICE Bodies will be running
soon on PA Pictures.

```
HSA581344 PAHOME     PA              12.33
```
POLICE Bodies Advisory
ATTENTION NEWS EDITORS AND CHIEF SUBS.
STRICTLY NOT FOR PUBLICATION
A neighbour of Timothy and Claire Barlow in Hillcrest Road,
Wilmsford, Manchester, has suggested that Claire Barlow had a lover
and may have been planning to leave her husband. We have been given
a name and are trying to contact the man for a comment.

```
HSA5811359 PAHOME    PA              12.57
```
POLICE Bodies (reopens)
Conservative councillor Christopher Taylor, chairman of Wilmsford
District Council's social services committee, denied today that he had
been having an affair with Claire Barlow.

'It's absolutely outrageous to suggest such a thing,' he said. 'I have
known Mrs Barlow and her husband for a number of years, but there
has been nothing improper about our friendship. It's appalling that
anyone should make such an allegation at a time like this.'

NOTE TO NEWS EDITORS AND CHIEF SUBS (not for
publication): Mr Taylor said he would be seeking legal advice in

connection with the allegations of an affair with Claire Barlow. Two other neighbours in Hillcrest Road say they know nothing about any such relationship. We are checking with our original source again.

HSA581400 PAHOME   PA   13.26
POLICE Bodies Advisory
URGENT. ATTENTION NEWS EDITORS AND CHIEF SUBS
Must kill POLICE Bodies time at about 12.55 regarding quote from Wilmsford councillor Christopher Taylor. Original source of story has now withdrawn allegations of an affair.

Every year I go and watch the Wilmsford pageant, although it's nothing like it used to be. When I took part as a little girl it was nearly a quarter of a mile long, with three bands, lorries decorated with beautiful tableaux, hundreds of children dressed up, the Mayor waving from an open Rolls-Royce. The *Messenger* printed dozens of pictures and there was even coverage in the *Manchester Evening News*. From the first time I was in it – as an elf in green crêpe paper for my school's entry in 1948 – I dreamt of being the Pageant Queen, wearing a long white satin dress, scarlet sash and golden crown, sitting with my attendants amid masses of flowers on the great brewery dray pulled by carthorses glittering with brass ornaments and ribbons. It finally happened on my fifteenth birthday in 1956, one of the hottest days of the year, and from the moment I woke up at half past five in the morning until Mother packed me off to bed at turned midnight it was the happiest, most satisfying, wonderful day of my life. Looking back, everything that has followed has been an anti-climax.

Isn't that dreadful? I have blamed everybody for it – my parents, my husband, fate – and all the time I know it's my own fault. I've compromised, given in, retreated, smiled and nodded when I should have fought, I've obeyed when I should have rebelled, colluded in my own destruction as an individual. You'll want to scream at me, slap me, shake me awake, you'll call me stupid and you'll despise me. Everyone I know – nearly everybody I have heard of – is happier than I am.

At least I'll keep the history brief; a wasted existence is bad enough without too much detail. Only child, possessive parents, not allowed to play with 'those rough children' in case I got my pretty clothes dirty, school told I was 'delicate', shy, wrapped in protective cotton wool that nearly suffocated me. Subtly, relentlessly drilled into me that there were strict limitations on what I could expect to achieve in life, that I had to conform like a good little girl. My mother read Barbara Cartland and my father boasted about living next door to a man who had once shaken hands with Robert Donat (if you're too young to remember him he was a famous film star who was born in Manchester). They were small people with small minds and they locked me in their cage, staring through the bars at the world outside.

It was a formalized, unquestioning, banal little world with fixed patterns and no sense of daring. Tinned peaches and ice cream; the front room kept 'for best'; a bottle of sweet sherry at Christmas, with the remains thrown away when another was bought a year later; *Family Favourites* on the radio at Sunday lunchtimes one of the highspots of the week; crocheted covers on the three-piece suite; *Reader's Digest* condensed books; insurance premium collected every Friday evening by a man wearing bicycle clips; a lamp filled with amber wax that melted and bubbled slowly when it was turned on; canasta; my father's pipe rack on the mantelpiece with 'A Souvenir of Morecambe' stamped on the base. That was home; that was a way of life. And I was not to question it.

I dreamt, of course; all prisoners do. For a while my fantasy role model was Shelagh Delaney, who became famous overnight when she wrote *A Taste of Honey* at the age of eighteen. She only lived a few miles away in Salford, in the sort of back-to-back house that my parents snobbishly looked down on. I read everything I could find about her; how she was meeting all sorts of important people as her play became a smash hit in the West End and New York, how she was making lots of money and had moved to London. If she could break out of her background, why not me? I knew I could never write a play, but the theatre offered other possibilities. I joined the Wilmsford Amateur Operatic Society, persuading myself that someone there would realize I was potentially a brilliant actress and I would be catapulted from the chorus to see my name in lights outside the Palace Theatre in Oxford Street (I didn't have the courage to think beyond Manchester). Stupid. My singing was never up to much and my upbringing had not given me the confidence to do anything other than exactly what I was told; I couldn't be creative. All that happened was that I met Tim and his mother.

Florence Barlow intrigued me. She was the same age as my own mother but seemed years younger, one of the stars of the company who was always given the leading parts. She was very pretty and vivacious, which seemed strange because she was a widow and I'd always thought they were sad, shrivelled women whose lives were over. She was different, and I made the fatal mistake of assuming that her son must be different as well, the sort of man with whom I could change. I convinced myself that beneath his quiet exterior there were all sorts of passions and fire. He was the only real boyfriend I ever had, and it just became accepted after a while that we would marry each other. I walked out of one prison straight into another. How obvious things become later – I was a child who married another child; he hasn't grown up and he's never allowed me to either. We're little, undernourished people and the worst thing is that he's contented and I'm not.

He's so different from his brother and sister. I first met Naomi when she came home from university (naturally my parents thought that such a place was not for the likes of me). We took one look at each other and disliked what we saw. She was casually arrogant, with long messy hair and tarty make-up, always wearing black and talking about how wonderful French films were. And she would deliberately say things to provoke and embarrass me.

'What sort of precautions do you and Tim take?' she asked me once. We were sitting in the living room in Tattersall Close; I'd called to see Tim, but he wasn't home and I was waiting for him to arrive.

'Precautions?' I genuinely didn't understand. 'What do you mean?'

'When you shag, of course.' She smiled triumphantly as I went as red as my cardigan and lowered my head.

'We're not married yet.'

'What's that got to do with it? There's no law against it.'

There was. There was my parents' law, so deeply embedded in me that I felt guilty whenever I let Tim feel my breasts.

'There's time enough for that later.' I mumbled my mother's standard phrase because I could think of nothing else to say.

'For God's sake, get with it.' Naomi pursed her lips suggestively. 'It's the only thing worth doing, and if the Russians drop the bomb you'll only have four minutes left to enjoy it. To learn how to do it in your case.'

I was floundering and bewildered, but fascinated by the implication of what she was saying.

'So have you . . . ?' I shrugged with acute self-consciousness. 'You know . . .'

She looked at me pityingly. 'Of course I have.'

'Who was he? Are you engaged to him?'

I don't think I've ever hated Naomi more than at that moment, because she laughed as though I was an idiot.

'Him? Engaged? You're totally square, Claire.' She leant forward in her chair, eyes brilliant with teasing. 'I don't just do it with one . . . you really don't know anything, do you? Want to guess my score?'

I couldn't cope with it any more. She was taunting me, sneering at everything I had been taught was right – and I was certain she was showing off, lying to me. Only prostitutes did what she was suggesting. I stood up, holding my handbag in front of me, the way my mother did when she was offended.

'I don't want to, thank you,' I said stiffly. 'Can you tell Tim I called, please? I have to be getting home now.'

She didn't say anything, but held up one hand, silently mouthing numbers as she opened and closed her fingers. Five ... ten ... fifteen ... I was weeping as I slammed the front door behind me and ran from the house. How could she be so cruel? I'd never done anything to hurt her, so why was she deliberately making fun of me in such a disgusting way? She knew nothing about me – she'd never shown the slightest interest in me as a person – so she couldn't know how much I longed to give myself to Tim but was terrified of doing so. Another girl would have understood and sympathized, perhaps helped me to overcome my own fears. Naomi just mocked me with her boasting dirtiness. She's changed now, of course; now she's the rich bitch with a phoney southern accent who boasts about all the people she's met rather than the men she's slept with. I just hate her for different reasons.

Richard, Tim's twin brother, is stinking rich as well – although he always complains that he's hard-up – and if that's what journalists are like you can keep them. At least he doesn't pretend to be anything but a bastard – unlike Naomi, who's always going on about how much she does for charity – but he's self-centred, conceited and nasty. If I wasn't related to him, he's the sort of person I'd have nothing to do with.

My mother-in-law is ... well, I've done my best. I've always tried to please her, wanted to be a friend as well as a daughter-in-law. It's not that she's ever unpleasant, but when we're together it's as though she would rather be spending the time with other people. As she's got older it's become a bit better, but in the early days it was as if she resented any attention she had to pay me and hardly ever accepted an invitation to come round for a cup of tea and a chat – which my mother did all the time.

Then, when I was feeling crushed and unwanted, just going through the motions of living, I had my darling Harry. When I first held him in my arms I felt that at long last I'd accomplished something. This was *my* baby, who'd love me as much as I loved him, who'd never let me down, who'd never belittle me, who'd grow up big and strong and clever ... dear God, I was so happy. I centred my life on him, but I wasn't being possessive. All I wanted was to give him what I'd never had. Freedom, independence, approval to climb mountains. It had been a struggle to have him, now nothing else mattered. I let Tim share him, of course; after all he had – finally – made him possible, but Harry was me.

He died a month after his third birthday. It was nobody's fault, although for a long time I screamed irrational accusations at everyone who came near me. He was running ahead of us across the playground in Wilmsford Park and fell as he reached the swings. His head hit the metal frame and he lay very still; I thought he'd just knocked himself out, but when I picked him up . . . The doctor described it as a mischance in a million; little children are not supposed to be badly hurt by accidents like that.

Tim was absolutely shattered. But he was very good; there's so much else I now blame him for that I must remember that. In all the agony and blame, we were close to each other. It's what happened afterwards that I can never forgive.

I had a very good friend at the time who was a Samaritan and she was still there when everyone else had gone away. She led me through my grief, absorbed my bitterness, listened to the same pain spill out over and over again. Only when I was ready did she gently suggest that Tim and I should go away where we could be alone and talk to each other in a place where Harry's little ghost didn't walk . . . she was holding my hand and speaking very softly but firmly . . . you're not the only ones, Claire, life has to go on . . . you always planned to have more children, didn't you? Tears were pouring out of me again, but I understood and nodded. She smiled and asked me to send her a postcard.

So we went away. And we talked. And we tried. And we failed. And we argued. And we kept failing until it became so bad that we stopped trying. And now I'm too old.

'Other people's babies, that's my life'; what a very sad Noël Coward song that is. At the day nursery I've got Sharon and Peter and Rupert and Jessica and . . . dozens of them. They call me Auntie Claire and sit on my knee, playing with my locket while I read to them; they bring little presents and kiss me; they draw pictures of me; they softly hurt me with their kindliness. Then they go away, but there are always others to take their places ... spare me your amateur psychology, I know exactly what I'm doing.

The sex thing is not talked about any more, and a mutual agreement to have separate beds avoided any further indignities. It doesn't bother me; if Tim couldn't give me more babies, then I wasn't interested. The magazines and videos he thought he'd hidden where I wouldn't find them sickened me, but I never mentioned them. That's not important because it didn't hurt. What hurts is that Naomi and Richard have children. I don't like the way they condescend to me as the slightly pitiful aunt and I resent their very existence, because their parents deserved them less than I deserved Harry.

Apart from my work in the nursery I have my fantasies, which compensate for the dead staleness inside me with romantic dreams of lovers. I've secretly started smoking. Tim would go mad – well, mad for him – if he knew, but I do it in the garden so there's no smell to give me away when he comes home. When things are really bad I stand on the patio and close my eyes and pretend that I'm on the terrace of some exotic continental hotel, beautifully dressed and incredibly elegant, casually displaying my good looks as I wait for my millionaire boyfriend. If anyone spotted me – and I think that busybody Mavis Goss next door did once – they'd see a middle-aged housewife guiltily puffing on a Silk Cut before going back indoors to peel the sprouts.

I could walk out, of course; Tim isn't man enough to stop me and I could manage on my own. Eventually I'd be able to divorce him, claim half the value of the house, be independent. I don't because I'm scared, not of being on my own, but of the very thought of doing something for *myself*. All my life I've existed as a part of someone else's existence. The lovable baby, the little girl treated like a pampered pet, the obedient wife, Harry's mummy, my husband's housekeeper. Endless roles devised for other people's needs. So now

I don't know how to behave unless someone makes the rules for me. The worst thing is that I think I could ... no, the worst thing is that I know I could but I can't. If Tim died it might be different because the last sheet anchor would drop and I could let the tide take me. I wouldn't care where, because it has to be somewhere better. But Tim won't die, not for years, and I'll just grow older and sadder and smaller.

Chapter Five: Charles

HSA581423 PAHOME PA   13.44
POLICE Bodies (reopens)

Elisabeth Kerr, a senior partner at City of London merchant bankers Kennet Bolingbroke, said that Charles Stansfield had been involved in the investigation into Stallion and Dupont, the Swiss-based conglomerate that collapsed earlier this year with liabilities of £1.7 billion.

'He suspected there could be a covert arms connection with the Middle East,' she said. 'He'd been approached by a former aide to Saddam Hussein now living in hiding in London who had indicated that Stallion and Dupont's oil and mineral interests were a cover for something else.

'Charles was very concerned about what he might be getting into and had raised the matter with MI5 and Special Branch. As a banker, he had no wish to become involved in the risks of probing arms deals that were breaking international sanctions.'

There have been reports that British and continental intelligence services have interviewed several people in connection with the Stallion and Dupont crash and that charges may be brought against leading business figures in London, Zurich and Vienna.

I started keeping a diary while I was at Marlborough; nothing in the Pepys or Evelyn league, but at least it's been consistently filled in. At the end of every day since I was sixteen – even the worst days – I've written something down about what happened, sometimes so briefly that many entries are now as incomprehensible as fragments of runes, but at the worst of times the

145

controlled act of writing could be a catharsis and the results now stand as vivid reminders. Only to me, of course; if Roberta or David read them after I'm gone they may know what happened but not how it felt.

I occasionally flick through the chronicle of frequently wasted time myself, unearthing traces of strange, forgotten things. Meeting times for the Cambridge University Communist Society; I didn't actually join the party, but that could have been embarrassing later if I'd ever wanted to enter politics. Somebody called Margaret was obviously important for several weeks in my first year, but I can't remember a thing about her now; however, I apparently took her to Grantchester one afternoon and undoubtedly quoted Brooke. And why on earth did I attend an interview with the Royal Shakespeare Company? Then there was National Service in Malaya, and I don't need the diary to remind me of that villager I shot; he was younger than I was.

The first really bad entries came when Sarah died; not for the grief, but for the sense of relieved guilt. My first marriage was a mistake and we both realized it very quickly. After the fallout from a series of blazing rows had settled, we agreed we would have to talk seriously about what we were going to do when she returned from New England. I never found out how she came to be in that private plane and the name of the pilot – Tony Merengo, the diary records – meant nothing to me. But I convinced myself, with no evidence whatever, that he was her lover, and now find the note of puritanical satisfaction in much of what I wrote acutely distasteful. What I could never bring myself to put down in words was that I had contemplated Sarah's death as the perfect answer. Divorce would have been messy and expensive, death clean and simple, avoiding having to lie – as I knew I would – to my parents and friends about where I had failed in the marriage. And death, which attracted sympathy instead of censure, was granted. There's a lot of selfishness in those entries, a quality that occurred again years later.

Then Naomi arrives; the first diary references are weeks apart, then they become more frequent and her initial is enough to identify her. 'To Gerald and Miriam's with N' ... 'N unwell. Send flowers' ... 'With N to Dollington. Father makes an enormous fuss of her and Mother is obviously impressed. Separate bedrooms, of course; the Parental Institution isn't ready for the liberated society. N is marvellous with them' ... 'N's birthday. Silver bracelet and dinner at Leopold's. The first time I actually say I love her. Why have I been putting it off? Have I finally let go of Sarah? N's reaction unexpected, almost as though she's frightened. Festina lente. The trip to Boston will give her time on her own' ... 'N accepted this afternoon. I knew she'd made up her mind the night before we came here. Father and Mother delighted.'

It was the best of times; such periods always are. Discovering another person, everything you do together having a newness about it, so much easy laughter. The only problem was her family, or rather that Naomi seemed determined to shut them out for as long as possible. After our engagement, my parents insisted that they must come to Temple Manor and ... Naomi's excuses became so ridiculous that I faced her with it.

'How long is this going to go on?' I demanded. 'Mother's started asking me if you're hiding something from them. From me as well. She's appalled that I still haven't met your family.'

'There's no problem, it's just that ...' She gestured round the library at Dollington where we were talking. 'It's all this. Whatever your parents think about me, my family's incredibly ordinary. Mother lives in a semi-detached and my brothers – well I've told you about Richard, of course – but Tim's only a junior school teacher and they're all so ... so middle-class, and I'm not sure how you'll—'

'Oh, for God's sake!' I snapped at her. 'Don't you know me better than that by now?'

'What do you mean?'

'I mean I'm not a snob. And I don't like you being one, particularly about your own family.'

'Am I being a snob?'

'Yes, and an inverted one, which is the worst sort. I realized a long time ago that I wouldn't find your family in Debrett's. It didn't stop me asking you to marry me.'

'What about your parents?'

'What about them? They're very fond of you and they know I love you. Anything else is irrelevant. You've got the problem, Naomi, not them.'

She turned away from me. 'All right. I'm sorry if I've been over-cautious. But remember one thing when you meet them. They're my family, they're not me.'

'What do you mean?'

'You'll see. But as long as you love me, it'll be fine.'

So I finally met them, and I did see although I've never understood. Naomi had been burying her own past. It must have taken an enormous effort, virtually an obsession, to have changed as much as she had done. And I could see no reason for it, certainly not to the degree to which she had taken it. This hadn't been ambition and self-improvement, this had been utter, deliberate rejection. If her family had been monstrously objectionable it would have made sense, but they weren't. They were perfectly respectable middle-class people and I've always got on with them. Once Naomi felt secure – which took about ten years of marriage and the arrival of the children – she became easier with them herself and the condescension towards her poor relations (even though Richard's worth a good deal) has disappeared. But I still didn't know what she had felt she needed to bury beneath her layers, and she would never tell me. Finally, I let it go. However close we become to another person, there's always a secret room to which only they have the key. I certainly have one; I keep what happened with Charlotte inside it.

She was my temporary secretary while Angela was on maternity leave. She was considerably younger than I was – of course – and it really was boringly predictable. A drink after work, careless innuendoes to inflate a middle-aged ego that she picked up on and then what somebody called the excitement of new flesh. I think I did it because it was expected that someone in my position would.

It lasted about six months, until the time I felt decisions closing in on me. Charlotte behaved much better than I did; she told me what all my excuses were going to be and that she accepted them. She added that if I started apologizing she'd throw something at me.

'Just go home to Naomi,' she said. 'I've always known you love her.'

'Then why did you . . . ?'

'Because I wanted to. You're an attractive man, but a lousy lover . . . sorry, I don't mean it that way. I mean you're a husband. Unfortunately for me, somebody else's.'

I escaped as easily as that; with the salient exception of Sarah, I've been lucky with the women in my life.

Another aspect of Naomi is that she can show immovable determination. I accepted it as part of her personality and for most of our married life it hasn't been important. Usually we agree with each other, and if we don't one of us just gives way. What rows we have had have often been over ridiculously trivial matters, except for the most recent – and vivid – occasion involving my father.

He'd coped with Mother's death in 1980 very well, selling off Temple Manor at the height of the property boom and buying a flat in Brighton, from which he travelled up to town to keep in touch with business and stay at his club. He often visited us, spoiling his grandchildren and being pampered by Naomi. He was perfectly sanguine about death, pointing out that his own father and two brothers had dropped dead from massive heart attacks, apologizing for the shock he anticipated causing us, but arguing that it was preferable to senility. Parkinson's disease was diagnosed in 1988 and a year later we moved him into the nursing home less than a mile from where we live.

I found it massively distressing. He'd remained active and mentally alert into his eighties; suddenly it was like watching a horror film in which a healthy body rots and half-disintegrates in seconds. His muscles went slack, his voice slurred and a terrible pleading sadness entered his eyes. Naomi went to see him most days, and I called in on the way home every evening, unless it was too late. I told him what had happened at work, how his shares were doing, bits of City gossip, and he nodded. I don't know how much he understood, but began to hope it was very little; it had been an important part of his world and he was now banished from it. The visits became increasingly painful.

'How was he?' Naomi asked as I walked into the kitchen one evening, a meaningless question we'd fallen into the habit of asking, ignoring its stupidity.

'Much the same.' The standard answer was automatic as well. 'What's for supper?'

'Beef bourguignon. It'll only take a few minutes in the micro-wave. Go and have your whisky.'

I went through to the sitting room, poured the drink and flopped into the chair by the fireplace. Naomi joined me with her wine, taking the chair opposite, running her fingers up and down the stem of the cut glass tumbler.

'It's becoming a burden, isn't it?' she said. 'I think he knows that.'

'I don't know what he knows.' I felt very tired. 'I talked to the sister tonight, and she says he's deteriorated noticeably in the past week.'

'So obviously we can't go away next month – and you need a break.'

'I'll survive.' I drank some of the whisky and gazed into the fireplace as I began to talk through an idea I'd had for some time. 'I've been thinking about moving him in here.'

'Here?' Naomi sounded startled.

'Why not? He could have the bedroom with the ensuite bath-room and we'll hire a full-time nurse. We can get her any special equipment she'll need.'

'But how will that help?'

'He'll see more of both of us. And . . . I think I'd like him to die in our home rather than where he is.'

Naomi looked down and shook her head. 'I don't want that.'

'It won't be for long,' I argued. 'The doctor says it could be a year at most.'

'No!' She stood up and crossed the room to the window, starting to draw the curtains even though it was still twilight outside. When she spoke again her voice sounded strained. 'Nobody can say exactly how long it's going to be, and I can't ... I can't have him so near me. I'm sorry, I just ... I love him ... I'll do anything to ... but not here.'

'But there'll be the nurse,' I repeated. 'Full time. It'll be no different from now.'

'Yes it will. I'll know he's in this house. Dying and ... Christ, supper'll be ready.'

She almost ran out of the room. For a few minutes I couldn't understand, then I realized and felt guilty for not thinking more clearly. I went through to the kitchen. Naomi was serving our evening meal and her hand was trembling.

'I'm sorry,' I said. 'I'm very tired and I'm worried about him. I completely forgot that you've been here before.'

'That doesn't matter.' She was becoming angry. 'It was forever ago. It's nothing to do with now. I just don't want to be alone with him in this house!'

'But the nurse will be—'

'Every moment? No days off?' Her anger was abruptly escalating into something that seemed like hysteria. 'She'll go out sometimes, right? And I'll have to be here. I couldn't cope with that!'

She dropped the ladle and pushed past me, knocking against the hand still holding my drink so that half of what remained spilled on to the floor.

'Finish serving it yourself! I'm not hungry!'

As I heard her pound upstairs and slam the bedroom door I began to feel angry myself. I'd made a mistake in not remembering what had happened with her father, but this was irrational. We'd been living with my own father's illness for years and had supported each other. What was so unacceptable about arranging for him to spend his last months in the home of those he loved – and for whom, as Naomi knew very well, he had done so much? I was in no mood to leave a cooling-off period and went straight after her. When I opened the bedroom door she was sitting at the dressing table with her back to me.

'You've always told me how much you love him,' I said accusingly. 'And I'm not asking you to do very much for him now.'

'I know you're not.' She looked at me through the mirror opposite her. 'I'm sorry.'

'Then give me a reason. One that makes sense.'

'I can't.'

'So there isn't one.'

'Yes there is.'

'Then what is it?' Her outburst had begun to affect me and both our voices were rising. I jumped as she picked up a silver-backed hand mirror and slammed it on to the dressing table.

'Don't push me, Charles!'

'I'm not pushing you! I just want you to start talking sense! About my father!'

'All right.' She turned round on the stool and looked straight at me. 'If I was alone with him in this house I wouldn't be able to go near him. Not even if he was screaming for someone. Satisfied? Now that's it. No more. End of conversation. Just leave me alone. Please.'

She stood up and walked into the small dressing room off our bedroom and I heard her lock the door. I stood there for a moment, then went downstairs, completed serving my own dinner and carried it through to the dining room. Naomi had set our two places as usual with glasses of mineral water and the post that had arrived after I'd left in the morning. The evening meal had long been an agreed and needed period in which to be alone together each day, the answerphone protecting us from callers, when we could core dump our days. When the demands of children from one generation and parents from another had crowded in on us it had been an oasis in which we could still touch each other. Now, when I needed her sympathy and support, I was there on my own.

Anger simmered into resentment as I read the post, scribbling odd notes on several letters to remind myself what action they required. By the time I finished I had calmed down. I went back into the sitting room, lit a cigar and sat by the fireplace again, trying to understand. The dying father motif was obvious, but Naomi's reaction had been too extreme. After more than thirty years, during which she had eradicated all traces of her childhood and changed her personality so much that I could only guess at what she might have been like then, why should her father's death still carry so much anguish? Because that had to be the parallel. I tried to recall what I knew. He had died in hospital, not at home, so there could be no memories of nursing him; in any event, there would be no nursing in this case. I'd never had any conversations with her family about her father's death; in fact Tim was the only one prepared to talk about him at all. At first I'd thought it slightly odd, then came to regard it as something that had happened so long before I met any of them that it was irrelevant.

'I'm sorry.'

I turned in the chair. Naomi was standing in the doorway, her face tearstained, a handkerchief crushed tightly in one hand.

'I missed you at dinner,' I said. 'It might sound ridiculous, but it's become an important time of day for me. I thought it was for you as well.'

'It is.'

'But you weren't there. In fact you were nowhere near me at all. And I needed you to be.'

'Don't,' she said. 'I'd rather you got angry and shouted at me. Call me a selfish bitch, tell me you hate me, but don't be so cruel by being so calm. It hurts because you're right.'

'Well, I'm not going to shout because it won't help,' I told her. 'What will help is if you sit down and tell me exactly what the problem is. I think I understand part of it, but there has to be more and I think I have a right to know. All I am suggesting is that my father is allowed the chance to die among those he loves – and who love him. I don't think that's too much to ask.'

'It isn't.' She came and sat opposite me again, uncrumpling the handkerchief, then staring down as she started to fold and unfold it. 'I can't ... explain it completely. You'll just have to trust me. You know I love Daddy very much and I hate what's happened to him. I don't want him to die and I want him to die at the same time. I go and see him as often as I can, and I'm not complaining in the least about that. But I cannot have him in this house, because ...'

I waited while the handkerchief was formed into a series of smaller and smaller triangles.

'Because?' I finally prompted. Naomi looked straight at me.

'I told you upstairs. Because there could be times when I'd be alone with him. I know there'll be a nurse, but it might happen.'

'It needn't. We can employ a back-up nurse.' She lowered her head again as I looked at her. 'You're making excuses. Why?'

'It's ... something about me. I can't be that near to death. Please. Try to understand.'

'That's what I've spent the past hour doing. I appreciate this has to be tied up with your own father's death, but—'

She stood up abruptly. 'I don't want to talk about it any more. He's your father and you must do what you want. But if you bring him into this house, then I'll leave. I'm sorry, Charles, but I mean that.'

She walked out of the room, and would never discuss the matter again. For a while I considered overriding her objections and facing her with a *fait accompli*, but then decided he should stay in the nursing home. I persuaded myself he was as contented there as anywhere and wanting to bring him to the house was perhaps more for my comfort than his. It wasn't the only time Naomi let me down, of course – and I've let her down often enough; marriages survive by amnesties over betrayals – but I was left with a sense of something disturbing, some unknown thing inside her. What troubled me most was that after knowing her for so long, there should have been so powerful a presence in her secret room and I had never before been aware of its existence. Over the next few weeks I wrote a lot in my diary about it. Mostly it was random, exploratory speculation, but one night I felt I captured my misgivings: 'I could accept Naomi lying to me. What is worrying is that she may be lying to herself. And I don't know why.'

When Roberta next visited I mentioned it to her; before I come to her reaction, perhaps I should explain my relationship with my own children. David is one of life's hedonists, intelligent and hardworking enough, but I'm afraid our efforts not to spoil him didn't quite work in that he will avoid anything that might cause him inconvenience or trouble. There is no sense of commitment to others because that would interfere with his self-indulgence. Roberta, on the other hand, is fascinated by people and has a very giving personality; the former she gets from me, the latter she must take the credit for. You should never differentiate between your children, but my daughter has become a person I like, my son one I'd probably find rather too selfish if I met him as a stranger.

At the moment, there's also an imbalance in Roberta's relationship to us following the break-up of her engagement to Martin. For several weeks, a sparky, confident young woman was suddenly our dependent daughter again, irrationally asking us to make it better. All we did was listen to what became, as it always does in such circumstances, a repetitive tale of despair, knowing all the time that she would find her own way out; the best thing was that she should lick her own wounds. She's fine now, except for the fact that she's carrying too much gratitude, because we didn't do as much as she thinks we did. For her sake, I want that to wear off; in the meantime, I bounce some of my problems off her so that a little role reversal will correct her perspective.

I didn't give her all the details, just what I'd suggested and that Naomi had refused. Roberta's first reaction was instant sympathy.

'Poor Daddy,' she said. 'I know how bad it is for me about Grandpa. It must be a million times worse for you.'

'Do you think we should bring him here?'

'I don't know. It's not my business, is it? I don't live here any more . . . how much do you want it?'

'Obviously not desperately, because Mummy saying no was enough to prevent it,' I replied. 'Perhaps Grandpa doesn't know where he is anyway, so it's academic.'

'But what's really concerning you is why Mummy dug her heels in. Isn't it?'

I smiled at her. 'There's my clever girl. Any suggestions?'

'Stop playing games,' she said. 'We both know the reason. It has to be tied up with her own father dying ... how much do you know about that?'

'Very little. He had a brain tumour or something and was unconscious for about a year before he died. The parallels are obvious enough, but I'd have thought after all this time they wouldn't have mattered as much as they appear to.'

'But you have to remember that Mummy and Tim and Richard were alone with him in the hospital when he died, so ...' She stopped as she saw my face. 'Oh, Christ. You didn't know that, did you?'

'No, I didn't. How do you know?'

'Grandmama told me once. Years ago. I'm sorry I've never mentioned it, but I assumed you knew.'

I shook my head. 'Mummy's never said anything about it ... and of course it explains why she doesn't want Grandpa in the house. She's afraid she might be with him when he dies as well.'

'But that wasn't the reason she gave you, was it?' Roberta pointed out. 'Otherwise you'd have known they were all there without me telling you. And why didn't she give that reason, Daddy? In fact, why has she never told you?'

For several moments neither of us spoke, then I asked, 'Does it matter?'

'It obviously matters to Mummy. Perhaps if I talk to her about—'

'No,' I interrupted. She was being too eager to help. 'Leave it with me. I'll think about it.'

For a while I did, but I never faced Naomi with it. It would have been a completely acceptable explanation, but she'd had nearly twenty-five years in which to tell me what had happened. If she –

and Tim and Richard – wanted to keep it to themselves, that was their business. Anyway, there are matters in my past that neither Naomi nor anybody else knows. Things like that aren't important.

Chapter Six: Richard

```
HSA581456 PAHOME    PA              14.00
```
POLICE Bodies Advisory

A short background piece on Richard Barlow to go with POLICE Bodies will be running shortly.

```
HSA581469 PAHOME          PA        14.14
```
POLICE Bodies (reopens)

Richard (Dick) Barlow (49) has been News Editor of the *Post* since 1976 and is one of journalism's most respected professionals.

He first made his name in 1970 with the exposé of a child prostitute ring involving senior politicians and show business personalities, an investigation that is alleged to have resulted in him receiving death threats. Two years later, he was named Journalist of the Year for what became known as the 'Wasted Britain' scandal in which he revealed Top Secret documents identifying potential nuclear waste dumps.

One former colleague said of his reporting career: 'When other newspapers heard that Dick Barlow was on a story they would send three reporters out just to try and keep up with him. Usually they failed.'

In a statement to the Press Association, Daphne Byron, Editor of the *Post*, said: 'Dick Barlow is one of the best operators I have ever worked with and his reputation is second to none. While we wait to hear from him, we are concentrating on doing the sort of job that he would do.'

A source at the *Post* said there was concern that Mr Barlow had not been in touch with them. 'However much he's personally involved in these deaths, Dick Barlow is the ultimate newspaperman and would want to be involved in covering the story'.

There's a lot of crap talked about how your father dying when you're young can screw you up; I've been there and it doesn't. All that happens is that kids you know look embarrassed when they say they're sorry and adults take a bit more interest in you for a while. But it passes and you're just a kid whose dad is dead and you've got your own life to live. In my case, that meant getting out of school as fast as I could and into journalism.

I landed a trainee reporter's job on the *Wilmsford Messenger*, our local weekly rag, and the old man's ghost actually helped. When I went for the interview the editor was wearing a Rotary Club badge and I casually mentioned that Dad had been president a few years earlier. It was no problem after that and I started working for them in January 1960. I moved out of Tattersall Close – Naomi had gone to university, but Tim was still at home – and found a bedsit over a shop in the town centre. I signed indentures for three years, but within less than two I'd learnt all the *Messenger* could teach me and broke them to join the *Evening Telegraph* in Blackburn, where I sold stories to the nationals on the quiet until the northern office of the *Daily Mail* offered me a job in Manchester. They didn't do me any favours – I spent the first six months on the late shift calling every police and fire station in the north of England every hour to check if anything was happening. But I kept my nose clean, bought drinks for the right people in the old Press Club in Albert Square, and made sure that anything I wrote was better than the opposition's version; impact was more important than accuracy. The result was that by New Year 1965 I was deputy night news editor, ordering about reporters who'd been in the business before I was born. The next step was obviously London, and I'd got it all lined up until the night I spiked some godawful piece of copy that turned out to have been written by a friend of the editor's wife and none of the bastards had warned me. Next thing I knew I was standing outside the *Mail* offices on Deansgate with a farewell cheque in my hand and the word was going round the grapevine that I wasn't to be offered a job anywhere else. Pissed off with the lot of them, I decided to spend some of the money taking away a bird I was knocking off. I wanted to go abroad, but she got all sentimental about how much she loved South Wales and I let her talk me into it; a bed's a bed whatever the view from the window. It turned out to be one of the best moves I ever made.

Remember the Aberfan disaster in 1966? Bloody great slagheap slipped all over the village school burying 144 bodies, most of them children, under it – and we were staying less than five miles away. I picked up a flash on the radio and, apart from the local press, I was the first journalist there. By the time the heavy mob arrived from Fleet Street I was on first-name terms with half the rescue teams. Christ, I got some great copy – there were quotes I didn't even have to make up – and was phoning in to everyone (except the *Mail*; I really stitched them up). On the second day, I was on to the *Post* when the copytaker said that the news editor, Stan Leatherhead, wanted to talk to me. He offered me a fortune for exclusives on everything I could give them and asked me to stay there for a few days, all expenses paid. After that, he wanted me to go and see him. I gave the *Post* stories that nobody else could touch – the best was the prayers of a weeping father kneeling in the rubble; if he'd existed, he couldn't have said it better than I wrote it. The girl I'd taken with me kept moaning, so I gave her the train fare back to Manchester and got on with more important things. When the excitement started to die down – even the best stories become boring after a few days – I packed up and went to London.

I'm not the sentimental type, but I can still remember the feeling as I walked up from Temple tube station and into Fleet Street for the first time. It was dominated by the black glass *Daily Express* building, and everywhere you looked you could see journalism, you could smell it in the air. Giant reels of newsprint being unloaded, photographers coming out of the PA and Reuters building, reporters hailing taxis, pubs where you might run into René McColl, Vincent Mulchrone, Sefton Delmer, Hannan Swaffer . . .

they even had the right sort of names in those days. At night it throbbed with the noise of presses and delivery lorries; even at eleven o'clock in the morning it hummed with tension. It's all been scattered now, of course, one of the few things in life I feel sorry about. I miss the sense of belonging it had.

The *Post*'s offices were in Bradley Court, just behind St Bride's Church, slick marble reception when you walked in and the usual mess in editorial on the third floor. Stan Leatherhead put me through what passed for an interview, but all we had to talk about was how much and when could I start before he took me off for a liquid lunch. On the way out we met the editor in the corridor who made complimentary noises about my Aberfan stuff and said he was glad I was joining them. Stan gave me some leads on where I could find a place to live and two weeks later I was sitting in a flat in Battersea reading my first by-lined piece for the *Post*. And if I'd taken that bird to the South of France like I wanted ... however good you are, you need a bit of luck.

It was obvious from the start that Stan was getting past it – spent too much time in the pub with other old farts reminiscing about how they'd reported the blitz – and his deputy was a wanker. When Murdoch launched the *Sun* and rewrote the Fleet Street rule book, Stan kept bleating on about responsible journalism and how tits on page three would never work, but when the *Post*'s circulation went into a tailspin he went down with it; mine was only one of the knives in his back, but they gave me his job. I was told I had twelve months to pull back 100,000 lost sales; I delivered twice that. Today I can make reporters shit themselves if they miss an angle or don't leave the opposition for dead. I've had a sign written for my desk that reads 'Nobody does it better than us – so don't fuck up.' I've been profiled on the Media page of the *Independent*; they said I was the latest in a line of legends stretching back to the great days of Fleet Street. That's what they called me in a poncy 'serious' broadsheet, whatever that means. The Prime Minister and most of the Cabinet have my private home number and Buckingham Palace press officers get nervous when they hear I've turned the *Post* loose on a story they'd rather keep quiet. When the head of Special Branch asked Daphne Byron, who's now my editor, if my bark was worse than my bite, she told him I didn't waste time barking. I could live, eat, breathe and sleep this job; there's nothing else worth doing.

My private life is fine. Civilized relationship with my ex-wife and two daughters who mean a lot to me, even though I don't see them as much as I should. Kathy's at Oxford reading English; that's where the brains in the family went. Emma's gone the other way, which worries me, but I don't know what I can do; perhaps it was a bad time for her when her mother and I split up. I gave her everything she could want – the fees for that school she was expelled from cost me an arm and a leg – and could have fixed her up with a job in the business, but she wouldn't have it. I've tried talking to her, even had her live with me for a while, but she kept drifting back to that bunch of deadbeats and acid heads she'd taken up with. I once went to see her in their squat; it wasn't my daughter living there, we didn't even talk the same language. I've tried everything I can to make her leave, but it's no good. At least she keeps in touch, though, and I manage to take her for a meal occasionally. I make sure she's got money, even if it means I'm probably paying for one of her friend's £60 a day habit; there's no way I'm going to see my daughter sitting in rags on the floor of an underground station being ignored by passers-by when she asks them for some spare change. And it'll be all right eventually; she'll come back one day. I just have to keep the line open.

Apart from the problem with Emma, I've got it made. Stephanie's been around for about three years now and there's no need to make the effort of finding an alternative. There are plenty of people who'd like what I have. Pushing £70,000 a year plus another ten grand in exes, top-of-the-range company BMW, free tickets for anything I want to see, plush mews flat in West London, the only job I want, independence, power, and a twenty-six-year-old brunette to keep me company at night. Nobody gave it me, I earned it, and nobody's taking it away.

The only other part of my life – not that it matters a great deal – is the family. With Naomi living in Hertfordshire, I call in occasionally, but the only time we're all together now is at the Christmas thrash in Brookmans Park. I don't know why we bother, but Naomi thinks it's important. Tim arrives in his clapped-out Sierra with Claire – the sort of woman who makes you want to burn every bed in the world – and they always bring Mother. What do I think of my family? Naomi I admire; she's got my determination and we've both come a long way. Perhaps we've not been completely honest about a few things, but honesty is a handicap. Tim's the one we left behind, mainly because he didn't want to move. When I go back to Manchester now – which is very rarely – it's an odd feeling that somewhere I was born and grew up in is such an unknown place; I've mentioned it to Naomi and she says the same. But Tim is still there, not just physically, but because he stopped at the nearest horizon he could see, a sort of flat earth mentality ... or maybe he simply didn't want to escape. I don't understand that, because there was a lot to get away from.

Then there's Mother. Tim thinks he knows her, but he doesn't. I've never grasped everything – she plays it very close when it suits her – but after Dad's death more happened in her life than she admits. I'm positive about Donald Barraclough, who lived next door to us in Tattersall Close, and I'm fairly certain there were others. Good for her; the old man kept her tied up too long. One day I might tell Tim.

Who else is there? Roberta, Naomi's daughter, who argues with me about journalism – she thinks ethics matter, but that's what you expect from people who work for the BBC – and her brother David, who looks a bit like his grandfather, cocky little bastard who think's he's God's gift to women. Perhaps he is; there's been enough of them. Charles is good for tips on the Stock Exchange, but we've not got much in common. When I try to get him to leak any dirt on the financial world he's very smooth at changing the subject.

The one thing I can't let happen is that something should frighten me, because that's weakness coming out and the weak go to the wall in my profession. I can still remember how scared I was in that hospital more than thirty years ago and swore I would never let that happen to me again. I didn't do it, but I was caught up in it and Naomi and Tim had control over me for the one time in their lives. Now they lie to themselves about it, even though killing the old man was probably the best thing they've ever done. It wasn't my idea, I just ... I just went along with it because ... because I did. He was better off dead – we were better off with him dead. Mum was better off. Anyway, he deserved it. Pompous, suffocating, adulterer – if it wore a skirt he was after it – hypocrite, stupid ... I hated the bastard and ... It doesn't screw you up, though. Would I be where I am today if it did?

Chapter Seven: Florence

HSA584600 PAHOME   PA   14.02

POLICE Bodies (reopens)

Donald Barraclough (78) who has lived next door to Florence Barlow in Tattersall Close, Wilmsford, for more than forty years, said she had been looking forward to the Christmas visit to her daughter's home.

'They've always been a very close family, even though they only get together once a year now,' he added. 'I was talking to her just before she left and she was full of the presents she had bought for everybody. There was certainly no indication that anything was wrong.'

Dawn Townsend, vice-chairman of Wilmsford Amateur Operatic Society, said that Florence Barlow was one of the longest-established members of the company and remained an active member.

'She doesn't play the leads any more, of course, but there are still occasional parts for her and she always wants to be involved,' she said.

'Somehow it seems worse that something so awful should have happened to someone who's always been so contented and blessed with a happy family. She's one of the most popular people I know, always laughing and full of energy.'

Mrs Barlow (74) was widowed in 1959.

Am I a wicked woman? I don't feel I am, not any more; I'm just different from how I was. So many things have changed in my lifetime that it's almost impossible to equate the world of my childhood and the one I live in now. I was born on St Valentine's Day, 1918, and grew up in a period when, despite the terrible turmoil of the Great War, people still clung to and accepted certain fixed rules of behaviour. Roberta cast her first vote when she was

18 – typically, for a very left-wing Labour candidate – while my mother was middle-aged before she won that right, and obediently voted Conservative, as my father instructed her. What would she think of how I've behaved? I simply wouldn't have been able to let her even catch a glimpse of it; she would have been horrified. You see, I sometimes think I was born in the wrong age, but lived into the right one. That's why I'm so close to Roberta; if I'd been born in the sixties I'd have been exactly like her. Brave, confident, sassy (I love some of the words we adopted from America), independent, and with a wonderful, natural enjoyment of sex. I eventually had that, but I was playing the second half by that time.

Donald Barraclough was my first lover, and it happened during the period when properly I should still have been in mourning for Harold; the first piece of clothing I allowed Donald to take off me was a black dress. It was less than three months after the funeral and when he started to say something I put two fingers of one hand against his lips and shook my head. He was a good lover – I very quickly realized that he'd had a good deal of practice on his trips away from home – but I can't pretend I really enjoyed that first time. It was in our bed one afternoon when his wife was shopping in Manchester. After he had left, I sat in the kitchen, drinking a cup of tea and smoking a cigarette – up until then my only vice, although in those days it was quite acceptable. I felt guilty about what I had just done and had to try and justify it to myself. I should have meekly accepted that I faced at least a period of abstinence; a second marriage was not out of the question, but not for a long time, and sex with a married man was certainly forbidden. I knew that what had been happening between me and Donald before Harold's illness had been leading up to it, but why had I allowed him to take me so soon? It suddenly occurred to me that it had been because I wanted to escape from my own past, to shake it off because . . .

I chain-smoked a second Players Medium – I really was on the slippery slope – as I tried to analyse it. It was more than resentment at the way my life had been organized for me, first by my parents, later by my husband. I was not just running away from dissatisfaction that stretched back years, but something more recent and specific. It was Harold's death – no, not his death, but the timing of it. Because ... because I had wanted my husband to die. What a terrible thing for the poor man. And had that wish been so strong that it had somehow brought about what happened, like an urgent prayer being answered? That sounds ridiculous, but you see – it's long enough ago now to admit this – I had more than wanted his death, I had even considered ... Donald worked for a drugs company and perhaps he would have been able to let me have something which I could somehow give ... Pain and worry give birth to all sorts of things in your mind. I hadn't even mentioned it to Donald, but the thought had been there and I felt guilty about it. Then, almost like a miracle, Harold had died, quietly, unexpectedly and in a way that the doctors had simply accepted, and everything was suddenly all right. His life assurances had paid out, what remained of the mortgage on the house had been cleared, I was not rich but quite comfortable and Naomi and Tim had been able to continue their education.

The children ... an inch of ash grew on the cigarette as I faced what was really in my mind, what I was really hiding from by letting Donald take me to bed. After so many months, had they also wanted their father dead? It was not the sort of thing children were supposed to think, but it would have been perfectly understandable. Nothing could be done for him, what he was living could not be called life and it threw a shadow across all their futures. Naomi and Tim had been concerned for me as well – I was less sure about Richard – and had kept suggesting what they might do to help. Both of them had said they would leave school as soon as possible and start work. They wouldn't earn a great deal, but it would be something. I'd told them they mustn't, that we'd manage somehow, but they knew I was just saying it, that I had no answers to the disaster that had struck us all. Then, one Saturday when they were alone with him in that side ward ...

No. Not that. Not even for love. It might have been a kindness to Harold and a lifeline for me, but it would have been too terrible for them. I accepted that my children had secrets from me, but I could not live with the thought that they carried one as dreadful as that. It was disproportionate, the sort of thing that happened in melodramatic Gothic novels, not to ordinary families living in semi-detached suburban houses. But respectable widows in such houses did not take lovers so soon after their husbands' deaths ... there are thoughts we do not have the courage to think.

The affair with Donald lasted nearly two years, during which I learnt a great deal, not least that adultery, like marriage, can be accompanied by unfaithfulness. It was a shock when I realized I wasn't the only other woman in his life, not because I was madly in love with him, but because it brought a new perspective. I had turned to him for comfort – yes, physical pleasure came into it as well – but it had never struck me that there was no reason why I should limit myself to him. When it became clear that he wasn't limiting himself to me I began to look at things very differently. All the children had left home, and with no real need to work – although I had a part-time job in Wilmsford Library to prevent my brain stultifying – I was a free woman. And the sixties were beginning, the time when freedom was to be enjoyed. At forty-two, mini-skirts would have looked ridiculous on me, but there were plenty of other fashions I could adopt, including sexual ones. Manchester was an exciting city in that period, with its own rock bands and gorgeous George Best playing for United; there was a social life filled with possibilities out there and I was ready for it. For nearly twenty years I'd been the passive, obedient wife; now I was an adulteress. Harold had first imprisoned me; his death had been my liberation.

The problem was keeping any hint of it from the children, who had a permanent image of me as their father's widow, very proper and respectable. Naomi was at university and Tim at teacher-training college, so I only had to worry about them during the holidays, and not long after starting work on the *Messenger* Richard announced that he wanted to move into a flat. I realized he expected resistance and had to be very careful not to reveal how much the idea appealed to me. He didn't move far – less than ten minutes by car – but he rarely visited me. I dutifully asked if he was eating properly and offered to do his washing, but he kept telling me he was all right. His bedsit – it looked as if a bomb had hit it when I once called unexpectedly – obviously had a constant stream of girls passing through; it amused me to think what would come out if we could ever compare notes.

But while I deceived my children I was still concerned for them, aware that they must have been affected by Harold's illness and death; he had been the strong influence in their lives and they had to adjust to that loss. It was interesting how they reacted. When Naomi returned for the Christmas break after her first term at Sheffield I hardly recognized her, thick, vivid make-up and tight black skirt; her father would have hit the roof. When she talked, it was as though a completely different young woman was imitating her voice. I was rather sorry, because she was very attractive and would have looked stunning if she hadn't resembled a Piccadilly tart. She gave a rather rueful grimace when I opened the front door and saw her.

'Hello, Mum,' she said. 'I've changed a bit.'

'So I see. It's ... well, it's certainly different.'

'It's what I like. You'll get used to it.'

And that was the extent of our conversation about her appearance. While she was in her room unpacking I made a pot of tea and wondered how each of us would behave. It was impossible for me to reveal anything about the affair with Donald and was unsure how much she would admit to having changed beyond her looks – because changed she must certainly be. When she came down, I asked about university and her friends, what clubs she had joined, how she was enjoying her studies. Then I gave her a carefully selected account of what I had been doing – the library job, amateur operatics, having the bathroom decorated; when she asked how the Barracloughs were I said how much I had enjoyed helping Cicely run the secondhand book stall for St Luke's Restoration Appeal.

We must have chatted for more than an hour before there was any reference to Harold, who had died less than six months earlier.

'I had a very nice letter the other day from that man who used to play chess by post with Dad,' I said. 'Just to say he was thinking of me as Christmas approached. It was very thoughtful of him.'

'More tea?' Naomi stood up and moved towards the kitchen without waiting for my reply. She didn't speak again until she called from out of my sight.

'That was nice. What was his name again?'

'Eric Summerville.' I was aware of staring into my empty cup. 'He lives in Hampshire.'

'Oh, yes. I remember . . . where do you keep the tea caddy now?'

'Usual place. Left-hand cupboard. Two level spoonfuls and half fill the pot will be enough.'

As I heard her lighting the gas to boil the kettle again, humming some pop song, I knew that she did not want to talk about her father – and perhaps I didn't want to either. I knew what my reasons were and wondered about hers. For the rest of the vacation we hardly mentioned him.

Tim was completely the opposite, the conventional student left over from the fifties in grey duffel coat and striped college scarf, as though the sixth former had done nothing more than change into another uniform. And he never stopped talking about Harold, in his weekly letters, when he telephoned, and especially when he came home. He commented on the smallest changes in the house, even those that were inevitable, such as Harold's overshoes no longer being in the well of the hallstand; it was as if he would have preferred the house to become a museum – no, more than that, a mausoleum for his father, with me as the faithful curator. He disapproved whenever he saw me in a new outfit and insisted that what had been his bedroom should remain exactly the same; the 1954 poster of Len Hutton, the former England cricket captain, remained on his wall until he married, when he removed it and took it with him; as far as I know, he's still got it.

His constant harking back to his father became irritating, even maddening, but I bit my tongue. It was obviously something he needed to cling to and it would have shattered him to learn that I considered it virtually irrelevant. I thought it was a phase that would pass, but it never really has. The first time he brought Claire to meet me he took her round the garden, explaining how Harold had laid it out, insisting that I dug out old photographs so he could show her what his father had looked like. She made all the right noises and asked questions about him because Tim clearly expected her to. I kept turning the subject back to her, but she seemed as dull as she looked.

'Claire really likes you, Mum,' Tim told me when he telephoned the following week. He sounded delighted.

'I like her as well.' I pulled an idiotic face at myself in the hall mirror. 'She seems a very nice girl.'

'Her parents want to meet you,' he added. 'They're only in Harper Close. I've given them your number and they'll be in touch.' My status as a prospective mother-in-law was being arranged for me in exactly the same way that I had become a wife, history repeating itself as farce.

And that just leaves Richard. Like Naomi, he hardly speaks about Harold, but then I hardly saw him after he moved out. Frankly, I don't care for him very much; I can't accept the fact that because he's my son I should care. To be honest, I rather think he feels the same about me. He patronizes me. So does Tim, but he's always done it in a suffocating way, as though on Harold's death I immediately became an ageing relic who had to be carefully pampered and, given the choice, I prefer Richard's offhand arrogance to his brother's cloying concern. Finally, none of my children understands me – and I'm not sure that I understand them. They are not the way they were.

Once a year, at Christmas, we are all together; it's become almost a tradition that we go to Hertfordshire. Naomi and Charles have such a beautiful house and are wonderful hosts. After she grew out of her student rebel phase, my daughter skyrocketed up the social ladder and became quite the lady of the manor (bitchy remark,

Florence, you know you enjoy being pampered in luxury). When the grandchildren were small it was wonderful; Christmas needs that sense of little ones' magic. But as they began to grow up their personalities emerged and began to clash. Now they are four young adults – and I find it unbelievable that one of them is going to make me a great-grandmother one day – they are a mixed brood. Roberta, of course, is my poppet, the one I would like to have been. Her brother, David, is so good at turning on the charm when it suits him, which I find slightly odd because physically he looks strikingly like Harold, and charm was not one of his characteristics. I don't like David because I'm not sure that I could trust him. Kathy and Emma, Richard's daughters, are chalk and cheese. Kathy has her father's coldness coupled with steely intelligence – no, intellectualism, which is a different thing – and is too ambitious for anybody's good; Emma is like a child who scrawls all over the wallpaper, not to get attention but to infuriate, a sort of meaningless, boastful defiance. I admire Richard for the way he's never given up with her – I wouldn't have had that much patience – and has managed to keep her part of the family, even if it's a constant embarrassment to everyone.

In the midst of all this I'm cast as the Aged Parent and dutifully fulfil my role while keeping a good deal to myself. The only time I have to wear all my hats is at Christmas, the one time of the year we're all together, even though it means Tim driving nearly two hundred miles; Claire, I know, would rather stay at home. The only one I haven't mentioned is Naomi's husband, Charles. I used to be a bit apprehensive about him – Marlborough and Cambridge, family straight out of *Country Life* – but he's very easy-going and has the ability to adapt to whatever company he finds himself in. One Christmas Eve he arrived home straight from a very high-powered meeting at 11 Downing Street but within minutes was chatting to Tim about the problems of primary school teachers. Breeding, as my mother would have said, always shows. He's very courteous to me but I sometimes think he suspects more about the real me than my own children recognize. He's exactly the sort of son-in-law Harold would have wanted.

Oh dear, why does Harold always keep appearing? For heaven's sake, he died in 1959. Looking back, I have to remind myself that I really was that docile wife and dutiful mother. I loved him – well, perhaps that wore off, but I always honoured and obeyed him – and I don't in any way regret what we had together. If he'd lived, my life would have been different, but he didn't live. So why is he so frequently in my thoughts? It happens when I'm with or thinking about the children, which means that ... I don't know what it means. It can't be long before I'm a great-grandmother to children who will grow up in the twenty-first century; I shall be too old, too tired and frankly too uninterested to worry about my own children. I shan't kick and scream if they want to put me in a home; they can get on with their lives and leave me with my memories. Perhaps I'll only think of Harold when they come to visit.

You see, the problem is that I don't like thinking about Harold because he's not been a part of my life for so long. And what I particularly don't like thinking about is his death. Even after all these years, all those lovers, the grandchildren, everything I've enjoyed, there are thoughts that still trouble me sometimes. And when I think the worst of thoughts, I have to tell myself over and over again that they can't possibly be true.

Book Three

Prologue

The tragedy of the Barlow family was at the top of BBC Television's lunchtime news bulletin on 27 December, the newsreader's voice deliberately sombre.

'Police are still questioning members of a family at a house in Hertfordshire where two bodies were discovered early this morning.' The screen blinked to film shot in Devon Lane, the camera tracking from the house and across the garden. 'They were called to the home of merchant banker Charles Stansfield and his wife, Naomi, in Brookmans Park at eight-thirty and found the victims in a downstairs room. Both had died from shotgun wounds. Mr and Mrs Stansfield had been entertaining several members of their family for Christmas' – faces appeared as names were spoken – 'including Mrs Stansfield's brother, Dick Barlow, news editor of the *Post* newspaper, and the couple's daughter, Roberta Stansfield, who works for BBC Radio news. Among the other guests were Mrs Stansfield's mother, Mrs Florence Barlow' – a ten-year-old still of Florence in costume for a production of *My Fair Lady* – 'and her other son, Timothy Barlow, and his wife, Claire' – a wedding photograph from 1963. The newsreader reappeared. 'A police spokesman said that other members of the family were spending Christmas at the house. The bodies of the victims have been taken to Barnet General Hospital. Police, who are not looking for anyone in connection with the deaths, say they will be named later today. The tragedy has shocked neighbours in the select area of Hertfordshire's stockbroker belt ...' The newsreader stopped as the picture changed to the Rev. Piers Lumley, Vicar of the parish church, his name superimposed at the bottom of the screen.

'Everyone is devastated. It's absolutely terrible and completely inexplicable. They are a very happy and close family who always spend Christmas together. Charles and Naomi brought Naomi's mother to my church on Christmas Eve and there was nothing wrong at all. I can't think of anything that could explain it . . .' The camera stayed on him for a moment as he lowered his head as if in pain, then the newsreader came back, tone of voice subtly altered. 'The latest ceasefire in Bosnia-Herzegovina was broken early this morning when artillery shells landed on . . .'

The clock on the wall of the conference room in Hertfordshire Police headquarters was stopped; it appeared to be the only thing that was still. Several reporters were talking to their offices on portable phones, passing on fragments of information and receiving instructions; television crews checked cameras set up in front of the table at one end of the room, ready to interrupt transmission with live coverage; photographers surrounded the press liaison officer, insisting that they needed to get into the house as soon as possible. Everybody wanted just two names, the human victims who would be the centre around which everything would be fitted. Background information was still being put out by the Press Association.

```
HSA581500 PAHOME        PA        14.22
```
POLICE Bodies Advisory
ATTENTION CHIEF SUBS, NEWS EDITORS AND
PICTURE EDITORS
First snap on police press conference following Hertfordshire double murder scheduled to be running by 15.05. Pictures of Chief Superintendent Michael Dundee expected to be available by 15.30.

```
HSA581507 PAHOME        PA        14.30
```
POLICE Bodies (reopens)
Trevor Webb, 33, who runs a squat in Bucklers Road, Hackney, London E8, where Emma Barlow lives, said: 'We're sure she's all right. Emma's always been able to look after herself.'

He denied that drugs were taken by members of the squat, although police are believed to have raided the house on several occasions.

POLICE Bodies (reopens)
Dr Mark Peters, whose private patients include Charles and Naomi Stansfield, spoke briefly to reporters outside their house in Devon Lane.

'It's absolutely dreadful in there, a nightmare,' he said. 'Everyone is in a state of shock. I've told the police that two of them should be taken to hospital for treatment as soon as possible, although they are not physically injured.'

Dr Peters confirmed that both victims were members of the family, but refused to identify them before the official police statement. He said that the room where the bodies were discovered was 'splattered with blood . . . like a slaughterhouse' and added that police did not suspect the deaths had been caused by an outsider.

'Like a slaughterhouse . . .' Good quote for a headline, particularly if we can get a pic of the room . . . superimpose the faces of the victims . . . have the artist do a graphic. Any word of an arrest? We don't bloody want one yet; it could screw up how much we can say. How about a family tree? Show how they're all related. The grandmother's been a widow for years, hasn't she? Forget the husband, then. Start it with her and work down. With mugshots. Highlight the two victims somehow. Black border round the edge? Something like that. Get someone on to it. What's the time? Right, we'll know in about ten minutes.

POLICE Bodies (reopens)
An ambulance took an unidentified woman on a stretcher from the house in Devon Lane at two-thirty this afternoon. She was accompanied by another woman for the short journey to Barnet

General Hospital, where the bodies of the murder victims were taken earlier.

A hospital spokesman refused to disclose the names of either of the women, but said that they were being treated for shock and would be admitted overnight.

MEMO TO PICTURE EDITORS: Horizontal colour picture of woman being carried into ambulance will be available on PA Pictures by 15.00 hours.

Chapter One

Except for Kate, Richard's elder daughter, who was spending the holiday in Somerset with her mother, all the family were together that Christmas. Her sister Emma had at first refused an invitation, sulkily telling her father she would be bored out of her mind, but at the last minute decided she had nothing better to do and at least it offered the prospect of free food. When Richard picked her up at the squat, he stayed in the car while Stephanie went in to collect her.

They started arriving in the middle of Christmas Eve afternoon, cars loaded with presents representing a sense of goodwill in some cases more obligatory than sincere. Over the years they had learnt to adjust to their differences, damping down resentments and jealousies, accepting qualities they would only tolerate from members of their own family. There was news to exchange, questions to ask, the novelty of being in each other's company again. The gifts were piled under the tree and everyone began to meld into a family party; Richard and Roberta argued about journalism; Tim and David played snooker in the cellar games room; Claire and Stephanie assisted with preparations for the following day's lunch and Emma reluctantly agreed to join them; in the evening, Florence went with Charles and Naomi to the Watchnight Service at the parish church. There were occasional faint scratchings of personalities, but nothing that hurt or left any trace of anger.

Christmas Day morning followed a pattern unconsciously established over previous years. Breakfast was minimal – Naomi spread a selection of cereals on the table and they helped themselves – then they gathered in the drawing room while lunch was cooking.

Charles put on a CD of carols by the choir of King's College and served sherry, although Richard asked for a whisky. They chatted in a desultory sort of way while waiting for what had become a tradition. When the children had been small, they had handed round everyone's gifts, and only when they had all been distributed were they opened. Although it had lost its childish appeal, Roberta and David had maintained the practice. Florence made her regular joke about looking forward to when there would be another generation to do it.

'The first one's for ...' Roberta twisted a parcel round to read the label, '... for Tim. There you are. This one's for Grandmama and this is ... oh, it's Kate's. Can you take it Richard? Thanks. Catch ... whose is that?'

'Yours,' her brother replied.

'That's my pile, then. Come on, or it'll take all day.'

'Uncle Richard, Kate again and ... Emma.' David passed them out.

'Mummy, David ... I can't throw this, it weighs a ton ... Claire ... Daddy ... this has got to be a bottle for ... where's the label? ... Mummy again ... love the paper ... two more for Daddy ... careful with that one. It's breakable ... Tim ... Emma ... what does this say? The writing's awful ... oh, it's Grandmama's ... reach that one for me will you? ... Richard ... no, that's a tree present for later. It must have fallen off ... here you are, Stephanie ... Roberta, hope you like the colour ... what on earth's this funny-shaped thing? ... it's for Mummy from Claire and Tim ... that Fortnum and Mason bag is hers as well ... Any more? ... God, this is indulgent ... thank you, dear kind brother ... Emma from Grandmama ... that's mine, mine, mine ... the tag's come off this. Anybody recognize it? ... David. Don't eat them all at once ... ah, I know what this is ... Richard. This has to be a book ... there's another one for Claire behind the tub ... is that it? Right, go.'

Discarded coloured paper and silky rainbow ribbons accumulated on the carpet amid expressions of pleasure, kisses of thanks and requests for admiration. Involved in their own discoveries, no one noticed Charles put down the Turnbull and Asser shirt from his daughter and pick up the long parcel that was obviously a box. He tore off the wrapping, removed the lid and took out a shotgun.

'Good heavens, what a surprise.' He smiled at Naomi.

'Did you know you were getting it, then?' Roberta asked.

'I had to go with Mummy when she bought it for me,' he replied. 'I'm the licence holder. However, I let her wrap it and promised not to open it until today. Thank you, darling.'

He held the gun up to his shoulder, pointing it at the silver star on top of the tree.

'Don't shoot that,' Roberta joked. 'It must be unlucky or something.'

'No, it's not. You wish on shooting stars,' David added.

'Not when you shoot them yourself.' Roberta pulled a sweater out of the parcel she was holding. 'Look at this! Richard, tell Kate I love her for ever. It's absolutely—'

'It's a gun!'

Everyone stopped what they were doing as Claire's outraged voice cut across the room. Fingers clasping a present she had been opening, she was staring accusingly at Charles.

'A shotgun,' Naomi corrected. 'Charles has been talking about getting a new one for ages, so I said I'd treat him.'

'For Christmas? It's meant to be a time of peace on earth, not killing people.'

'It's not for killing people,' Naomi snapped. 'Don't be stupid. Charles shoots pheasants with it. For heaven's sake, you've eaten them here enough times and never complained.'

'That's not the point. Do you realize that while we're sitting here there are innocent children being killed with guns?'

'Oh, Christ,' Roberta murmured to herself. 'She's flipped.'

'Claire!' Florence glared at her daughter-in-law. 'What's got into you? Naomi can buy Charles anything she likes as a present. It's nobody else's business. Now just be quiet. You're spoiling things for everyone.'

'I don't like guns,' Claire repeated stubbornly. 'And I think it's—'

'Nobody's interested in what you think!' Florence interrupted.

There was a silence before Claire replied. 'No, they don't. They never do.' She sniffed slightly. 'All right. I'll apologize. I'm sorry, Charles. I'm sure it's a lovely shotgun.' She glanced at Tim, who looked away.

'It doesn't matter, Claire,' Charles told her. 'I'm sorry it upset you.'

'Heavy,' David whispered to his sister sitting next to him on the floor.

'Help me cover it up,' she whispered back, then leapt to her feet and hugged Florence. 'Grandmama! These are gorgeous! Where did you find them?'

Florence smiled at her appreciatively. 'They're not very much, dear, but the woman in the shop said they were all the rage.'

'They're perfect.' Roberta leant forward and whispered as she kissed her, 'And I'm smoothing over the row.'

'I know you are. Well done.'

The unwrapping continued, but after a few minutes Claire stood up and left the room without saying anything. Nobody made any comment until Charles was pouring sherry again.

'Do you want to take one to Claire?' he asked Tim quietly.

He shook his head. 'She'll be back in a minute.'

'I think you should go and make sure she's all right.'

Tim went reluctantly; he had never been able to handle family rows. Claire was in their bedroom, staring out of the window at the frost-covered fields on the opposite side of Devon Lane.

'All right? Are you coming down?'

'I expect I have to.' She continued to look out of the window. 'After all, I mustn't spoil Naomi's Christmas, must I?'

'It's everybody's Christmas.'

'No, it's not. It's hers. We're the privileged peasants invited to a stately home. Know our place and mustn't be rude to the lady of the manor.'

'That's ridiculous.'

'Is it?' She shrugged indifferently. 'Well, if you can't see it, I'm not going to waste breath trying to explain. All right. I'll bite my tongue and not embarrass anybody while I'm counting the hours until we get out of this bloody place.'

'You are coming down, then?'

'When I'm ready. Don't worry, I won't say anything else that people don't like. I'll be there in a few minutes.'

'We'll be having lunch soon.'

'I'll try to remember which knife to use and not say "serviette".' She turned to face him. 'All right?'

'There's no need to make a fight of this.'

'No, there isn't. But I didn't start the fight in the first place.' She stared him out of the room, then sighed heavily before opening her handbag and starting to repair her make-up.

As Tim reached the foot of the stairs, Charles was coming out of his study.

'I've put the shotgun away,' he said. 'Where's Claire?'

'Just coming. I'm sorry about—'

'There's nothing to be sorry about,' Charles interrupted. 'It upset her, but it's over. Everyone's forgotten it.'

Nobody had forgotten it, but at least they gave the impression of having done so as they waited for Naomi and Florence to finish preparations for lunch. Flicking through the biography of Rupert Murdoch from his elder daughter, Richard did not notice when Stephanie went and stood next to David, who was looking out of the window through the Fujinon binoculars his father had given him. The previous Christmas, when she and David had first met, there had been occasional ambivalent looks and quiet private remarks between them. Nothing more, but she had been unexpectedly disappointed that he had not found a way to contact her again – or perhaps had not bothered. Richard, for all his defiance of growing old, was starting to bore her. The initial excitement of an affair with the news editor of the *Post* had been replaced by a sense of the widening gap between them; he had no time for Guns N' Roses, she thought Status Quo were dead. A relationship that offered little outside the bedroom was beginning to decay.

'You're at university in Leeds, aren't you?' she asked. 'It's my home town. In fact, I'm going back for a visit next month.'

'Whereabouts?'

'Headingley.'

He lowered the binoculars. 'I've got a flat in Hobbs Road. Do you know it?'

'Yes . . . can I look through them?'

'Sure. You can see the time on the church clock.'

'Which way?' She took the binoculars and held them to her eyes. 'I can't even see the church.'

'Here.' He took hold of her left hand and moved it slightly to one side. 'Got it?'

'No. I'm hopeless with things like this.'

He stood close behind her, hands now on the sides of her head, moving it gently. 'Watch for the square tower . . . got it?'

'I think so . . . but it's blurred.'

'Hang on.' His hands reached forward. 'They need focusing.' As his fingers rotated the ridged wheel, their bodies touched and Stephanie deliberately pressed backwards against him, only slightly but enough.

'Your hair smells nice,' he murmured.

'Thank you.'

'See it now?'

'Yes.'

'What time is it, then?'

'A long way to bedtime.'

They moved apart as Florence came back into the room to announce that lunch was ready. David's hands brushed the front of Stephanie's sweater as he lowered them; each of them knew what had started.

The frisson caused by Claire's return was covered by the activity and little ceremonies of the meal. They pulled Harrods crackers to win carved wooden novelties, teased Emma until she agreed to wear her paper hat, then began to eat: pears in tarragon sauce before the main course of Italian-style roast ham in a pastry case and turkey, with glazed onions, carrots paysanne and roast and croquette potatoes. There was Christmas pudding blue-flamed in brandy or orange chiffon cream to finish. Florence protested she had eaten so much she would not be able to get up and leave the table.

After lunch Charles and Naomi left with Roberta and David to visit Charles's father in the nursing home, Florence began to doze in her chair and Tim suggested walking off lunch. Claire refused, but Richard, Stephanie and Emma agreed and they set off across the fields, chilled, silent and empty under a low, claustrophobic sky, heavy with the threat of snow. They were an uneasy quartet, Richard with the first hints of whisky-induced aggressiveness, Tim uncomfortable over Claire's behaviour, Emma and Stephanie with nothing in common but their sex and a sense of boredom.

'Claire was bloody rude,' Richard told his brother bluntly as they reached the first gate off Devon Lane.

'What about?'

'Charles's present, of course. Nobody's asking her to go out shooting things. She isn't becoming a bloody vegetarian now, is she?'

'She doesn't like guns.' Despite regretting what his wife had said, despite all that was wrong with their marriage, Tim still felt a need to defend her, particularly when attacked by his brother.

'I don't like her, but I keep quiet about it. Stupid cow.'

Anger flared in Tim's face, then he turned and opened the gate, walking ahead of the others, shoulders hunched and hands thrust deep in the pockets of his quilted jacket. They followed, walking in silence because none of them could be bothered to speak, until they caught up with him, kicking stones across a narrow concrete service road leading to a group of farm buildings on the far side of the first field.

'Which way do you want to go?' he asked. 'I'm going right. It's longer, but it's a good walk.'

'I'm going left, then,' Richard replied. 'It's too bloody cold to hang around out here. Come on, you two.'

'I don't want to go back yet,' Stephanie said. 'I'll go with Tim.'

Richard looked surprised for a moment, then shrugged. 'Suit yourself. I don't give a shit what anybody does. Emma?'

'OK. I'll come with you. You're right. It's fucking freezing.'

Never together from the moment they had set off, they physically separated as well. Stephanie and Tim hardly spoke; she had no interest in her lover's brother and he had always found her confidence and sexuality disturbing. He repeatedly fantasized about her in terms of the magazines he bought, oiled and eager nakedness that confused feelings of guilt and something unexperienced and desirable.

Walking with her father, Emma felt she ought at least to show some interest in him. 'Sorted that new guy at the *Post* yet? The one from the *Sun* who you said was a pain in the butt?' She looked at him with a flicker of concern as he remained silent. 'What's the matter?'

'I've not sorted him. He still remembers how I screwed him up on a story years ago.'

'So?' she sounded dismissive. 'You've seen off better than him.'

'I know, but he's putting the acid in all over the place.' He looked at her. 'He's out to get me.'

'Well, he can't.' The statement sounded part encouragement, part insistence that such a thing could never happen; for all her rejection, Emma Barlow needed to know her father's strength was there. 'You've always told me that the secret is to be a harder bastard than the others.'

'Yeah.' He pulled up the collar of his coat. 'But they're always waiting for you to slip up.'

'Slip up? You? Balls.' Emma did something she had not done for years; she put her arm through her father's. His depressed mood concerned her because she had never imagined that he might one day need her support, and had as little idea how to give it as he knew how to ask for it. 'Come on. Don't let me down.'

'Am I letting you down?'

'You will do if you go under ... but you won't. Will you?'

Richard did not reply as he stared at a sinking fireball sun blazing through the black lace of winter trees on the horizon.

'Not if I can help it . . . come on, let's get back.'

Florence sat up in her chair as Claire walked into the room with the tea she had asked for after waking up.

'I hope you realize how ill-mannered you were about Naomi's present for Charles,' she said. 'It embarrassed everyone, and you are a guest here.'

A cup rattled against a saucer as the tray in Claire's hands trembled. 'It's over and done with. I said my piece – and apologized for it.'

'But if you hadn't said anything in the first place there would have been no need to apologize, would there?' Florence took her cup. 'Thank you . . . it was nothing to do with you and nobody in this family criticizes you.'

'Nobody in this family takes any notice of me.'

'Don't be ridiculous.'

'I'm not being ridiculous. And you've all patronized me for years. Don't think I don't know it.' Claire gestured round the room. 'Look at this place. Naomi's always flaunting how rich she is at me.'

'What on earth are you talking about? Naomi and Charles may be rich, but my daughter is not a snob, and—'

'Not a snob?' Claire interrupted sarcastically. 'You really can't see it, can you? If you weren't her mother she'd have nothing to do with you. You wouldn't be posh enough for her.'

'How dare you!'

Claire put her cup down very deliberately and leant forward in her chair. 'How dare I? Why shouldn't I? I could tell you a few things about Naomi. She married Charles for his money and underneath all this she's as common as I am. In fact she's a damn sight more common. I never did anything I'd have been ashamed to tell my own mother about.'

'What do you mean by that?'

'What you don't know won't hurt you.'

Florence stood up and smoothed her skirt. 'I think there must

189

be something seriously wrong with you, Claire. If I were you, I'd go and see the doctor when we get back to Manchester. Anyway, I'm not going to sit here and listen to this. I'm going to my room.'

As she closed the door behind her, Claire collapsed back in her chair and burst into sobs. For the first time in her life she had challenged someone from her parents' generation and had only been able to do it emotionally because she had been conditioned to believe that they always knew best. Instinctively she wanted to blame her change of life, but knew she would just be reaching for what had become a standard excuse to avoid something that went back years, the terrible human loneliness brought about by a sense of utter failure. There was nothing that she valued, nothing that brought a sense of satisfaction or achievement, least of all herself.

For all of them the day was divided. The enjoyment – however spurious – of exchanging presents and lunch over which they could escape into traditional family jokes and memories of previous Christmases had sunk into anti-climax. A sense of stagnation caused by eating too much; the realization that they had to spend the rest of that day and the following one together; a feeling of being trapped in a house in midwinter. And Naomi, Charles and the children brought back from the nursing home a depressing aura of impending death.

'How is your father?' Florence asked Charles as they walked in. She had come back downstairs when the others had returned from their walk, but was pointedly ignoring Claire.

'Much the same,' Charles replied. 'He was happy to see us.'

'No, he wasn't. He hated it.' Roberta sounded on the edge of angry tears. 'He knows it's Christmas and he wants to be here instead of stuck in that place.'

'I don't think Grandpa really knows anything any more, darling,' Charles told her. 'And he was happy to see us.'

Roberta looked at her father's face, then kissed him. 'Yes. All right. Of course he was. Sorry, Daddy.'

'It's so ironic, isn't it?' Florence smiled at Roberta sympathetically. 'The grandfather you never knew ended his life in much the same way.'

'Will someone help me make tea?' Naomi said abruptly. 'Then we can cut the cake and hand round the tree presents.'

'I'll help.' Richard's voice was fractionally too precise as he stood up, keeping hold of the whisky he had poured for himself. 'I've done sod all so far.'

He followed his sister into the kitchen and took instructions about where to find trays, cups and saucers and side plates as she began to slice the fruit cake, white icing decorated with tiny green trees and a Santa Claus on a sledge.

'Charles's old man is becoming a burden, isn't he?' Richard said. 'How long do they give him now?'

'It could be any time ... and I don't want to talk about it. No, not that tray. The one with the flower decoration. And there's a linen cloth for it in that top drawer.' Naomi returned her attention to what she was doing.

'It's not a problem we had, is it?'

'Shut up, Richard.' Her hand trembled slightly as she cut another slice. 'You've been drinking.'

'So? If I'm still standing up I can't have had that much.'

'You've had more than enough. Pass me those plates.'

He leant against the kitchen unit, watching her cut and arrange the pieces with a silver cake slice.

'I'll give you this,' he said. 'You've done bloody well for yourself.'

'What on earth are you talking about?'

'All this. Big house, rich husband, right sort of friends. When you think of what it was like when we were kids—'

'Richard!' Naomi straightened up, the slice pointing at his chest. 'What's got into you?'

'For a start, I'm sick of playing this happy families farce every Christmas.'

'You don't have to come.'

'Yes I do. Face it, Naomi. We've been putting on an act for more than thirty years. The devoted children rallying round the widowed mother. Tim's made it a lifelong obsession, you play the successful daughter generously sharing out her fortune, I'm the high flier who remembers his roots ... well, something like that, anyway. Whichever way you cut it, we're all bloody liars.'

'Liars?' Naomi repeated in disbelief. 'Oh, that's rich coming from you. You earn your living being a liar.'

'Well, I learnt how to do it early on, didn't I?'

Naomi suddenly realized that the kitchen door was half open. Even though everyone else was in the drawing room at the far end of the hall, they might be overheard. She closed it firmly, then stood with her back to it.

'Now listen,' she said. 'I don't know what's brought this on – apart from the whisky – but you stop it right now. Understand? What are you trying to do? Put on a hair shirt after all these years?'

He stared at her for a moment, then rubbed his hand across his eyes. He kept his head lowered as he spoke.

'Just tell me something.'

'Tell you what?'

'That it wasn't my idea.' The words were mumbled, like a guilty confession.

'What?' Naomi crossed the kitchen and put her hands on his shoulders. 'What wasn't your idea?'

'Killing the old man.'

Richard's facade crumbled and Naomi was looking at a person she did not know and whose existence she had never suspected. She heard someone in the hall and whirled round, alarmed that whoever it was would come into the kitchen, but the footsteps went up the stairs. She turned back to her brother urgently.

'Stop it!' She shook him violently. 'Sober up!'

'Don't blame the drink.'

'If it's not that, then what the hell is it?'

He raised his eyes and there was a terrible pleading in them. 'I don't know what's brought it on now – perhaps it's Charles's father being the way he is, or ... it's not important. The point is that this has been crucifying me ever since ... I still have nightmares about it. Only the other week Stephanie had to wake me up because I was screaming.'

Naomi's mind tried to cope with her horrified realization that the strong brother could be fatally weakened. 'But it doesn't matter now. We're all right.'

'You may be. I'm not.'

She drew in her breath deeply. 'Then start getting right. For God's sake, we've all had to come to terms with it. Do you think I'd be where I am today if I'd let guilt get to me?'

'You've still not told me.'

'Haven't told you what?' In her confusion and alarm, she had forgotten he had asked her a question.

'That it wasn't my idea.'

It was the almost childish begging for assurance, so alien to the image that Richard Barlow presented to the world, that hardened Naomi's fright into anger.

'Don't be stupid!' she snapped. 'Of course it was your idea! Do you think we'd have done it if you hadn't suggested it in the first place? Don't try loading your guilt on to me, Richard. I can't be doing with it.'

He stared at her for a moment, then walked out of the kitchen without another word. Naomi realized that her hand, tight round the ivory handle of the cake slice, was sweating.

Chapter Two

The holly was from the hedge in her own garden, but Naomi had picked the mistletoe off low-hanging trees further along Devon Lane. Now it hung from the four-branched chandelier in the hall, dull green leaves and leprous white berries brightened by a chain of golden balls and glittering threads of tinsel. Stephanie did not notice it until the evening of Christmas Day, when it caught her eye as she was coming down the stairs. The family were scattered about the house, some watching television, Tim back in the cellar, playing snooker on his own, Roberta helping Naomi in the kitchen, Emma finishing a joint in her room, opening the window to puff out smoke, then instantly closing it again against the cold. As Stephanie reached the last step, David came out of the downstairs cloakroom.

'I've just seen the mistletoe,' she said. 'And nobody's kissed me under it.'

'We'd better do something about that, hadn't we?'

'I ought to go and find Richard.'

'I wouldn't bother. He's half-asleep in a chair.'

'Not much use to me at the moment, then, is he?'

'No ... but I am.'

David Stansfield had the conceit of the young, wealthy, handsome and self-confident; Stephanie Phillips was completely aware of the effect that her sort of looks had on men. Neither had a character inconvenienced by conscience. They made it clear to each other that the kiss was the prelude to a great deal more as soon as it could be arranged. They were so engrossed in putting the message across to each other that they did not see Emma reach the turn of the stairs from the landing and step back hastily.

'That's enough for now,' Stephanie whispered. 'We don't want anyone wondering where we are.'

'OK ... you know that my bedroom's next to yours and Richard's, of course.' David wiped her lipstick off his mouth with his handkerchief as he walked towards the drawing room.

'You conceited bastard,' Stephanie murmured to herself. She sounded approving.

After a few moments, Emma peered cautiously round the banister; the hall was empty. She came down and joined the rest of them watching television; Stephanie was sitting on the floor at Richard's feet, arm resting on his knee; David had joined his grandmother on the settee, offering her a selection from a box of chocolates. Emma admired their coolness as she thought about how she might use what she had learnt.

In the kitchen, Naomi dropped a cut-glass stemmed goblet that shattered on the red quarry tiling.

'Mummy, that's not like you. You're always so careful with things.' Roberta opened a cupboard door and took out a brush and dustpan. 'Stay still so you don't tread on it. I'll clear it up.'

Naomi looked down at her daughter's head as she swept around her feet. She never dropped anything, at least not anything that mattered. Possessions were important to her, tokens not so much of wealth as of security; Naomi Barlow could only have dreamt of possessing something like this, Naomi Stansfield owns half a dozen of them. Therefore Naomi Stansfield is not ...

Since Richard's outburst, Naomi Barlow had come vividly back, frightened, guilty, haunted and haunting. Tim's tree present had been a paperback book of cricket cartoons and he had commented how much his father would have enjoyed them. Naomi had choked on a mouthful of wine and dashed out to the kitchen with an urgent assurance that she'd be all right if they just left her alone. But she hadn't been all right. Standing against the sink unit, chest and stomach heaving, she had seen her reflection in the darkened glass of the window in front of her. Some trick of the light masked lines of age and change, making the image younger, like she had looked when ... her body bent, she had retched in agony. What was it about this Christmas? What combination of events and emotions were coming together to shake the walls of what had seemed secure defences?

'Move your foot a bit.' Still crouched in front of her, Roberta tapped her mother's right shoe with the brush. 'That's it. Nearly done.'

It will be all right, though. Richard was just drunk; in the morning he'll have a hangover, but he'll have forgotten. He won't want to talk about it again; he'll be too interested in the prospect of getting back to his precious *Post*. And everyone else will go away and it'll be just Charles and me again with Roberta and David visiting us when they like. Charles's father can't live for much longer – and next Christmas we'll tell them all we're going away. That will break the pattern. Mum will be disappointed, but the others won't care. Get out of here, Naomi Barlow. You don't belong.

'If Daddy notices I'll tell him it was my fault.' Roberta straightened up and winked at her. 'Another little family secret.'

'What do you mean?'

Roberta was startled by the sharpness in her mother's voice. 'I mean that he doesn't have to know you did it ... what's the matter?'

'Nothing ... I just ... tell him anything.' She turned away, unable to meet her daughter's concerned look, and caught her reflection again. 'God, I look a sight. I'm just going upstairs to fix my face. See if ... see if anybody's hungry. There's cold turkey and sesame seed rolls – or you can cut some more of that ham ... I'll be down to help in a minute.'

Roberta wrapped the broken glass in newspaper and dropped the package in the waste bin. She had sensed something wrong about her mother since they had returned from the nursing home; she had become nervous and brittle, brusquely correcting Florence at one point, shaking her head furiously at Charles when he suggested more drinks. It was so unlike her, especially in her role as the perfect hostess . . .

'Hi.'

Roberta snapped out of her thoughts. 'Hi, Emma. Anyone hungry in there?'

'Don't know.' She smiled slyly. 'Well not for food, at any rate.'

'What? Talk sense for Christ's sake. I'm not in the mood for games.'

Her cousin crossed the kitchen and hitched herself on to the work surface under the fitted cupboards, helping herself to a date from a half-empty box. The enmity between her and Roberta went back to childhood; Roberta was six years older, and by the time they had been old enough to play together had insisted on having her own way, often using childish violence to get it. And Roberta had been the pretty little girl who grew into the slim, vivacious young woman; Emma, the pudding baby, was now the podgy teenager with the bad complexion. She had first resented her older cousin and had then started to despise her; one of the reasons she had rebelled against convention was that Roberta had become so conventional, studying hard, going to university, landing a good job. Emma relished her rare opportunities for revenge.

'I mean that your brother's hungry.' She chewed the date suggestively. 'Very hungry.'

'Spit it out, Emma,' Roberta said impatiently. 'I'm not in the mood for . . . you disgusting little bitch!'

'You told me to spit it out.'

'I didn't mean that. Now pick it up.'

'Pick it up yourself . . . or are you going to twist my arm to make me?'

'Christ, grow up.' Roberta said wearily, then used the brush and dustpan again to sweep the date stone off the floor. 'Now what do you mean about David?'

'He wants to get his rocks off.'

'What on earth are you talking about?'

'He and Stephanie want to screw.'

'Oh, for God's sake,' Roberta said irritably. 'Just get your mind out of the gutter for once. All right? I know that the crowd you hang around with have what brains they've got in their crotch, but some people actually manage to get through life without thinking of sex every minute of the day and night. It's called being mature. Ever heard of it?'

Emma shrugged. 'They still want to bonk. I don't blame her. David's quite dishy.'

'She happens to be your father's girlfriend.'

'Yes, but the old man's getting past it, isn't he? You can't blame her for wanting someone more her pace.'

Roberta stared at her, then shook her head. 'What the hell are you on at the moment? Ecstasy? You're starting to have hallucinations.'

Emma shrugged as she slid off the work surface. 'Then I must have hallucinated that I saw them French kissing in the hall with his hand squeezing her bum. Anyway, I'll go and see if anyone wants more food pushing through the bars.'

Roberta's body flopped as Emma walked out of the kitchen. She had good memories of Christmas stretching back to her childhood, now it was becoming a time of strain. She was still distressed after seeing her grandfather, and concerned for her mother; now Emma was maliciously stirring for no other reason than to make waves. It was ridiculous that there could be anything going on between David and Stephanie. Of course, David regarded himself as God's gift to women and had the moral standards of a bent lawyer, but surely even he wouldn't be so stupid as to start something with Stephanie right under Richard's nose? Roberta dismissed it. She had more important things to worry about.

By the middle of the evening a collective sense of tedium had settled on everyone when Florence brightly suggested a game of charades.

'We always used to play it,' she said. 'Why did we stop? It's great fun.'

'Of course, Grandmama.' Roberta jumped at the idea as anything to break the deadly monotony. 'I'll go first.'

She stood in front of the fireplace and thought for a moment, then held both palms together face upwards before making a gesture like someone holding a movie camera.

'A book and a film,' Florence announced, for anyone who hadn't grasped it. Roberta held up two fingers. 'Two words in the title.' She pointed to the second finger. 'Second word.' Roberta tugged her ear. 'Sounds like . . .' Roberta touched her toes.

'Aerobics,' David said.

'Fit,' suggested Tim.

'Showing off.' Charles grinned at his daughter, who scowled back at him affectionately. She held her arms out as if holding a stick, then pushed both of them downwards.

'Break,' said Florence. Roberta shook her head and made the gesture again, this time more slowly.

'Bend.' Roberta pointed at Stephanie and nodded.

'Sounds like bend,' Tim said. 'Lend? Send? Shorter than that? End? Something end.'

'Journey's End,' said Florence.

'It wasn't a book, was it?' Charles queried. 'It was a play originally.'

'I think it was,' Florence agreed. 'What else is there?'

Roberta indicated the first word, then tugged her ear again before miming someone cringing in fear.

'Sounds like bad acting,' David said. Roberta stuck her tongue out at him.

'Frightened . . . terrified . . . . fearful . . . scared . . . timid . . . Timid End? . . . what sounds like timid? . . . limit? . . .'

'Coward,' Naomi put in. '. . . Howard's End.'

'Mummy's got it,' Roberta said. 'Come on, your turn.'

Naomi went forward reluctantly. She was not in the mood for party games, but it had been her mother's suggestion and she did not want to disappoint her. Her mind was blank and David started a mock slow handclap as they waited.

'Just a minute,' she protested. 'I'm thinking ... all right.'

She mimed a book and a film again, then held up four fingers, indicated the first word and held the first finger and thumb of her right hand close together.

'Short word,' said Tim. 'A? An? The? Right. The something. Third word ... another short one. But? To? And? Of? OK. The something of something.'

'The Darling Buds of May,' Claire said instantly.

'That's five words,' Roberta corrected. 'Go on, Mummy.'

Naomi hesitated, then went back to the second word with the sounds-like gesture before outlining the double curve of a female figure with her hands.

'I must see this film!' David called out.

'Woman ... female ... sexy ... very sexy ... girl ... thirty-eight, twenty-four, thirty-six ... what the hell rhymes with that? ...' Naomi shook her head and outlined a square, then a triangle. 'Woman by Picasso ... eternal triangle ...' Naomi added a rectangle and a circle. 'Her sister by Picasso ... fat woman with a box on her head ...'

Naomi gestured them to stop and indicated the last word. Richard was sitting nearest to her and she glared at him in fury, raising both hands, fingernails scratching towards his face. Confused by drink, he had only been half aware of what was going on and he jumped.

'Hate,' someone called out. 'Kill ... attack ... destroy ... murder.'

'*Stop it!*' Richard leapt up and staggered. Whisky spilled from his half-filled glass and stained the carpet. There was a stunned silence.

'It's only a game, Richard,' Naomi pleaded urgently. 'It's all right.'

'It wasn't a game, it was ...'

'No!' She pushed him violently and he stumbled against Charles's chair.

'Naomi!' Charles said sharply. He helped Richard to his feet. 'Sorry about that, Richard. Come and sit down.'

Everyone was watching them except Tim, who was staring at his sister. Her face had gone dead as she recognized the subconscious significance of the charade she had chosen. Rhymes with shapes, last word wrath. *The Grapes of Wrath*. By John Steinbeck, now unfashionable, but one of the first serious authors her generation of teenagers had read. An author whom the sophisticated Naomi Stansfield dismissed as second rate, but Naomi Barlow had devoured . . . she ran out of the room.

'It's all right, Roberta,' Charles said as his daughter started to move. 'I'll go. I think she's just very tired. Sorry about that, everyone. David, see if anyone wants a nightcap will you?'

He went upstairs, positive that Naomi would have fled to the privacy of their bedroom. She was lying face down on the bed, sobbing.

'Leave me alone!' Made the instant he opened the door, the muffled demand was shot through with an almost childish temper.

'Not until you tell me what's wrong.' He sat beside her and tried to stroke her hair. She shook his hand off furiously.

'Don't touch me!'

'All right. I'll just sit here.'

Naomi found her husband's calm, concerned presence an additional torment. On their silver wedding anniversary earlier that year they had made a sentimental journey back to the church where they had been married and another visitor had taken their photograph standing together again in the porch. The framed picture now stood on Naomi's bedside table and she had regarded it as the final proof that what she had set out to achieve in a Sheffield garden one afternoon in 1962 could never be reversed. As she had burst into the room a few minutes earlier that picture had leapt out at her and she had had to stifle a scream. Built on lies and deceit, her protective world was collapsing and the fact that Charles was still holding out his hand to her amid the ruins was agonizing. He didn't know what was happening, but his love for her was as immovable as her security was false.

'I'm sorry,' she mumbled. 'I'm not feeling well . . . it's nothing

'... I'm just ... go down and tell them ... I can't talk about it, not now ... I'll be all right ... please ...' Her voice disappeared as she swallowed. 'I love you.'

'I love you.' Charles touched her hair again and this time she did not resist. 'You stay here and I'll be up shortly.'

Roberta was waiting for him in the hall. 'What is it?'

'I'm not sure, darling. She says she's not well, but there's more to it than that. She's got into a state about something. You must have noticed.'

'Of course I have.' She nodded towards the closed door of the front room. 'It's become a poisoned day. You could carve up the air in there and use it for chemical warfare. What's the matter with everybody?'

'Perhaps it's a Christmas too far,' said Charles. 'We've all got past the stage of wanting to be together. Anyway, it'll be over soon. Anyone heading for bed?'

'Grandmama certainly, and I think Claire's had enough. And bloody Richard ought to lie down before he falls down – he's still drinking like it's going out of style, incidentally.'

'Come and help me make appropriate noises.'

As he spoke, the drawing room door opened and Florence appeared. 'I'm going to bed ... and I've suggested that everyone else does the same. How's Naomi?'

'Lying down,' Charles told her. 'She's been overdoing it. She's sorry about that outburst.'

'Well if her own brother hadn't been so drunk ...' Florence pursed her lips disapprovingly. 'He's incapable of apologizing at the moment, so I'll do it for him. I'm very sorry, Charles.'

'It's not important ... goodnight.'

'Sleep well, Grandmama.' Roberta kissed Florence's cheek.

'Goodnight, my dear. Thank you for a lovely Christmas Day.' She went upstairs.

'Let's go and drop broad hints to the rest of them,' said Charles.

Their return triggered vague enquiries about Naomi which Charles dismissed before Claire and Emma said goodnight. Claire was obviously displeased that Tim did not accompany her, with the excuse that even the house's three bathrooms could not cope with everyone at once. After about ten minutes, Charles wanted to get back to Naomi and said no more than slightly caustically asking that the last one should turn out the lights. Roberta followed him out into the hall.

'Why don't you just tell them to bugger off to bed?' she demanded in an angry whisper. 'It's your house.'

'And they're my guests. It must be something to do with the way I was brought up.'

'You're tired as well, aren't you? And worried.' She kissed him sympathetically. 'Go and see how Mummy is. Give her my love. I'll sort them out in there.'

When she returned she deliberately started to tidy the room, sharply refusing Stephanie's half-hearted offer to help.

'It won't take long,' she said. 'I don't want to keep anybody up ... don't you need your beauty sleep, David?'

She was furious with her brother. He had not seemed unduly concerned about their mother and had completely failed to give their father the support he needed. Roberta had always known David was selfish, and the older he became the worse he got. Emma's remark in the kitchen came back to her; was his mind really only occupied with how he could get together with Stephanie?

'OK,' he agreed. 'Sure you don't want any help, sis?'

'Yes ... but you're not giving it.' She continued filling a tray with used plates and empty glasses.

'What do you mean?'

'Forget it. Just go to bed.' Before he could say anything else she walked out and through to the kitchen. She hoped he would follow her ... but she heard him going upstairs, humming to himself.

'Self-centred sod,' she muttered as she loaded the washing-up machine. 'I'll sort you tomorrow.'

Only Tim and Richard remained when she went back to the front room.

'Stephanie's gone up,' Tim explained unnecessarily. Roberta

doubted that Richard was aware of the fact. His face had gone puffy and he appeared to be trying to focus his eyes with as little success as he was able to operate his brain.

'And when you two go, I go,' she said. 'Come on, this is getting—'

'Wanna talk to Naomi.' Richard's voice was so slurred that it was almost impossible to understand him.

'What?' Roberta demanded.

'Naomi,' he repeated, then made a visible effort to speak with drunken patronizing impatience, as though they were being deliberately obtuse in not understanding him. 'It's important. We need to talk. Where is she? I'll go and . . .' He half-stood up then reeled dizzily.

'Get him to bed, Tim,' Roberta ordered tersely. 'I don't want him anywhere near my mother in this state.'

'Not your mother,' Richard mumbled. 'Our sister. Was our sister long before . . . years and years . . . when the old man was alive. Always the three of us . . . the terrible threesome they called us . . . got up to all sorts of—'

'Richard, be quiet!' Tim snatched the whisky glass out of his brother's hand. 'That's enough. Roberta's right. We're going to bed.'

He tried to take his arm, but Richard clumsily pushed him away.

'Gotta see Naomi first . . . talk . . . she thinks it was my idea. You don't think that, do you? I just went along with you. I never wanted to . . .' Roberta gave a little scream as Tim hit him.

'Stop it! You've had too much. For Christ's sake be quiet!'

Richard's eyes bleared at him. 'You hit me . . . bastard. You can't do that . . . I'll knock your fucking teeth out . . . come here.'

Tim gave a choking sound as Roberta grabbed hold of his shirt collar and pulled him backwards, then stepped between him and his brother. She was weeping with rage.

'I don't know what the hell this is about, but I'm stopping it right now,' she warned. 'How *dare* you? This is our home. Daddy's worried sick about Mummy, half the bloody household is on tenterhooks, and you two are behaving like pigs! Now I may not be very big, but you'd better believe I can fight very dirty. So either you both cool it right now and get to bed or I am going to start kicking in the balls. Got it?'

'He hit me,' Richard repeated sullenly. 'He can't . . .' He yelped in pain as Roberta kicked his shin.

'I warned you, Richard. And next time I aim higher.'

He stared at her in dismay; Naomi had once kicked him like that, in the garden shed at Tattersall Close, and after all these years he could still remember it. His chest heaved and a gurgling sound spluttered out of his mouth.

'If you throw up . . .' Roberta snatched up a linen napkin she had overlooked when clearing the room and pushed it into his face. 'Just get upstairs.'

Richard suddenly seemed to have entered a state of sobered confusion. Holding the napkin against his mouth, he nodded then crossed to the door with delicate caution.

'Now you,' Roberta said as he walked out. Tim was rubbing his throat just above the tear in his shirt and blinking rapidly. 'I don't know what your excuse is, because at least you seem to be sober. Anyway, I don't want to hear it. Just piss off like your bloody brother!'

'I'm sorry, Roberta. We shouldn't have . . . I can't explain it.'

'Don't waste your breath trying. Goodnight.' She turned her back on him, arms folded across her chest, determined to remain standing until he left. A violent headache stabbed into her and she began to cry again, no longer in rage but in a stream of painful release. As she heard Tim close the door, she had to grab hold of an armchair as her legs gave way.

'Christ Almighty,' she sobbed. 'Just get the hell out of here. All of you.'

Chapter Three

In the night, it was as though nothing would ever move again. Ice silently locked the surface of the ornamental pond in the garden and frost sealed windows and laid a gritty silver sheen across brittle glass and metal of the cars in the drive. The branches of trees became fossilized, bone-white and rigid. Inside the house everything also appeared still, but there were little private movements. Naomi moaned in her sleep and Charles put his arm around her; Florence half awoke, still angry and embarrassed at her son's behaviour; Roberta turned over restlessly, disturbed and seeking explanations for what had happened; Tim stared at the ceiling, blinking nervously. Richard snored in an alcoholic coma, occasionally spluttering unintelligible half sentences. Stephanie had pretended to be asleep when he had come up, contemptuously listening to him curse as he stumbled out of his clothes and flopped down beside her with an ugly belch; what would the *Post* think now of their super-efficient news editor reduced to the repulsive state of a pitiful wino? As he groaned and settled, she edged away in case he started to maul her, but he was unconscious almost immediately. After a few minutes she quietly slipped out of bed, put on her dressing gown and crept out on to the landing; there was a glow showing beneath David's door. As she pushed it open and stepped quietly into the room he glanced up from the book he was reading.

'Hi,' he said casually. 'I'd nearly given you up. How's Richard?'

'Dead to the world.' She closed the door. 'Incidentally, I hope you're prepared for this.'

He opened the drawer in his bedside cabinet and took out a packet of condoms, casually dropping it beside him on the duvet.

She could see it had already been opened. 'Never travel without them.'

'Sure of yourself, aren't you?'

'Yes.'

'God, you're so bloody conceited. I'm not one of your student pushovers, you know.'

'But you're here.' He looked at her with confident amusement. Stephanie realized that if she walked out he would laugh to himself indifferently and return to his book. He really was . . . suddenly he had the additional attraction of a challenge. She unfastened the belt of her dressing gown and let it slither down her body to the floor. The expression on his face changed.

'That got to you, didn't it?' she said drily. 'Now are you going to say you're glad to see me or do I walk out of here?'

He nodded slightly. 'I'm glad to see you.'

'That's better.' As she stepped towards him his hand reached towards the lamp on his bedside cabinet. 'No. Leave it on. I want to watch your face.'

Waking out of brief, troubled sleep, Roberta looked at her alarm clock; it was twenty past four.

'Jesus,' she groaned as she fell back on to the bed. In a few hours they would all wake up and would the frictions carry on where they had left off? How soon would it be before Richard started hitting the whisky again? What the hell was there to do on Boxing Day except remain imprisoned in the house with everyone just wanting to get away? Merry bloody Christmas. But at least there was only one day to survive; on the 27th Tim would want to start back to Manchester as soon as possible and Richard would be racing back to the *Post*, dropping Emma and Stephanie off on the way. Roberta promised herself she would spend time talking to her mother . . .

She felt wide awake and her mouth was dry; amid the emotion of bedtime she had forgotten to take up a glass of water. Sighing resignedly, she got up. Familiar since childhood with her parents' home, she did not need to turn on the landing light, which meant she instantly saw the gleam still coming from beneath her brother's door. Nothing registered for a moment, but then she paused at the top of the stairs. Why was he awake, unless ... her face went bitter as she remembered what Emma had said, and was about to walk into his room when she stopped herself. If she found what she suspected, she would explode and wake half the household – but she still had to know. Softly she opened Richard's bedroom door and looked inside; snoring noisily, he was alone in the bed. Roberta leant her head against the door frame, weeping as she whispered to herself.

'You bloody, inconsiderate, selfish, randy ... *shit*!' At that moment she hated her brother more than she had ever hated anyone. Sleeping with Stephanie was not the point; Roberta had never had any illusions about her uncle's girlfriend. She was physically oversexed and morally retarded. If she wanted something going with David, fine. But that her brother should be so callously unaware of everything that was happening around him that he hadn't waited until they could be more discreet about it ... Roberta went downstairs, determined to play hell with him the moment she had the opportunity.

She made herself a cup of tea in the silent kitchen; she felt exhausted but had no desire to go back to bed. Instead, she went into the drawing room, turning on only the tree lights for illumination. Naomi had decided that this year's decorations would all be shades of red, pinks, crimsons, rose, vermilion, cherry gleaming amid the dark pine leaves. Roberta smiled sourly at the lurid impression it gave of a brothel. She lit one of her rare cigarettes – bad sign, she told herself, too much tension – and began to try to make sense of it. Richard had been pissed, but there had been more than sodden rambling about him; Tim had actually hit him; her mother had been on a knife edge. All three of them seemed to be cracking up, unable to control themselves even for the sake of good manners ... it was disturbing because it was so unlike them. Still, just one more day to get through, then ... she fell asleep, cigarette burning in the ashtray. Later the house began to wake up.

★

'What are you doing down here?'

'Mmm?' Roberta blinked sleepily. 'Oh, hi, Mummy. Sorry. I woke up at God knows what time and wanted a cup of tea. I must have nodded off . . . what time is it?'

'Nearly eight o'clock. I'm going to start breakfast.'

'God, it's like feeding the five thousand . . . I'll give you a hand.' She rubbed her eyes and stood up, looking at her mother carefully. 'How are you feeling?'

'Fine.' Naomi tightened the belt of her dressing gown.

'No you're not. You look dreadful.'

'Oh, thank you very much. You're no oil painting yourself at the moment.'

'Don't joke about it. I'm worried about you . . . what was it all about last night? Tim and Richard nearly had a bloody fight in here.'

'What?' Naomi sounded startled. 'What about?'

'God knows. Richard was pissed as a rat, of course. He kept going on about wanting to talk to you. I had to kick him to make him shut up.'

'Don't . . .' Naomi turned away. 'Don't get involved, darling. We . . . he and I had a row earlier . . . it's not important. He'll have forgotten all about it this morning. Let's just get today over and . . . come on, if you're going to help me, let's get on with it.'

'I'm going back.' David stirred drowsily as Stephanie got out of bed. 'Richard'll play hell if I'm not there when he wakes up.' She pulled on her dressing gown and kissed him briefly. 'Best Christmas present I've ever had. See you later.' He was already asleep again.

She peered out on to the landing, then hurried back to the next room. It smelt of whisky fumes and Richard was still snoring. She climbed in beside him, feeling warm and satisfied. David Stansfield might be infuriatingly conceited, but she could put up with any man who made love like that . . . she pulled the duvet closer around her body, reliving the sensuousness and satisfaction, already planning when it could be repeated.

'I want to go home today,' Claire said. 'I've had enough of this.'

Tim shook his head. 'We can't. It'll disappoint Mum. You know how much she enjoys coming here.'

'Yes. And we know why as well, don't we?'

'What do you mean?'

'She's just lapping up all the luxury as though it was her right. If your sister hadn't married money, your mother would never have got her foot across the doorstep of a house like this.'

'For God's sake—'

'For God's sake nothing! She makes me sick the way she sits there like a cat with the cream while you and I are humiliated. Can't you see how she changes when we bring her here? Roberta sucking up to her all the time, David treating her like bloody royalty. It makes me sick. And as for your brother last night . . .'

'Claire . . .' Clumsily, he tried to put his arm around her shoulders, but she pulled him away violently. She had dreaded the annual trial of sharing the same bed again and the experience had been as bad as the anticipation. She had repeatedly woken up, aware that the sleeping man beside her was her husband; after so long, it should have been a natural state of their marriage, comfortable in their physical closeness with countless moments of passion to remember and repeat more quietly and deeply. It should have been a warm, sustaining, secret place of love, not a permanent torment reminding her of how much she lacked. Her rejection made him sag under another defeat and he became sullen.

'We still can't go,' he repeated. 'There's only one more day to get through. For God's sake, you can manage that.'

'All right, but next year you can come if you want, I'm staying at home.'

'Good morning Charles.'

'Florence. Sleep well?'

'Not very, I'm afraid. I'm going to speak to Richard later and tell him he must apologize to you. His behaviour last night was inexcusable.'

'I'd rather you didn't. It's not important and there's no need ...'

'Yes there is. He embarrassed everybody and obviously upset Naomi ... how is she this morning?'

'She seems all right. She's in the kitchen preparing breakfast.'

'As if she hasn't done enough ... I'll go and help her.'

Without the traditional established pattern of Christmas Day, they drifted down as they felt like it; at eleven o'clock Emma had still not appeared and Richard said he would go and get her up. She was wide awake with the curtains open, lying on the bed and staring blankly at the ceiling.

'Are you coming down?' he asked.

'What for?' She didn't move.

'You can't just lie there all day.'

'Why not? There's fuck all else to do.'

'Come on, Em. Do it to please your old man.'

She turned her head and looked at him coldly. 'And what's my old man ever done for me?'

'What does that mean?'

'What it sounds like ... all right, I'll be down in a bit ... how's Stephanie this morning?'

'Stephanie? She's all right. Why?'

'Just wondered ... perhaps she's found a way of enjoying herself in this bloody house.'

'What are you talking about?'

'Nothing. Go on ... I said I'd come down.'

Roberta had made a deliberate effort to look good that morning. She washed her hair and brushed it into a short shining hood of chestnut, and put on the beige wool crêpe skirt of the Emporio Armani suit that her parents had given her for Christmas with a washed silk Nicole Farhi blouse. Examining herself in the mirror, she determined to try and lift the mood of the house. As she walked into the kitchen, the first person she saw was Claire – permed hair, heavy patterned cardigan, dark tartan skirt, flat shoes – who took one look and immediately stared down into her tea.

'Good morning, Grandmama.' Roberta kissed Florence.

'Good morning. You look very nice. I read in one of the papers that long skirts were fashionable again.'

'Very trendy.' She whirled round on her high heels. 'Wait till they see me in this at the Beeb. I'll be fighting them off.' She grinned impishly. 'Just like you, Grandmama.'

'That's enough from you, young lady. I'm a respectable lady of rather more than a certain age.'

Roberta pulled a disbelieving face. 'Really? Tell me about it.'

Claire silently hurt at the glances they exchanged. Little private jokes between people close to each other mattered so much. If Harry had lived, she could have had grandchildren by now and they might have grown up to become her friends.

'Where was Richard off to in the car?' Roberta asked as she began to make herself a cup of coffee.

'He's gone into the village to buy a copy of the *Post*,' Florence told her. She liked the way Brookmans Park still referred to its high street.

'He'll get all the others that are out today as well, then. God, the social embarrassment of having the *Sun* in the house. At least it'll keep him busy. What are the rest of us going to do? Claire?'

Claire stood up. 'I'll do what I'm told, Roberta. Like I always do.'

Roberta gave a low growl of anger as her aunt walked out. 'I didn't need that, Grandmama. I'm trying to cheer people up around here.'

'I know you are, darling. But it's always uphill work with Claire.'

'I know it is, but . . .' Roberta sat at the table opposite Florence. 'What *is* the matter with everyone? They piss me off. Mummy's worked so hard and all they're doing is shitting on everything. Sorry, I don't usually use that sort of language to you, but—'

'It's all right,' Florence interrupted. 'If there's any more nonsense like last night, you may hear me using it. Richard was disgusting.'

'He wasn't the only one.'

'What do you mean?'

'It doesn't matter.' Roberta reached across and took her grand-mother's hand. 'You and me against the rest of them? For Mummy and Daddy's sake?'

'Of course. We'll be all right.'

The day was too empty, too many vacuums to be filled with anything that would relieve the tedium. And there were things that people felt had to be said. Florence began it when she found Richard alone in the drawing room.

'Have you apologized to Naomi?' she asked.

'What for?'

'Last night, of course ... and please put that newspaper down. You were drunk and you embarrassed everybody.'

Richard lowered the *Daily Mirror* but kept hold of it. 'She hasn't said anything.'

'Well, I'm saying something. I expect my children to behave better.'

'I'm not your bloody child. I'm nearly fifty years old.'

'You certainly didn't behave like it last night. I won't have it, Richard.'

'Won't have what?' Head splitting from a hangover, Richard snapped with anger. 'If Naomi wants to give me a bollocking that's up to her. Stop treating me like a kid. I don't like it.'

'I'm not interested in what you like or don't like. You were disgusting. If your father could have—'

'Shut up!' The *Mirror* fluttered and fell apart as he threw it towards her. 'What the fuck's he got to do with it?'

Florence's face hardened. 'Fuck you, Richard! That surprised you, didn't it? But never talk about your father like that again! If you can't do anything else, at least show some respect for him.'

'Respect? For that hypocritical, self-satisfied, pompous bast—'

'Richard! Stop it! Have you started drinking again already?'

For a moment they stared at each other, then the door from the hall opened and Naomi came in.

'What on earth's going on in here? The third world ...?' She stopped as they turned towards her. 'Oh. I didn't realize it was you.'

'I'm sorry, Naomi,' Florence said stiffly. 'I was just telling Richard that he should apologize for his behaviour last night, but he appears to be in a very odd mood this morning. However, I've done my best. Perhaps he'll be less hysterical with you. I'm going to my room for a while.'

'Thanks, Mum, but you didn't have to ...' Naomi sighed as Florence walked out, then turned wearily to Richard. 'What the hell was all that about?'

'It doesn't matter. She just got up my nose.'

'By asking you to apologize?'

'No, it was ... forget it. And OK, I'm sorry. I made a pig of myself.'

'Yes ... and I've been thinking about this, Richard. Unless you promise to behave in future, you're not welcome in this house any more. I can't stand another episode like last night. You've never liked coming here anyway. As you said, perhaps it's just a pretence that we keep up for the wrong reasons. Let's just let it go.'

'Can you do that?' he asked quietly.

'Don't start that again,' she warned. 'I don't want to know. Just ... just ... sort it out for yourself. Like Tim and I have. And don't ask me to carry your bloody burdens. Right?'

'But you said that—'

'Shut *up*!' Naomi closed her eyes and shuddered. 'What I said, I said. What I said, I meant. That's it. Now for Christ's sake just hack it for yourself.'

She turned and walked out of the room. Richard stared after her for a moment, then went and poured himself another drink.

Separated by less than a second, two explosions crashed and echoed through the silence of the woods, fading amid the flapping of frantic wings as winter birds fled into the sky. Hidden in the undergrowth, a muntjac deer scampered away in terror. It was early afternoon, the sun making a token effort as cold pale light turned chill mist lemon yellow and sparkled on frost and ice. Charles lowered the shotgun and broke it, expelling the spent, smoking cartridges; he had not been trying to kill anything and had fired at a high branch on a dead tree.

'Ever used one of these?' he asked.

'Not for a long time,' Richard replied. 'I was taught the basics on a freebie PR weekend about ten years ago.'

Charles reloaded and held the gun towards his brother-in-law. 'Try again. The recoil's not as violent as you'd expect.'

He stood behind Richard as he locked the barrels and pointed them into the empty sky. Stephanie covered her ears with the sheepskin mittens Naomi had lent her and thunderous detonations ripped the silence again.

'It's enough to wake the dead,' she complained.

'Don't worry, the nearest house is more than a mile away,' Charles assured her. 'Do you want to try it, David?'

'OK.' He took the gun from Richard and loaded it himself.

'What does it ... I mean they're not like bullets, are they?' Stephanie asked. Now that David was holding the gun, she became interested in it.

'No, it's shot.' David looked round the clearing in which they were standing. 'See that tree trunk?' He held the gun at waist level and fired. The thick mat of fallen leaves against the edge of the log erupted and fragments of wood were torn off and hurled into the bushes beyond. 'Come and see.'

Stephanie crossed the clearing with him and they crouched down; the bark was peppered with tiny holes. David picked up a pellet of lead.

'Just imagine you're a bird in the way of a few of these.'

'I'd rather imagine something else,' she replied softly and ran her fingers along the barrels of the shotgun he was still holding. 'They're

215

very . . . Freudian, aren't they?'

'Not now,' he murmured.

'Later, though . . . and I want both barrels.'

'Christ, you're insatiable. I like that in a woman.' His lips barely moved, then he straightened up and turned back towards his father. 'You're right about the recoil, Dad. You can hardly feel it.'

'Come on, it's time we were getting back,' Charles said. He had suggested that they test his present as a means of escape from the suffocating house, but now he wanted to get back to his wife. As they walked towards the car, Richard put his arm round Stephanie's shoulders and felt the controlled reluctance of her body.

Chapter Four

Neighbours had been invited in for drinks on Boxing Day evening, outsiders who had to be given an impression of happy family enjoyment.

'Yes it's nice to have everyone all together ... we've been coming to Charles and Naomi for years now. They always give us a marvellous time ... You're a teacher? You must talk to Tim ... Try one of these. They're delicious ... We haven't been able to print it, but we know that before he died, Maxwell ... Just outside Manchester. Not far from Lancashire's cricket ground. Do you know it? ... Is she your first grandchild? How lovely ... Do you like it? My niece bought it for me ... Claire, this lady knits as well ... we'll be going back tomorrow morning ... nice to meet you ... goodbye ...'

As Charles and Naomi closed the front door behind the final departing couple an emptiness descended and they separated from each other again. Florence, for whom the previous two hours had been exactly how she felt Christmas in Hertfordshire ought to be, sat with the library book she had brought with her; Claire, who had found the neighbours snobbish, read the *Daily Mail* from Richard's pile of newspapers; Tim idly looked through the dozens of cards around the room. There were desultory conversations, meaningless talk to fill the silences. Stephanie asked if she could borrow a drier and went upstairs to wash her hair; Charles said he had some urgent work to do in his study.

'This is dire,' Roberta whispered to her mother. 'We've got to do *something* with them.'

'There's a film on BBC2 shortly. They can watch that.' Naomi appeared exhausted. 'I'm going to the sitting room to write some letters.'

Roberta was aware that her parents were abandoning their duties as host and hostess, as though they had given up on their guests. At least it was nearly nine o'clock; less than three hours and everybody should be in bed. The film came on and provided another escape; a slick Hollywood production that was bound to have a happy ending ... Richard suddenly remarked that Stephanie had not returned from washing her hair and said he was going to find her. Roberta instantly registered that David had left the room about fifteen minutes earlier.

'No, it's all right,' she said hastily. 'I've got to go upstairs anyway. You stay there.'

Filled with renewed anger, she ran up the stairs two at a time, irrationally convincing herself that if she expected the worst it would somehow not be happening. Richard and Stephanie's room was empty, and the hair drier she had borrowed was still in its case on the bed.

'You bloody well are, aren't you?' she said to herself, then stepped across the landing and hurled open the door of her brother's bedroom. Urgent coupled bodies abruptly stopped moving and there was a brief, tense silence as they slackened and separated. David had taken off his trousers and underpants, but was still wearing his shirt and socks; Stephanie's skirt and knickers lay crumpled on the floor and her sweater and bra were pushed up under her neck, exposing her breasts. Partial nakedness made them look sordid and furtive.

'Don't you know it's polite to knock?' David asked sardonically.

'Jesus, you're ... pigs!' Roberta spat the word at them. 'Just get dressed right now and come downstairs. Separately. Incidentally, I know you were at it last night as well. Would it be too much to ask you to behave until you leave? After that you can screw each other's brains out, but doing it in this house is gross.'

'Butt out, sis. It's not hurting anybody.'

'Not hurting ... ?' She shook her head in disbelief. 'Have

you no bloody idea at all what's going on around you, David? Everybody's at each other's throats, Mummy's cracking up. It's like a bomb waiting to go off, and all you can think about is getting your end away with this slag!'

'What?' Stephanie sat up, eyes blazing. 'You sanctimonious cow! Take that back right now or . . . oh, *fuck!*'

She fell back on to the bed and stared at the ceiling. Roberta realized that David was looking past her on to the landing and turned round; Richard was standing behind her.

'No!' Roberta grabbed hold of Richard's arms. 'Don't start a row. Please . . .'

She staggered as he savagely pushed her aside and David jumped back on to the floor as his uncle lunged at him across the bed; he fell across Stephanie then scrambled off the other side, intent only on reaching his nephew.

'Bastard! Just let me . . .'

Half-naked and vulnerable, David snatched a book from a shelf and hurled it at him; Richard stumbled as he ducked and it hit the wall, then he caught David's ankle as he tried to dash past him.

'Stop it!' Roberta ran to the struggling bodies, desperately trying to pull them apart. 'Stephanie, for Christ's sake help!'

Richard hurled her off and clawed at David, fists wildly punching towards his face. Roberta grabbed his right wrist and managed to hold it for a moment before he wrenched it free and hit David in the mouth. As he raised his fist again, Stephanie threw her arms round his neck and fell backwards, her weight dragging him with her; David shuffled away awkwardly, like a terrified crab, swearing as he held his hand to his split lip. Roberta stood between the two men, sobbing.

'That's *enough*! Stop it! You're disgusting! Both of you.'

'Don't talk to me about disgusting.' Richard's face was flushed with rage. 'Tell your bloody brother.'

'Then hit her as well,' Roberta snapped. 'He didn't exactly have to tie her down.'

'No, he didn't.' Richard turned to Stephanie, who had let go of him and was picking her skirt from the floor with one hand as she pulled her bra and sweater down with the other. 'Which of you started it?'

'Does it matter? It happened.'

'It happened last night as . . .' Roberta stopped herself as emotion loosened her tongue, but it was too late.

'Last night?' Richard exploded. 'Do you mean they were——?'

'No!' She crossed the room and closed the door. 'I don't know. I just saw . . . I was probably wrong.'

'Saw what?' Stephanie demanded. 'Just a minute, you said that before. For Christ's sake, were you watching?'

'Don't be sick! I noticed a light under this door. I didn't know what was happening, but . . . sorry, I should have kept my mouth shut.'

'Of course.' Richard stood up, rubbing the knuckles of his right hand. 'When I was pissed.' David shrank back as he stepped towards him. 'Don't worry, I'm not going to damage your precious good looks any more . . . but I am going to get drunk again.'

'Don't Richard.' Roberta's eyes begged him as she remained with her back against the door to prevent him leaving. 'I'm so sorry, but . . .' She began to cry again. 'But it's so awful. I don't know what's wrong with everybody. It's like living on the edge of a volcano. Can't you at least just put on an act until the morning? Please.'

'I've been putting on an act all my bloody life and I'm tired of it.' He rubbed his hand across his forehead. 'OK. I'll make no promises, but I'll try. There's enough shit in this family as it is.'

'What do you mean?'

'It doesn't matter.'

She stared at him in bewilderment as she let him move her aside and walk out; she had known him all her life and he was a stranger.

'I'm bleeding.' David sounded childishly petulant.

'Shut up and get dressed.' Roberta felt sick with distaste. 'Then come down and act normally for the rest of the evening. Tomorrow you can piss off and do what the hell you want. But for now I want you two to behave. All right?'

'If you hadn't burst in here none of this would have happened.' David had taken a tissue from a box by the bed and was dabbing his lip with it. 'We were going to keep it quiet. You've just screwed it up for everybody.'

Roberta looked away from him. 'If that's what you think, David, then I can't talk to you any more.'

She left them and went into her own room, where she had to lean against the wall as she felt dizzy. Deep inside her was the additional personal hurt of what had happened with Martin. She hadn't actually seen him in bed with Suzanne, but for a long time afterwards she had been unable to prevent the torment of imagining what they must have done to each other's bodies. The fleeting sight of her brother and Stephanie, panting and obsessed, had brought back the jealousy and hatred and the sense of humiliating worth-lessness.

'Let it go!' she said aloud. 'That doesn't matter. Just get through the rest of tonight.'

She cleaned up make-up smudged by tears, then sat very still for a few minutes, forcing calmness into herself before returning downstairs. Stephanie was already back in the living room, sitting on the floor by Richard's feet. Roberta felt it was taking the act too far, but they were not touching each other. She was surprised to realize that the incident had taken so little time; she had been out of the room less than a quarter of an hour, her absence covered by communal concentration on the film as though everyone was determined to keep everything around them at bay. Florence was the only one who looked up and smiled at her before returning her attention to the screen.

David was coming downstairs as Naomi left the little sitting room.

'What on earth have you done to yourself?'

'What? Oh, this.' He gingerly touched his lip where the split was covered by a sticking plaster. 'I slipped in the bathroom. It's all right.'

'There's a bruise as well ... let me see ...'

'Forget it, Mum.' He stepped backwards as she approached him. 'It's OK.'

'There's blood soaking through that plaster. Just let me ...'

'Back off! I'm not a kid!'

Offended by his rejection, Naomi glared at him. 'You're not acting much like a grown-up, either. Anyway, if you want to bleed all over the place, that's your business. I've got enough to contend with without you. Is everyone still watching the film?'

'As far as I know they are.'

'Well, perhaps you can come and help me be hostess? Roberta's done more than her share.'

Saying she was going to write letters had only been an excuse. For the previous hour, Naomi had sat alone, persuading herself that her protection was secure and could not just be torn away to expose her. She would have to meet Richard in town as soon as possible and discover what had suddenly weakened him, restore her defences by rebuilding his. Perhaps she needed to talk to Tim as well; after thirty years it could not all be lost. In the meantime, there were the last stages of Christmas to get through. She'd managed years of them without any problem; why should this one be different? All she had to do was treat everyone normally, like in any other family; she did not need her son being aggressive about her concern.

As the film's credits rolled, there was a sense of apprehension at the prospect of having to try to relate to each other. It was just after eleven o'clock and Florence immediately said she was going to bed.

'We've got a long journey tomorrow and the forecast said there could be snow in the Midlands, so we should set off early.' She went to Naomi and kissed her. 'Thank you. It's been a lovely Christmas. As always. Where's Charles?'

'He's still working. He's got an important meeting tomorrow.'

'I'll thank you both again in the morning, then.' Florence looked round the room. 'Is anybody else coming up?'

'Yes,' Claire replied. 'You're right about the weather. We'll need to leave as soon as possible. Tim?'

'I'll just finish this.' He held up his glass.

'Don't take too long about it.'

Craving for a joint, Emma followed almost immediately, but Richard said he wanted to watch the late news and made it clear that Stephanie was to remain with him; Roberta stared at David until he got the message and left.

'I'll just go and see if Daddy's finished,' Naomi said.

As soon as she left the room, Stephanie got up from Richard's feet and sat apart from him. Roberta sighed inside herself. She remembered what he had said about putting on an act all his life and wondered what he had meant, but there had been so much about people's behaviour in the previous two days that didn't make sense. She suddenly felt sorry for him, a strong man who couldn't cope with having to spend the night in the same bed as the girlfriend he had seen with another lover. But it was impossible to arrange separate rooms; there wasn't the space in the house and it could lead to difficult questions from Naomi that he might be drunk enough to answer. Because he was drunk again, with a quiet deliberateness that seethed with rage.

'I'm going to bed,' Stephanie announced abruptly. 'I'm tired.'

Richard ignored her, but after she had left he turned to his niece. 'You go as well, Roberta.'

'Don't tell me what to do in my own house.'

'Do it,' he said. 'I want to talk to Naomi and Tim. Alone.'

'I'm still not going to—'

'I'm putting on the act like you wanted,' he interrupted. 'Now I want you to go to bed. If you don't, I might say things you'd rather I didn't.'

'What are you talking about?' Tim sounded puzzled and slightly apprehensive.

'Roberta knows,' Richard replied. 'That's why she's going to bed.'

She had felt sorry for him, his ludicrous middle-aged chauvinism

223

damaged and his arrogance deflated by the almost farcical events earlier. Now she detested him, raddled and telling her how to behave. The worst thing was that she had to accept it; if she didn't, he would say what she desperately wanted to keep quiet from her mother and father.

'All right,' she agreed. 'But don't ever threaten me again, Richard. Goodnight, and as I don't particularly want to see you in the morning, goodbye as well. Happy New Year when it comes.' She stalked out of the room; at the end of the hall the kitchen light was on and she realized her mother must be in there.

'Goodnight, Mummy,' she said from the doorway.

'Goodnight, dear . . . what's the matter? You look furious.'

'Richard wants to talk to you and Tim, so he's just sent me to my room.'

'What? He can't have meant it like that.'

'Yes he did.' Her anger began to come out in tears. 'I'm sorry, Mummy, but apart from you and Daddy and Grandmama I hate everyone and everything in this house at the moment. It's been the worst Christmas in the history of the world.'

'Oh, darling.' Naomi put down the glass of water she had just filled and put her arms round her daughter. 'I know it's been awful and thank you for being there and helping.'

'But what is it?' Roberta sobbed as she leant against her. 'Why is everyone being so awful?'

'They're not.' Naomi stroked her hair. 'You know they're not. Grandmama's the same, isn't she? And Emma. And David.' She looked startled as Roberta violently pulled away.

'David's a selfish pig!'

'Why? What's he done?'

'It doesn't matter . . . I didn't mean to say that. Forget it.' Roberta rubbed away tears with the back of her hand. 'I'm going to bed now . . . where's Daddy?'

'He's already gone up. He's very tired.'

'I'll go and say goodnight to him, then.' She stepped towards Naomi again and kissed her. 'I love you.'

'I love you too, darling. Don't worry about anything. It'll be all right. Goodnight.'

That it was hurting Roberta affected Naomi most. Having convinced herself that her own childhood – Naomi Barlow's childhood – had been damaged by her father, she had always determined that her children should be happy, understood and given attention. She was proud of Roberta and David, successful, well-adjusted, complete, representing another aspect of how she had changed into the woman she was; damage to them threatened her. Having gone through fright and worry over Richard, she was now angry with him. By the time she returned to the drawing room, he had poured and half drunk another large whisky, crossing from alcoholic rambling to aggression.

'Good,' he said as she walked in. 'I want to talk to you.'

'So Roberta told me.'

'Roberta? Oh, yeah. Had to send her to bed.'

'Which was inexcusable, but I'll talk to you about that when you're capable of understanding. Anyway, what do you want to say that's so important?'

'You know.'

'No I don't . . . do you, Tim?'

'He's been rambling on about Dad and—'

'That's it,' Richard interrupted. 'The old man. Want to tell you something about him. You two don't know this, but—'

'Just help me get him to bed, Tim,' Naomi said sharply. 'He'll have forgotten it all in the morning.'

'Oh no.' Richard stood up and moved away from the door. 'Not until you've heard about . . . what was her name? Welsh tart with big tits. Worked at Coombes Brothers.'

'Coombes Brothers?' Naomi repeated in disbelief. 'For God's sake, Richard, how drunk are you? What are you trying to do?'

'Tell you something . . . just listen. She was called . . . not Myfanwy. Something like that . . . Megan! That was it. Megan Williams. The old man was knocking her off. Didn't know that, did you?'

'Don't be stupid!' Tim sounded outraged. 'And don't say things like that about ...'

'Tim, he's out of his tree.' Naomi gestured impatiently. 'And I'm not going to listen to any more of this. At the moment, Richard, I don't want to speak to you ever again. You're disgusting.'

'Disgusting? Second time I've been called that tonight.'

'I'm not surprised. Who by?'

'Roberta. Just because I was sorting out your bloody son.'

Naomi turned to Tim. 'What's been happening?'

'Nothing,' he insisted. 'We've all been watching television. I don't think Richard and David even spoke to each other.'

'There you are, then. He's so drunk he thinks he's had a row with David this evening, so you don't need to take any notice of anything he says about Dad. He couldn't even spell his own name at the moment. Leave him here. He can pass out on the floor for all I care.'

She turned towards the door, trembling. To be alone with her brothers and the ghost of their father after so many years was terrifying.

'Nimmy ...' Tim began.

'Don't call me that!' She whirled round on him. The childhood name had conjured up Naomi Barlow and she had to be instantly attacked and destroyed again through him. 'For Christ's sake, grow up. Look at you. Little schoolteacher who can't even control a class of seven-year-olds. Going on about tacky Chinese restaurants as if they're the Dorchester. Dressed like something out of an Oxfam shop. Clinging to Mum like a bloody kid. Don't you realize how pitiful you are? All you're good for is laughing at, Tim.

'And as for you, Richard ... well, I thought I had two brothers, but all I've got is two weak sisters. A drunk and a case of arrested development. Neither of you has been any help to me since we ...' She choked on words she was no longer able to say, gulping and beginning to sob. 'Just get out of here. Go away. You're ... you're ... what are you trying to do? Destroy everything I've got?' She stared at them accusingly, then ran out of the room.

'What do you mean by ... ?' Tim's fists were clenched as he shouted after her. He turned to his brother. 'Did you hear that? After all I've done for Mum while she was turning herself into Lady Muck and you were kicking your way through Fleet Street.'

'Lady Muck?' Richard repeated sarcastically. 'Christ, I haven't heard that for thirty years. Naomi's right, you've never grown up. You're just the same.'

'Thank God I am. At least I'm honest.'

'Are you? Come on, none of us is honest, Tim. We daren't be.' He lit a cigarette and drank the last of his whisky through half-expelled smoke. 'I want to ask you something I asked Naomi earlier. Whose idea was it?'

'Whose idea was what?'

'You know what I'm talking about. Who first came up with the idea of killing the old man?'

'What?' Tim shook his head. 'Jesus, Richard, you know that. It was yours.'

Richard paused, then nodded as though suddenly understanding something. 'I get it. You've sorted it out between you.'

'What the hell are you on about?'

'You and Naomi. You can't handle it, so you blame it on me. Easy, isn't it? Everyone says I'm the hard bastard. Lets you both off the hook.'

'It was you,' Tim insisted. 'Right from the start. You worked out how we could do it, then persuaded us to join you. And as soon as you could you ran away from it and became what you are. You let us ruin our lives because all you were interested in was yourself. I loved Dad and—'

'Crap. You hated him as much as we did.'

'Don't ever say that again, Richard. I'm warning you ... and what the hell were you saying about him and some woman at Coombes Brothers?'

'I told you. He was knocking her off.'

'Liar!' Tim stepped towards him threateningly. 'He wasn't! Dad would never have done anything like that. What are you trying to do? Find an excuse for the fact that you helped to kill him?'

'Don't be stupid. I wouldn't have killed him for that. It just showed what a hypocritical sod he was. I bet she wasn't the only one. Can't say I blame him, though. She had the biggest pair of . . .' He staggered backwards as his brother pushed him like a small child trying to fight an older bully. 'Back off, you prat! If you don't like the truth don't ask me about it.'

'It's not the truth! You're—'

Richard grabbed hold of his shirt. 'Listen, dickhead. He was screwing the arse off her. You can kid yourself as much as you want, but I know.'

'No . . . no!' A shirt button broke loose as Tim struggled free and backed away. 'You've been telling lies too long, Richard – that's what they pay you to do – you can't believe anyone can be decent. Not even your own father.'

'All right, don't believe me. But let's ask Mum. She's never said anything, but she must have known something was going on. She's always been sharp as a needle.'

'Don't you *dare* say anything to Mum!'

'Why not? It doesn't matter now. And she's had a perfectly good time in bed since then. She thinks nobody knows, but remember Don Barraclough who lived next door? Rep for a drugs company or something. Years ago, when I was working on the *Messenger*, I called round one afternoon unexpectedly and they were upstairs together. Mum shouted down that he was helping her fix something, but she didn't ask me to go up and help. In fact she told me to wait until she came down. When she did, it was written all over her face what they'd been up to. She tried to hide it, but I knew. And I'm bloody positive he wasn't the only one.'

Tim had begun to shake and tears of rage and betrayal ran down his face. He was breathing deeply and jerkily, and for a moment looked as if he was going to fall down. He swallowed with difficulty and when he spoke, the words came in painful gasps.

'No . . . no . . . no . . . Nimmy's right . . . you're sick . . . Dad would never have . . . Mr Barraclough was . . . don't do it, Richard

228

... stop ... it's cruel ... not Mum ... you've got to love ...'
Fragments vanished beneath a massive sob. 'You're evil!'

Richard laughed. 'And you're pitiful, just like Naomi said.
Perhaps you'll believe it when Mum admits it. Now piss off to your
sodding awful wife like a good little boy. I'm going to stay down
here and finish this Scotch. There's nothing for me to go to bed
for.'

Still sobbing, Tim turned and ran out of the room as fast as his
sister had. After a lifetime of lies, there had suddenly been too much
truth.

Chapter Five

With other murders that Michael Dundee had investigated, the victims had been in locations that mirrored the ugliness and brutality of the crime – a burnt-out car, a filthy tower block council flat taken over by junkies, sprawled in a litter-strewn, badly lit underpass smelling of stale urine. The house in Devon Lane was all wrong; it was the sort of address the police might visit in connection with motoring offences, perhaps high-class fraud, but not to find two hideously violated bodies, slaughtered like animals amid the elegance. The woman's hand must have knocked over the tall Chinese vase on the gleaming grand piano as she fell, silk flowers scattering around her body so that they looked as if they had been placed there by grieving friends.

But everything had been disproportionate. When Charles Stansfield had opened the front door that morning he had behaved impeccably correctly, shock and horror masked by a proper level of responsibility. Nothing had been disturbed, he assured Dundee. After he had been woken by the shots, he had gone downstairs and found them, instantly realized they were both dead and had immediately telephoned the police before calling a doctor. He had even asked Dundee's permission to pour himself a brandy before giving a lucid, controlled statement. Now that Dundee had to talk to him again, his calm still covered anguish and blame.

'Your shotgun, Mr Stansfield. First of all, why wasn't it locked in a secure place? I'm sure you know the terms of your licence.'

'Of course I do, and normally it would have been, Superintendent. I am very much aware of how much I'm responsible for what's happened and ... well, that's something I have to live with.

It wasn't in its proper place – I'll show you where it should have been in my study if you wish; it's perfectly secure – because yesterday afternoon I went out to try it. I've told you it was a Christmas present from my wife. When I came back, something distracted me and I leant it in the corner by the front door. It's inexcusable, but afterwards I simply forgot about it.'

'And did you leave ammunition with it?'

'I'm afraid so. I had a couple of cartridges left in my pocket and just put them on the hall table.'

Dundee made no criticism; Charles Stansfield knew what he had done, that it had been dangerous and had resulted in tragedy. He would never forgive himself.

'Apart from yourself, who in the house would have been able to load the gun and fire it?' he asked.

'My son, David, whom I taught myself. My wife, although she gave up the sport a long time ago. My brother-in-law – Mr Richard Barlow, that is – although I didn't know until yesterday that he had done it before. I don't know of anybody . . . oh, I'm sorry. Roberta was interested once, but that was years ago.'

'And you're positive you didn't leave it loaded?'

'Absolutely. I've been unforgivably careless, but I haven't been stupid.'

'I appreciate that, sir, and I'm not accusing you of it.' Dundee allowed him a look of quiet sympathy before continuing. 'Of course, once the gun had been loaded by someone who knew how to do it, another person could have fired it.'

'Obviously . . . but there's something I've been thinking about. If an intruder had entered the house and—'

'I'm afraid not,' Dundee interrupted. 'I realize that would be better for you all, but there's no evidence to support it. The patrol officers who arrived first say there had been a slight snowfall at about seven o'clock, not a great deal, but enough to cover the ground. And they noticed that the only tyremarks on your drive had been made by the doctor arriving just before them. After that we checked round the outside of the house. Nobody could have approached without leaving footprints. There weren't any.'

'But someone could have come before it started snowing.'

'Possibly, but how did they get in? You're clearly very security conscious. Every door and window is fastened and nothing's been forced. In any event, if someone did break in during the night, why were they still here at eight o'clock in the morning?' Dundee smiled bleakly. 'I'm sorry, sir, we're not dealing with impossible murders that turn out to have ridiculous explanations. They only happen in books. This was done by someone in this house. I just need to know who it was, and unless I get a confession I'll probably find that out through something as simple as fingerprints. In the meantime, we need to establish other information. The question that most interests me at the moment is why ... had there been any arguments between members of your family over Christmas?'

Charles Stansfield sighed. 'I'm not sure if you'd call them arguments, but there has been a certain amount of tension. It was something that ... I felt my wife knew more than she was prepared to tell me.'

'Unfortunately Mrs Stansfield isn't in any condition to tell us anything at the moment,' Dundee said. 'Except for ... you might be able to help me here, sir. Since the police arrived, your wife has said only one sentence. One of my officers was trying to persuade her to speak. Naturally she called her Mrs Stansfield, but then your wife suddenly said, "I am Naomi Jean Barlow." That's all. I know of course that that was her maiden name, but why should she use it again now?'

'I don't know, Superintendent, but she's terribly shocked and you can hardly expect her to be rational. I can't see that it's important, anyway.'

'Neither can I,' Dundee agreed.

'And when will you let me see her? I appreciate your authority over everyone's movements is very considerable at the moment, but keeping us apart is becoming intolerable. Where is she?'

'She's still here, sir. The doctor's with her. I'll take you to her or

232

bring her here as soon as possible. Tell me more about this ...
tension, I think you said.'

For more than an hour Naomi Stansfield had not taken her eyes off
the window opposite, but it was as though she could see nothing.
Her face looked as if the slightest movement of a single muscle
would unleash a terrible dam of grief and horror that she was
holding inside; apart from the single sentence Dundee had told
Charles about, she had not said a word since the police had arrived.

'Naomi. Just swallow these.' Mark Peters urged as he pressed the
tablets against her lips, gently trying to prise them open. 'They'll
make you feel better. Come on. Please.'

Her lips stiffened as he pressed harder, then she shook her head
violently and pushed his hand away.

'Naomi, this isn't doing any good.' He sighed as she continued
to stare at the window. 'I can't help you unless you'll let me. It's
just a couple of tablets ... look, I'll leave them here with the water.
Promise you'll take them.'

He put the pills and the glass on the table next to her chair and
looked at her sadly for a moment before leaving her with the silent,
watching policeman in the sitting room. A policewoman smiled
sympathetically as he stepped out into the hall.

'Still no go?'

'No, and I want her to take them before we move her to hospital.
If she keeps on like this I'm going to have to give her an injection
... but that means somebody will have to hold her down.'

'We can help you with that.'

'Thanks. I'll give her a few minutes to see if she takes them
herself.'

'You look exhausted,' the policewoman said. 'I've found my way
around the kitchen now CID have finished in there. Come and have
a cup of tea. You've done all you can for them for the time being.'

He followed her and lit a cigarette as he sat at the table. The
policewoman switched on the kettle and added sugar to the tea bag
in a mug.

'You've known them a long time, haven't you?'

'I was Naomi's doctor when she had both Roberta and David. In fact, I'm David's godfather.'

'I thought this was more than just another family who've had a tragedy. I'm awfully sorry. This is bad enough without a personal connection as well . . . what do you think happened?'

The doctor looked at her shrewdly. 'Is this a formal questioning?'

'No.' The kettle turned itself off and she poured water into the mug. 'I'm not CID. I'm just interested in what you think. I don't think you'd say anything to me that you wouldn't repeat to my colleagues.'

'What can I tell them, anyway? Charles called me straight after it happened and I got here to find the police, two bodies and . . . what is it? . . . eight people in a state of shock. Nobody else seems to know exactly what happened so why should I? What does your Mr Dundee think?'

'I'm only the local beat bobby. They don't confide in me. But from what I've overheard, they can't get a coherent story out of anyone. Hardly surprising. Most of them were still asleep when the shots woke them.'

'And no . . . no indications about what led up to it?'

'Not that I've heard, but it must have been something dramatic. I could believe a drunken row that got out of hand last night, but not at that time in the morning.'

'No.' For the first time, Peters was able to think objectively. 'That means that they got up, stone cold sober, came downstairs and . . . good God. It makes it even worse, doesn't it?'

'And how many people got up?' the policewoman added.

'Surely just the two of them. One has to be suicide. It was obvious the barrel of the gun had been put in his mouth.'

'But did he put it there himself?'

'He must have done. You don't just let someone shove a loaded shotgun in your mouth.'

'Unless you'd been knocked out first – and there's nothing left of his head to disprove that.'

'Is that what the police think?'

'Until they know exactly what happened, the CID think everything and they certainly aren't going to talk to me about it. But there aren't going to be any rational explanations for this, Doctor.' She handed him his tea. 'How are the others?'

'Mrs Barlow – Naomi's sister-in-law – collapsed and has been taken to hospital. Your CID don't want to let anybody else go unless it's absolutely necessary. They've still got a lot of questions to ask. The rest of them are more composed than you'd expect. It's shock, of course. They'll go to pieces afterwards.' He swallowed half the tea at one gulp. 'Incidentally, can't you get rid of those bloody reporters? They were on me like wolves when I went out.'

'They're on a public highway and they're not causing an obstruction,' she replied. 'And by their standards they've been quite well behaved.'

'And all they're waiting to do is splash it all over their front pages.'

'Of course they are. It's what their readers expect.'

Anticipation stiffened among the waiting journalists as Dundee walked into the conference room, accompanied by the deputy chief constable and the press liaison officer, and sat at the table in front of the cameras. There was a short pause while he was fitted with a lapel microphone.

'First of all, I'm sorry there has been some delay in holding this press conference,' he began. 'But we have had a great many enquiries to make which are still continuing. I shall first read a statement, copies of which will be available immediately afterwards from Sergeant Davies.'

His eyes moved down to a sheet of paper he was holding. 'At eight-thirty this morning, Hertfordshire police officers went to a house in Devon Lane, Brookmans Park, following a 999 call.

'In a downstairs room, they found the bodies of two persons who had died as a result of shotgun wounds. They have been identified as Miss Roberta Stansfield, aged twenty-three years, and her uncle, Mr Timothy Barlow, aged forty-nine years. Miss Stansfield was the daughter of Mr and Mrs Charles Stansfield of that address. She lived in Muswell Hill, North London. Mr Barlow was Mrs Stansfield's brother, of Wilmsford, Greater Manchester.

'A third person had also suffered minor shotgun wounds. Police are examining a double-barrelled shotgun that was found at the scene.

'Apart from Mr and Mrs Stansfield and the deceased, there were six other persons in the house. With one exception, all were members of the family. These persons are still being questioned. The police are not looking for anyone else in connection with this crime.'

He looked up. 'That completes the official CID statement, ladies and gentlemen. You will appreciate that there are details that at this stage I cannot reveal, but I will answer what questions I can ... Yes?'

'Has anyone been charged, Superintendent?'

'No.'

'But charges are imminent?'

'I'm not yet in a position to say.'

'But they would be against someone in the house?'

'If they were made, yes.'

'Can you tell us who else was in the house? We already have some names.'

'I can confirm Mr and Mrs Stansfield, but I would prefer not to comment on others.'

'Are any of the names that have been published wrong?'

'I don't know all the names that have been published. I will just repeat that all but one were members of the family who had been spending Christmas together.'

'Who was the exception?'

'A friend of one member of the family.'

'A girlfriend?'

'Yes.'

'Can you tell us anything about the nature of the victims' wounds?'

Dundee paused, considering his reply. 'Miss Stansfield had wounds to the upper part of her body. Mr Barlow had sustained wounds to the head.'

'Had both barrels of the weapon been fired?'

'They had.'

'Superintendent, regarding Mr Barlow's head wounds. Could they have been caused by the gun being placed in his mouth?'

'That is certainly possible.'

'Are you saying it *had* been put in his mouth?'

'No. I'm saying it's possible.'

'If it had been, did he place it there himself?'

'As we don't know if that happened, I obviously can't answer you.'

'You've said that a third person was wounded. Who is that?'

'I can't reveal that at present.'

'But they must have been there when it happened.'

'Yes. And have given a statement.'

'Was it a man or a woman?'

'I'm sorry, I don't want to go even that far.'

'Who called the police?'

'Mr Charles Stansfield, the owner of the house.'

'Was he the one who was wounded?'

'I will not be drawn on that question.'

'Have you any idea of the motive?'

'We are . . . pursuing various lines of enquiry. We have been told of . . . certain disagreements that had occurred.'

'What about?'

'You can hardly expect the police to reveal that.'

'*When* had these deaths occurred?'

'From what we have been told and from medical examination, it appears to have been not long before police were called to the house.'

'At eight-thirty?'

'That was when the first officers arrived. We received the call at' – Dundee held a brief whispered conversation with the press officer – 'at eight-fourteen. A police patrol car was at the house some fifteen minutes later and the first CID officers arrived by nine o'clock.'

'So it happened at . . . what? Eight o'clock?'

'Around that time.'

'Were the victims dressed?'

'They were in their nightclothes.'

'Can you describe them? The nightclothes.'

Dundee recognized an instant tabloid instinct for possible salaciousness. 'Perfectly ordinary. Both were also wearing dressing gowns.'

'So they weren't naked?'

'No, they were not . . . next question, please.'

'Mr Dundee, there have been reports that Charles Stansfield may have been involved in an illegal arms deal. Could there be any connection?'

'I know nothing about that. However, at this stage, we have no evidence of any outside influence in this case.'

'How did the shotgun get into the house?'

'It was a Christmas present for Mr Stansfield from his wife.' Dundee felt the suddenly heightened interest in the room. 'Mr Stansfield is a licensed owner and the weapon had been purchased from a registered dealer.'

'So it was his own gun – bought by his wife – that killed his daughter?'

'I'm afraid it was.' Dundee nodded and stood up as the chief constable touched his arm. 'And I think that's as far as we can go at present. I only want to add that the police appreciate that so far there has been no undue intrusion by the media and hope it will remain that way. We know that you have a job to do, but trust you will recognize that this has been a terrible tragedy. Should charges be brought against anyone, the Press Association and other agencies will be informed immediately. Thank you.'

HSA589569 PAHOME   PA   19.36
POLICE Bodies URGENT
Hertfordshire Police spokesman said that Richard Barlow is being
questioned in connection with the deaths of his brother and niece.

HSA589574 PAHOME   PA   19.45
POLICE Bodies (reopens)
Richard Barlow, news editor of the *Post* newspaper, was tonight being
questioned following the deaths of his brother, Tim Barlow, and his
niece, Roberta Stansfield.

   Mr Barlow (49) was spending Christmas at the home of his sister
and brother-in-law, Charles and Naomi Stansfield, in Brookmans
Park, Hertfordshire. Other members of the family who were guests in
the house have also been helping with police enquiries.

HSA589577 PAHOME   PA   19.50
POLICE Bodies Advisory
ATTENTION NEWS EDITORS, CHIEF SUBS AND
PICTURE EDITORS
A new picture of Richard Barlow now available on PA Pictures. Police
have not indicated any objection to publication. A colour picture
(upright) of victims Roberta Stansfield and Timothy Barlow together
is also available. We are trying for interviews with other members of
the family and watching for possible charges.

Chapter Six

What Richard Barlow told Hertfordshire CID was not the truth, because he was protecting himself from his past. It remains a story from which he has never deviated, either when talking to the family or being interviewed by members of his own profession.

The sequence of events began at about half past two on the morning of 27 December. Richard had remained downstairs, finishing the whisky before he fell uneasily asleep. Drink had a depressing effect on him, and when he awoke he was overcome by an overwhelming sense of failure. His job at the *Post* – the success, power and importance upon which his self-respect centred – was threatened to the degree that it was only a matter of time before he lost it. His girlfriend, an essential assurance of fading vitality, had betrayed and humiliated him. His brother and sister had destroyed a lifetime of self-delusion about their father's murder, which he had hidden behind. His personal support systems in ruins, he had to face himself and could not tolerate what he saw.

He half remembered seeing the shotgun by the front door. Hazy and confused, he went and collected it, picking up the cartridges that Charles had left on the hall table. It is impossible to say whether he really meant to shoot himself at that point, but the gun presented the physical manifestation of the option of suicide, an option that a great many people at least consider at some crisis in their lives. Loading it strengthened the option, feeling its weight in his hands was like balancing its attractions of instant death against self-pitying misery and defeat. At one point, he actually put the barrels in his mouth, but it made him retch and he pulled his head back; he had placed his hands carefully away from the trigger in any event. The melodramatic gesture was another form of deceiving himself. I want to do it ... I could do it ... it will be instant death ... why not? But then, why? Why let them beat you? If the *Post* got rid of him, another paper would snap him up. There were plenty more available young women. He had the means of hitting back at his brother and sister; Naomi could be told about David and Stephanie, Tim could be made to face the truth about their parents. So suicide was stupid. Feeling somehow reassured, he put the shotgun on the floor, then lay back in the chair and slipped again into alcoholic unconsciousness.

Tormented by what his brother had said about their mother and father, Tim had hardly slept. At first he had convinced himself that it was just Richard's lies, but he had threatened to face Mum with it, which would be unforgivable; the subtext of his fears was the appalling thought that it might also be true. Another life lived on deceit was under siege. Shortly after seven-thirty, he could stand it no longer and went to find his brother. Seeing Stephanie alone in bed, he crept downstairs; Richard was snoring in an easy chair, his neck awkwardly bent to one side.

'Wake up!' Tim shook his shoulder violently. 'Richard! Wake up!'

'What?' Richard half shouted and jumped as he was jerked into consciousness; the sudden movement sent pain shooting through his head. 'Jesus!' He held his head in his hands as nausea washed into the back of his throat.

'Wake up,' Tim repeated urgently. 'I've got to talk to you.'

'Fuck off. Leave me alone.'

'Not until you promise.'

'Promise what?'

'Not to say anything to Mum about ... you know what about. About Dad.'

Richard groaned. 'What time is it?'

'That doesn't matter!' Tim shook him again. 'Listen to me! You mustn't say anything! It's all lies! If you don't promise, Richard, I'll ... I'll ...'

'You'll what?' Richard thrust his brother's hand away impatiently. 'Don't come bursting in here like … like … I don't know what like. Sod off and leave me alone.'

Tim was panting with agitation. 'But you've got to promise! Scout's honour.'

'*Scout's honour?* Christ, you're not real. Or are you as pissed as I am?'

'You've had time to sober up.'

'Well, I'll soon do something about that. Where's that bloody Scotch?'

Tim pushed him back into the chair as he started to stand up. Physical attack outraged him and he leapt to his feet, slapping his brother across the mouth.

'Keep your fucking hands off me! I'll tear your bleeding face off!' He blinked, almost as if in surprise, grasping the wing of the chair as he went dizzy, then recovered and staggered slightly as he walked towards the drinks cabinet, muttering to himself.

'Stupid little prat. Scout's bloody honour!' He fumbled with the handle of the cabinet door before opening it and picking up an empty lead crystal decanter. 'Shit. There's none left.'

'Richard!'

'Oh, for fuck's sake, just shut up and—' As he turned round impatiently his body jerked with fear. Tim had picked up the shotgun from where he had left it on the floor by his chair and was pointing it at him. 'Put that down, you stupid bastard!'

'Not until you promise.'

Richard recognized the level of hysteria in the demand. 'All right! I promise, for God's sake! I'll promise anything, but just—'

'Of course you will!' Tim stared at him, as though something had just become clear. 'You'll always promise anything. But you won't keep it, will you? You never do.'

'What do you mean?' Richard felt a paralysis of panic at the look on his brother's face. 'All right, Scout's honour! Cross my heart and hope to die. How the fuck can I make you believe me?'

'You can't.' Tim shook his head. 'I hate you, Richard. I hate you because you hate everybody else. You're a destroyer. It was your idea to kill Dad, now you want to destroy Mum and me with your lies. You're ... you're not fit to live with decent people.'

'Hey, come on. Cool it. Look, I'm sorry for anything I said about ...' Richard's eyes flashed frantically round the room, looking for places where he could find protection behind furniture. However he had been moments before, he was wide awake now and aware that his brother was moving out of control. 'Look, just put that thing down and—'

'*Tim!*' Both men whirled towards the door. Awakened by their shouting, Naomi had come down. 'What are you doing?'

He pointed the gun back at his brother. 'He's going to tell lies to Mum. About Dad. He mustn't do that.'

'For Christ's sake talk some sense into him!' Richard pleaded.

'Please, Tim,' Naomi said softly as she stepped forward. 'It's all right. Come on. Give that to Nimmy.'

He backed away, shaking his head. 'No. You know what he's like. He's wicked. He was the one who killed Dad.'

'I didn't! You did ... she did ... we all did!' Richard snatched up the empty decanter and hurled it across the room, but it missed his brother and crashed into the branches of the tree, shattering Christmas decorations.

'Oh my God!'

Naomi turned round as she heard the voice behind her. 'Stay there, Roberta. No, go and get Daddy.'

'But what's happening?'

'Tim's upset and ... just get Daddy.'

'Is this thing loaded?'

'Stop asking questions!' Naomi shouted.

'I know how to find out,' Tim said quietly. As he raised the shotgun again, Richard dived behind the settee and started scrambling on his hands and knees towards the door. 'Get someone! He's cracked! Call the bloody police!'

Tim dashed past Naomi, pushing her to one side. 'It's no good, Richard. You can't keep running away.'

'*Stop it!*' Roberta stepped forward and stood by the grand piano, at the point where Richard was about to emerge from his hiding place. Naomi gasped in terror. 'Tim, put that down. You don't know what you're doing. You aren't going to shoot Richard.'

For a moment Tim hesitated, then Richard leapt up immediately behind his niece in a panic dash for the door. Tim swung the gun to one side, following the movement; Roberta instinctively moved with it, then everything in the room shook as there was a shattering explosion. Roberta caught the full blast and was hurled backwards along the curved edge of the grand piano, her right arm knocking over a vase before she fell to the floor. Richard yelped as he clasped his hand to his cheek where three stray pellets had struck him.

'No! No! *No!*' Naomi screamed and raced to her daughter, dropping to her knees beside her and clasping her body against her own.

Tim stared down at his niece, aquamarine dressing gown torn to shreds, face ripped open and unrecognizable, then looked at the shotgun in his hands as though trying to understand something incomprehensible.

'I didn't mean . . .' Still holding the gun, he walked forward and knelt beside his sister. 'I'm sorry, Nimmy. It was . . .'

Stunned with shock and disbelief, he made no resistance as Naomi gently laid Roberta down and took the shotgun from him. Without hesitating, she turned it round and held it almost touching his face. Unable to move, Richard closed his eyes as she blew Tim's head off. Then she put the gun down and cradled her daughter in her arms again, as though they were the only people in the entire world. On the carpet beside them, the pink and lavender silk flowers spilled from the vase darkened as their petals soaked blood.

Richard became conscious of footsteps hurrying downstairs and stepped into the hall just as Charles reached the door.

'Don't go in there!' He grabbed his brother-in-law's arm urgently. 'Just call the—'

But Charles had already passed him. He stopped in the doorway for a moment, then went into the room. Richard leant against the wall and closed his eyes again, then opened them as David raced down the stairs.

'What the hell was that?'

'There's been an accident. With the shotgun.'

'Christ. Has anybody been hurt?'

'Yes ... look, your father's in there at the moment and ...' Richard flinched as Florence appeared on the stairs, followed by Claire. He turned back to David. 'Nobody must go in that room. I'll close the door while you stop them, then I'll come back and help you. Don't stand there, get on with it.'

David moved towards the frightened questions coming from the stairs as Richard went back into the drawing room. Charles had unclasped Naomi's arms from Roberta and was helping her to her feet.

'Will you take her, please, Richard?' he said. He showed no hysteria, just rigid calm and stunned concern. 'I'm going to call the police.'

Naomi's body felt as if it was dead as her brother put his arm round her shoulders and led her away, closing the door behind them. Charles Stansfield's face was immobile as he looked down at the body of his daughter, then he crossed the room and picked up the telephone.

'Police, please ... police? My name is Stansfield and I'm calling from eleven Devon Lane, Brookmans Park. I'm afraid there's been ... an accident. Two people have been killed. Can you come immediately? No, nobody is in danger now ... that's right, number eleven. It's called The Larches. I'll make sure nobody leaves the house ... yes, please call an ambulance. Thank you.'

He rang off and dialled another number. 'Mark? It's Charles Stansfield. I'm sorry to call you, but can you come here immediately? Roberta's been ...' A painful choke trapped the word. 'She's been shot. I'm positive she's dead, but perhaps you can do something for Naomi. No, nobody else is hurt, apart from ... just get here, Mark. Please. At once.'

He put the phone down and did not look at either body again

as he walked out of the room to join the rest of the family.

That is what really happened.

Considering that he had been a witness to two violent and bloody deaths, Dundee felt that Richard Barlow was almost uncannily composed, but he put it down to a powerful personality. During the day, his officers had discovered a great deal about the reputation of the *Post*'s news editor. Holding a copy of his statement, Dundee took the chair opposite him at the table in the interview room.

'I'd just like to clarify some points in your statement, Mr Barlow,' he explained.

Richard nodded. 'What do you want to know?'

'You say . . .' Dundee glanced at the first page, '. . . that on Boxing Day night you did not go to bed but remained downstairs in the front room. Why was that?'

'I'd been drinking and fell asleep in the chair.'

'Didn't anybody try to persuade you to go to bed?'

'No . . . I'd been drinking a lot and I'm afraid I'd become rather objectionable. I think everyone just wanted to leave me alone.'

'I see . . . and you were asleep in the chair all night?'

'I vaguely remember waking up a couple of times, but went off again.'

'Until your brother woke you at . . . what time was that?'

'I'm not certain, but it must have been some time around eight o'clock.'

'And you immediately started arguing?'

'Yes. We'd had a row the night before – just before he went to bed, in fact – and he was taking it up again.'

'First thing in the morning? It must have been something serious.'

'It was to him. It concerned our father.'

'Your father?' Dundee looked at the statement again. 'I thought your father was dead.'

'He is. He died in 1959.'

'So what were you arguing about after all this time?'

Richard lit a cigarette. 'It's a long story, but basically I told my brother that our father had had an affair when we were teenagers. He knew nothing about it and was upset when I told him. He accused me of lying. I told him I wasn't and that I was sure our mother had known about it. I suggested we could ask her in the morning.'

Dundee leant back in his chair. 'And first thing next morning – apparently, the moment he got up, in fact – your brother was still ... agitated about this? Something that happened more than thirty years ago?'

'Yes. You have to understand something about Tim. After our father's death he became very close to our mother, very protective towards her. He obviously felt that if I mentioned what I knew it would upset her.'

'Would it have?'

'Frankly, I don't think it would. I think she probably knew.'

'So your brother's reaction seems extreme in the circumstances.'

Richard shrugged. 'He loved our mother very much indeed. He felt I was threatening her in some way.'

'Would you have told her? About this affair?'

'Probably not. I was drunk when I told him about it last night.'

'I see.' Dundee picked up the statement again. 'You say that when he woke you up he was holding Mr Stansfield's shotgun.'

'That's right. Charles had left it by the front door in the hall.'

'But Mr Stansfield insists it wasn't loaded when he left it there.'

'I'm sure it wasn't. I went to the woods with Charles yesterday afternoon when he tried it out and I remember him breaking it and carrying it over his arm as we walked back to the car. I didn't see him reload it after that.'

'So how was it loaded? Your brother didn't shoot, did he?'

'He did once. Some years ago he was attending a teaching conference in London for a few days and stayed with me. One afternoon I'd been invited to the press opening of a shooting club and took him with me. He learnt the basics there, although I don't know if he ever did it again.'

'When was this, Mr Barlow?'

'I'm not sure . . . ten years ago? Twelve, perhaps.'

'What was the name of the club?'

'I can't remember.' Richard tapped ash into a saucer on the table. 'It was somewhere in Surrey, I think. Or it might have been Kent. I never went again.'

'So you're saying that your brother could have loaded the gun.'

'I can't see why not. It's not very difficult once you've been shown how.'

'Very well. What happened next?'

'It's all in my statement.'

'I'd still like you to tell me again.'

Richard lit another cigarette from the end of the first before stubbing it out in the saucer.

'Tim became very agitated. He was shouting at me and waving the gun in all directions. I tried to calm him down because he'd obviously lost control of himself. Of course I didn't know then if the gun was loaded, but I wasn't going to risk trying to take it off him. The noise must have disturbed Roberta and she came downstairs. I don't know why, but seeing her seemed to make Tim worse.'

He paused. 'The next minute or so were very confusing because I was so scared, for Roberta as well as for me. She and I moved near each other. We were both trying to talk to him at the same time, begging him to put the gun down. I had an idea that if we could move nearer the piano, I could drag her with me under it. It doesn't sound the best idea now, but they weren't the sort of circumstances in which you think clearly. The trouble was that it meant moving towards the door into the hall. He really became hysterical then, so we stopped. He was crying – he even laughed once – and I realized something must have snapped inside him. Then Naomi came into the room and screamed at him. That did it. He pointed the gun straight at us both and I knew he was going to fire. I grabbed Roberta to drag her on to the floor, but . . .'

He hesitated again, this time for several moments. When he spoke again, he sounded guilty.

'I should have just pushed her down and fallen on top of her. What I did meant I was almost holding her like a shield. Apart from this – ' he touched his face where his minor wounds had been dressed by the doctor – 'she took the full blast.'

He lowered his head and Dundee waited through the silence.

'I appreciate this is very difficult for you, Mr Barlow,' he said finally. 'It's just that we have to . . .'

'I know.' Richard looked up again. 'It's all right. Getting facts is my business as well. There isn't much more anyway. Naomi screamed and dashed over to Roberta. I was too stunned to do anything except stand there. Tim . . . let me think. He didn't move for a moment, then walked over and stood next to them. He said "Nimmy" – it was a nickname he's had for her since childhood – and she just looked up at him. She was holding Roberta against her. For a moment they just stared at each other, then he turned the gun round in his hands and put the barrels in his mouth. That was it. He didn't hesitate, and there was no way either of us could have stopped him.'

Dundee nodded. 'Thank you, Mr Barlow. There are just a couple of points. Your fingerprints were found on the gun. Did you pick it up afterwards?'

'No, but they'd have been there from when I went out with Charles the previous afternoon. You may have found his son's on it as well.'

'And Mrs Stansfield's? Did she go out with you, or pick up the gun after the shootings?'

'No, but she bought Charles the gun as a Christmas present. He had to go with her as the licence holder, but she kept it for him to have on Christmas Day. It sounds silly, but that's what they did. She'd have handled it when she wrapped it up, of course.'

Dundee was aware that Richard Barlow had a complete answer for everything. It was perfectly possible, but such recall immediately after so traumatic an event was unusual.

'I've just received an initial pathologist's report,' he said. 'The injuries to your brother do not appear to be absolutely consistent with him having held the gun in his mouth.'

'He certainly put it in his mouth,' Richard repeated. 'But I remember that his hands were trembling. As he pulled the trigger, it could have jerked back and gone off in his face. I know I closed my eyes when I realized what he was going to do.'

'So your statement is that your brother killed your niece accidentally while he was in some sort of uncontrollable rage with you, then shot himself.'

'That's what happened. I don't know what my sister has told you, but I don't imagine she's in a state to talk about it coherently.'

'Not at present,' Dundee confirmed as he stood up. 'I think at this stage, Mr Barlow, we have no further reason to detain you and you must want to get back to your family. However, I must ask you to be available should we wish to question you again . . . when were you planning to return to London?'

'I was going today, but I'll stay for a while.'

'Well we have your address there in any event. Thank you, Mr Barlow.'

In his office, Dundee read through all the statements, written words stripped of the tears and anguish that had accompanied them. There was nothing that cast doubt on Richard Barlow's story; there had been disagreements, tensions, too much drink. Charles Stansfield said he had been aware of considerable friction involving his wife and her brothers, although he had not been able to ascertain the cause. The statement that was missing was that of Naomi. The problem there was that it was as though she had gone into a catatonic trance, refusing to speak to anyone; the family said she had been like that since Richard had led her out of the drawing room. Her doctor had insisted that she was in no state to be questioned and could not suggest when she might be; she had been sedated and taken to hospital.

'Well?' Dundee said to his sergeant. 'Accident and suicide? Murder and suicide? Two murders? Take your pick.'

'What do you think, sir?'

'It's so excessive, you could think anything. Nice, respectable, law-abiding family spend Christmas together and end up with two of them blasted to pieces. Not the sort of case where you can see what happened. I'll tell you one thing, though. Harmless, middle-aged schoolteachers don't start waving shotguns around without a damned good reason. I'd like to know what that reason was.'

'He'd had a row with his brother.'

'About an affair their father had in the fifties?' Dundee said dismissively. 'There's got to be more to it than that. The problem is that once families like this one close ranks, it's bloody difficult to get through. At the moment, our one eyewitness gives a plausible story that fits what facts we have.'

'What about this illegal arms deal thing Stansfield is said to have been mixed up in?'

Dundee shook his head. 'Forget it. Special Branch say he went to them the moment he started suspecting something and he's completely clean. Anyway, if there was a connection they'd be out to kill him, not his daughter and brother-in-law.' He tapped the papers on his desk. 'And Richard Barlow's version is as acceptable as anyone can come up with.'

'Do you believe him?'

Dundee shrugged. 'I'm not sure. I'll be very interested in what Mrs Stansfield tells us when she's fit to talk. In the meantime, we pursue our enquiries. Perhaps it was the way he told it.'

HSA581702 PAHOME   PA   21.04
POLICE Bodies (reopens)
Chief Superintendent Michael Dundee said tonight that Richard
Barlow had been released after questioning. A statement to the Press
Association added that police had been given an explanation for the
deaths and that the matter was now in the hands of the coroner.
Enquiries are continuing, but no arrests are expected.

The inquest reports into the deaths of Roberta Stansfield and Tim
Barlow contain the official explanation for what happened; both

are based almost exclusively on what Richard told the court. On each occasion, he was closely pressed by the coroner but did not deviate from his statement to the police. Naomi, the only other witness, was in the psychiatric wing of a private hospital in Hampstead and medical evidence was given that it was impossible for her to be called. After the verdicts, Michael Dundee was instructed to close the files on both deaths; he often thinks about them, but has never found a reason to reopen the investigation.

Naomi remains in the hospital. After she was admitted, staff noticed that she became agitated when they called her Mrs Stansfield; these outbursts ceased when Charles suggested they should call her Naomi Barlow. She still does not speak, but occasionally will stop someone apparently at random – a nurse, a cleaner, a visitor, once a man who came in to repair a light – and say a single, urgent sentence: 'I murdered my father.' However skilfully she is questioned, she refuses to say anything more. Her psychiatrist has discussed this with Charles, who has told him what little he knows. They are both intelligent men and have decided it must be caused by some confusion in her unreachable mind involving Harold's death when she was a susceptible teenager, the trauma of what happened to Roberta and Tim, and possibly the fact that Charles's father was dying at the time. When Charles mentioned this to Richard, he agreed, adding that he felt nothing his sister might say could be relied upon.

Florence is living in Devon Lane; when Charles sells the house he plans to buy her a flat near the hospital where Naomi is. She visits her daughter every afternoon, the two of them sitting in her room or walking arm in arm through the grounds when the weather is good. She constantly talks to her, but there is never any response; it is not certain that Naomi even knows who she is. Florence has discovered that as her grief becomes less agonizing, her depth of guilt increases. She was so sure that she and Harold brought their children up properly, but feels that anything so terrible must somehow be her fault and blames herself for not paying them more attention after their father's death.

Claire no longer has any contact with her husband's family and has allowed herself to fall in love with a man whom she has known for several years; one day she will tell him. She has not grieved for Tim and now there is nothing in her home to remind her of him; even the photographs of little Harry have been thrown away. Nobody can understand, and several friends think she must either be going mad or has become unforgivably cruel. But the children at Wilmsford day nursery unquestioningly adore Auntie Claire.

Richard is still with the *Post*, but he is no longer its news editor. Daphne Byron was overruled by the board of directors when she wanted to fire him and instead he was made associate editor, a title that impresses outsiders, but in journalism is recognized as a meaningless position for senior executives who have become irrelevant. He is expected to make no more than token appearances in the office and spends most of his time drinking with his contemporaries, recalling long-forgotten stories and reminding themselves that once they were the lions. He is patronized by his successor and hates it. In their different ways, all of Harold Barlow's children are dead.

For several weeks after Christmas, Charles's father appeared confused and distressed that Naomi and Roberta no longer visited him, then he lapsed into a deeper twilight and gently died. His son and grandson were the only mourners at his funeral. Charles Stansfield has stopped filling in his diary; there is now nothing in his life that he feels is worth recording.

The Dying of the Light

An idyllic Cornish setting is the background to Maltravers' fourth case. The violent death of Martha Shaw, a local sculptress, seems to be accidental; Maltravers suspects otherwise...but can he prove it?

'Augustus Maltravers, most intellectually sensitive of sleuths, is on the spot to winkle out the heart of an ancient mystery. Fascinating and colourful' - *Mail on Sunday*

£3.50 0 575 05091 8

Sleeping in the Blood

A chance to interview his teenage idol, singer-turned-actress Jenni Hilton, turns sour for Maltravers when he uncovers a hitherto unsuspected murder and unleashes a torrent of hatred.

'Tense, well-written, wickedly accurate on modern ad-world and Sixties foibles' - Marcel Berlins, *The Times*

'Maltravers as smart and entertaining as ever' - William Weaver, *Financial Times*

£3.99 0 575 0 5319 4

The Lazarus Tree

Nasty things have been happening in the ancient Devon village of Medmelton. Maltravers faces a hostile community as he delves into murder, myth and magic, and discovers secrets best left hidden...

'X-certificate cosy' - *Guardian*

'Richardson in sombre vein, fermenting a rich, heady brew of past indiscretions, present revelations' - *Sunday Times*

£3.99 0 575 05522 7